AKy

Forever
Charmed

ROSE PRESSEY

PRAISE FOR ME AND MY GHOULFRIENDS BY ROSE PRESSEY

"Rose Pressey spins a delightful tale with misfits and romance that makes me cheer loudly."
Coffee Time Romance

"Her characters are alive and full of quick witted charm and will make you laugh. The plot twists keep you turning the pages non-stop."
ParaNormalRomance

"I absolutely loved this book! It had me chuckling from the beginning."
Fallen Angel Reviews

ROSE PRESSEY'S COMPLETE BOOKSHELF

The Halloween LaVeau Series:
Book 1 – Forever Charmed
Book 2 – Charmed Again

The Rylie Cruz Series:
Book 1 – How to Date a Werewolf
Book 2 – How to Date a Vampire
Book 3 – How to Date a Demon

The Larue Donovan Series:
Book 1 – Me and My Ghoulfriends
Book 2 – Ghouls Night Out
Book 3 – The Ghoul Next Door

The Mystic Café Series:
Book 1 – No Shoes, No Shirt, No Spells
Book 2 – Pies and Potions

The Veronica Mason Series:
Book 1 – Rock 'n' Roll is Undead

A Trash to Treasure Crafting Mystery:
Book 1 – Murder at Honeysuckle Hotel

The Haunted Renovation Mystery Series:
Book 1 – Flip that Haunted House
Book 2 – The Haunted Fixer Upper

DEDICATION

This is to you and you know who you are.

ACKNOWLEDGMENTS

To my son, who brings me joy every single day. To my mother, who introduced me to the love of books. To my husband, who encourages me and always has faith in me. A huge thank you to my editor, Eleanor Boyd. And to the readers who make writing fun.

CHAPTER ONE

My mother had been downright giddy when I was born on
Halloween night. It was honestly like she'd won the
supernatural lottery. She'd even *named* me Halloween, as if
Halloween LaVeau was an easy name to walk around with.
I guess she figured having that auspicious birth date meant
my witchcraft talents would be extra special. That I would
boost her social status by out-magicking all of the other
witches in Enchantment Pointe. Unfortunately for her—
not to mention for me—my skills were nothing to get
excited over. In fact they were far from spectacular.

Whatever. I'd always been fine with my so-so magic.
Never mind that the local coven had published a pamphlet
based on my life entitled *How to Screw Up Witchcraft in Ten
Days or Less*. Even my mother had done her best to hide
her disappointment. She ignored my botched potions and
substandard spell-casting until, at the age of fourteen, my
painful lack of talent could no longer be brushed under the
magical rug.

That was around the time I'd got mixed up in a minor
cupcake-related incident involving a partially destroyed
kitchen and a couple singed eyebrows. My mother's
eyebrows, to be specific. She has to pencil them in to this

day, bless her heart. I tried to remind her of the bright side of being eyebrow-free—she never had to use tweezers again—but apparently this wasn't much consolation.

Despite my witchy failings, my life had been kind of normal, some might even say out-and-out boring. I attended school with the non-magical townsfolk, and went to my high-school prom with a date conjured up by my mother who turned back into a garden gnome the minute my curfew was up. All things considered, I had a fairly typical upbringing.

But my boring days were over when I inherited LaVeau Manor.

Several months ago, at the young age of one hundred and twenty, my great-aunt Maddy LaVeau had left this world. She had no children, other than the cat that now owned me, and she'd left a mysterious message in her will about me "taking my place in the world." Apparently, that "place" required owning her creepy old manor.

It was my mother's idea to turn the place into a bed-and-breakfast. "Who knows, maybe you'll snag yourself a husband," she'd said. She was always trying to snag me a husband, with little success—her prospects were generally warlocky and covered in warts. I'd assisted in her Bewitching Bath and Potions Shop for many years and she returned the favor by helping me establish my little venture, getting both the licenses from the state and approval from the Coven board who were always sticking their nosy wands into everything.

No matter how imposing and eerie the mansion was, I was thrilled to finally have a place of my own. I'd spent days exploring the various rooms, studying the intricate details, the tall ceilings, and stunning hardwood floors. The manor had been built by my great-great-great-grandfather, a famed alchemist within the witchcraft world. Stories about him had been passed down through the generations, how he just disappeared one day, never to be heard from again. Rumors still floated around town that he was buried in the basement, or his old bones stashed away in a trunk in the attic.

By my third week as mistress of my new home, I'd already cleared out most of Aunt Maddy's things, saving that spooky attic for last. But with my bed-and-breakfast about to officially open for business, I could put it off no longer.

That afternoon, I began my ascent up the staircase which led to the upper floor of the manor. Each step was steep and narrow, and creaked ominously under my feet. I turned the antique knob and the door creaked open. After taking a deep breath and blowing it out, I stepped inside the space. The attic was surprisingly empty. It was dim, illuminated only by the small window on the wall across from me. A stream of sunlight shone through, highlighting the old, scratched floor. Shadows lingered in the corners, waiting to jump out. I looked around for a light switch, but that was an upgrade Aunt Maddy had neglected to add. As I knocked a cobweb out of my way and moved further into the room, dust motes floated through the sunbeam. I gave the window a good heave to air out the musty smell.

It was early autumn, the days warm in the middle, but crisp around the edges. A breeze wafted into the room, carrying the scent of damp soil and burnt leaves. Drooping branches from the tall oak trees shaded the back lawn, and beyond that, the river lay a few hundred feet away. A raven took flight from the treetop, drifting across the sky in rhythm with the water below. The flap of its wings and caws floated across the air. I looked down, watching the river run steadily past. Beneath one of the oak trees sat a small family cemetery enclosed by a black wrought-iron fence.

The sun dipped toward the horizon, the last faint color of the day lingering in the sky. It would be dark soon, and I needed to sort through the old boxes and get back downstairs before my imagination about discovering my great-great-great-grandfather's bones got the better of me. Instinctively, I looked around for the old trunk.

Three boxes formed a neat stack to my left and a couple of brown vintage suitcases set to the right. An old wingback chair with a bureau pushed up next to it took up space at the back of the room. I'd have to find someone to help carry them down. After popping open the suitcases, I sifted through their contents. One contained what I assumed was my great-aunt's clothing, velvet and satin with lots of feathers. The other held hundreds of postcards from around the world, some blank and others from people I'd never heard of, addressed to her with indecipherable personal greetings. The boxes were full of old books, dishes, and stuffed animals. She was eccentric like that.

I stacked everything up ready to take it downstairs and started to move toward the door when something stopped me. I wasn't sure what that *something* was, but my feet froze to the spot. A strange force compelled me to look to my left. Out of the corner of my eye, I spotted it. An old book, stashed behind a beam. My feet carried me to it, a peculiar power pulling me to the mysterious tome.

I plucked the heavy volume from its hidden location and blew the dust from the stained and weathered cover. Fear placed its icy arms around me, and cold shivered up my spine when I touched the leather binding. My heart rate increased. A panic attack, I thought. Inheriting the house was a big undertaking and the anxiety had caught up with me, that was all. Goosebumps emerged on my arms.

As I held the book, a dark sensation, evil just beyond its edge, nagged at the boundaries of my thoughts. But I couldn't release my grip. I opened the cover and a rich scent of leather stirred in the air around me. An unrecognizable foreign language covered the thick, yellowed pages, not French, definitely not Spanish. With each flipped page, my fingers tingled. Nothing about the book's contents offered a clue as to what it was about, no owner's name inside or even initials, but the symbol on the front was strangely familiar: a twisted knot circled by fancy scrolling. Had I seen it before in my mother's Book of Shadows? If this was a spell book, it was unlike any I had seen before.

"Anyone home?" a familiar singsong voice called out.

I jumped three feet in the air, almost tossing the book across the room. I slammed it shut, as if I'd been caught reading someone's diary.

"I'm in the attic. Come on up." My voice wavered. I'd forgotten my best friend Annabelle Preston had agreed to stop by.

"There's no way in hell I'm coming up there! It's creepy. You come on down here."

I rolled my eyes. It had been all I could do to convince Annabelle to come over in the first place. She thought for sure the house was haunted. Even so, I told her, ghosts wouldn't hurt her. But being non-magical, she got a little on edge when around the supernatural and she wasn't buying my reassurances.

"I'll be right down," I called back.

I tucked the book under my arm and made my way to the door. With my hand on the knob, I paused and looked back, sure that I'd heard footfalls behind me.

Now Annabelle's paranoia was getting the better of me.

My best friend stood at the bottom of the stairs, peering up at me with wide, mascara-rimmed blue eyes.

"I don't know how you can live in this place all by yourself. At least get another cat or ten, for heaven's sake." She looked around for my black cat, Pluto. He'd been scarce since the first day at LaVeau Manor.

"Great, so then I can officially be the weird cat lady in the big old creepy house." I moved down the first few steps.

"Okay, how about a dog?" she asked with hope in her eyes. Annabelle was obsessed with animals. She had two dogs, three cats, a hamster, and too many fish to count. I'd had to stop her from getting a monkey. When I'd told her about the diaper-changing she'd changed her mind right away.

I nodded. "Fine. Maybe a dog, but I doubt Pluto will take too kindly to a new resident."

"What are you doing up there all by yourself, anyway?" She gestured with a tilt of her head. "I'd be afraid I'd get trapped and never get out."

"I wanted to know what was up there," I said.

"A trunk full of bones, that's what's up there." She rubbed her arms, warding off a shiver.

I made my way to the last step of the wide, winding staircase. "Sorry to foil the urban legend, but I found no trunk, no bones. Just a bunch of old crap."

"This place is the epitome of creepiness. I could have sworn I saw a man standing on the front porch when I pulled into the driveway." Annabelle looked over her shoulder toward the front door.

A bang echoed through the foyer and Annabelle screeched, wrapping her arms around my neck.

"Oh my God, we're going to die!"

CHAPTER TWO

I peeled her arms from around my neck. "It was just the cat. Take a deep breath and calm down."

She clutched her chest. "I guess I'm a little jumpy, huh?"

"A little," I said, pinching my index finger and thumb together. "I can't believe you saw a strange man at my front door and you're just now telling me." My voice raised a level.

"Well, upon closer inspection, I think it was just the shrubbery." She tucked a blonde strand of her hair behind her ear.

"No one could accuse you of a lack of imagination. Remember when you watched *Pride and Prejudice* and then insisted we all had to speak with a British accent and have four o'clock tea every afternoon?"

"Never mind that," she huffed. "You're never going to let me forget about that, are you? I happen to think England is a beautiful place."

I laughed. "I think it's beautiful too, but you have to admit my accent sounded more like *Pirates of the Caribbean* than Princess Di. And it's not like you ever let me forget about that time I wanted to join the circus."

"You're not the traveling type. You freak out when you have to drive to New Haven." She shook her head. "So you didn't find a body in the attic?"

"No body. You've officially become paranoid."

"You probably didn't look hard enough." Annabelle paused, peering up at the staircase with distrust.

We moved across the foyer, the sound of our footsteps echoing across the old wood floors.

"What's that?" She pointed at the book tucked under my arm.

One thing I loved about Annabelle was that she had never judged me, unlike the other non-magical folk in Enchantment Pointe. We'd been best friends since the day we shared our finger paints in kindergarten, and she'd stuck by me through thick and thin—burned-down kitchens and all. She knew about my ancestors and my witchy background, but it never fazed her.

"Um, an old book. I'm not sure what it is. I can't read it. It's written in a weird language." I was still feeling strangely unsettled by it. After stepping through the open French doors leading into the library, I sat down in one of the red velvet-upholstered chairs opposite the large ornate fireplace. The room's walls were covered with wood and floor-to-ceiling bookcases with my great-aunt's old hardbacks lining an entire wall. A large crystal chandelier hung from the ceiling.

"Can I see it?" Annabelle asked.

I hesitated for a moment, then handed the book to her.

She flipped through a few pages and then shoved it back in my direction. Her abrupt movement surprised me. It was as if she thought she shouldn't be looking at it. Maybe she sensed it had otherworldly qualities—she'd always been uncomfortable around magical objects.

Just as I opened my mouth to ask her why she seemed so freaked out, the sound of movement caught our attention—footsteps echoing through the walls. We remained seated in front of the fireplace, neither one of us moving an inch. The footfalls sounded as if they'd come from the bedroom directly above us. I shook off my fear: this was *my* home now, and if there was an intruder, I'd deal with it like the witch I was.

Jumping up, I tiptoed over to the staircase. Annabelle followed, but stopped short at the library entrance, pressing her back against the wall. The hair on the back of my neck prickled. The footsteps sounded again, this time coming across the hall toward the landing. An undeniable presence emanated from the top of the stairs, but I saw nothing. I knew something was there... I felt it. A cold misty sensation sent chills down my arms.

Slowly, I placed my foot on the step in front of me and forced the other one to do the same. The stairs made a creaking noise with the movement. Annabelle rushed over, grabbing the back of my shirt so I almost tumbled backward. A ghost hunter she was not.

"You can't go up there," she whispered, still holding my shirt.

"Why not?" I whispered back.

"Because it's dangerous, that's why. Can't you do some kind of spell and get rid of the spirits?" Her voice wavered.

"Ghosts are supposed to be living with me here, Annabelle. It's their *job*. Their whole purpose is to make spooky noises and make us think we're losing our minds. They haunt creepy old manors. I can't ask them to leave. Besides, witchcraft doesn't work that way. Don't you know that by now?"

I hoped she would never ask how witchcraft really worked, because there was no way in hell I could explain. *I* had no idea how it worked. If I had, I wouldn't have been named Worst Witch of 2009 at the local fête.

"If I see bones coming down those stairs I will probably pee my pants," she whispered, still holding my shirt.

I pulled the fabric from her grasp. "Let's go up there and see what happened. Maybe it was just the wind."

Okay, even I couldn't say that with a straight face. There was no way the noise we'd heard was the wind.

Annabelle shook her head, stepping backwards toward the door. "I just remembered. I told my mother I'd take her shopping for yarn."

I turned around to face her. "Yarn?" I raised an eyebrow. "Since when does she know how to knit?"

"New hobby. She's quite good actually. You should see the lovely scarf she's making." She chuckled nervously.

"I can't believe you're leaving me here with a ghost. You're supposed to be my best friend!" I closed the space between us.

She grabbed my arms and looked me straight in the eyes. "I don't want you to stay here. Get out while you can. This place is haunted and it's creepy. They shoot spooky movies in houses like this one."

"You are officially in panic mode."

"You're damn skippy I'm in panic mode. And you'd do well to turn on that switch too. Join me in my freaked-out state, won't you?" If possible, her eyes widened even more.

"Take a deep breath and tell yourself that everything is fine. Repeat after me: 'I ain't afraid of no ghosts.'"

"Okay, now you're just making fun of me." She crossed her arms in front of her chest.

"What? Me? Make fun of you? Never."

The look in her eyes told me that she wasn't remotely convinced by my false bravado.

Annabelle shook her head. "Fine. But don't come crying to me in the middle of the night when some ghost wakes you up and you freak out. I'll be sleeping."

I used my index finger to draw an imaginary cross over my heart. "I promise."

I wasn't about to let her in on the fact that I was more than a little creeped out. That would only cause her more terror. As far as Annabelle was concerned, I had always been fearless. My witchcraft ancestry made me invincible. I didn't want to burst her paranormal bubble. Heck, I wouldn't dare tell Annabelle about the pull that I'd felt from the book. The yearning desire I had to understand every single word between its old covers.

As she hurried toward the door, she called over her shoulder, "I was just joking about calling me, you know? You can call anytime you want."

I nodded. "I know. Go help your mother with the yarn. I'll be fine. What's the worst that can happen?"

CHAPTER THREE

Thunder cracked and rolled across the night air, making me sit straight up in bed. Rain pounded against the window. Another crash of thunder rang out, but that wasn't the only noise. I could hear a strange pounding coming through the wall. Was something happening up in that old attic? Had the old bones come to life?

I'd looked around upstairs after Annabelle left, and I'd found no intruders, no ghosts—nothing that could have made those creepy sounds. Maybe it really was the wind. But I could have sworn I heard a baritone voice whispering in my mind, calling out my name.

Halloween LaVeau, Halloween LaVeau...

Now I was imagining things? Hearing voices? Great. Insanity had officially set in.

The pounding echoed through the room. I caught my breath, then slipped out of bed, shoving my feet into my slippers and grabbing my silk robe. As I inched along the hall and down the stairs, the knock rang out again. Someone was at the front door.

Who would be visiting at this time of night in the pouring rain? A deranged killer, no doubt. I eased over to the door and peered through the tiny peephole. A dark figure stood on the stone veranda in front of the entrance. My chest clenched as I swallowed hard.

I couldn't make out any features, but could tell by its size that it was a man. My heart thumped, warning me I shouldn't answer, but responding to strangers was a big part of running a bed-and-breakfast. Turning away customers wasn't exactly the best way to make my business successful. Maybe this was some poor man whose car had broken down. He probably just needed a place to crash.

Yeah, I could tell myself that all night long, but believing it was a different story. He'd probably hack me to death the second I opened the door.

A stone fence separated my property from the main road and a crushed pebble circle drive spanned the length of the manor. Beyond the veranda, swirls of fog cascaded along the ground. Through the peephole it looked like a scene straight out of a hokey vampire movie. The mist purred its way down the street and straight up my driveway.

Ignoring my gut instinct to bar the door and go back to bed, I called out, "Who is it?"

As if this man would come right out and tell me if he was a psychopath: *Hello, single vulnerable woman, I've come to chop up your body, stuff it in an oil drum, and bury you in the back yard. Would you let me in?*

"I saw your sign for a bed-and-breakfast. Do you have a vacancy?" he asked.

His voice was strong and smooth. He certainly didn't sound like a killer, but what did a killer sound like? Once again, a mysterious pull willed me to open the door—this strange, yearning feeling that had become all too common since I'd moved into LaVeau Manor. I had to start learning to ignore my gut instincts—nine times out of ten they got me into trouble.

"I have a room," I choked out.

Feeling like a crazy woman, I unlocked the massive carved walnut door with a turn of the old key and swung it open. He wore black. What else, right? He was dressed like a walking cliché: all that was missing was a cloak. The cut of his short, black hair emphasized his strong jaw, chiseled features and brilliant blue eyes. His gaze seemed to hold an electric charge. I wondered for a moment if I was dreaming. Had a mysterious handsome stranger really just emerged out of the misty night?

I thought again of turning him away, but instead I continued to move as if controlled by a force outside myself, stepping aside to allow the man to enter my home. He shook out his umbrella and walked in, placing the umbrella in the stand.

Light fell across his face. If I didn't know better, I'd suspect my mother was involved in bringing Mr. Tall, Dark and Handsome to my doorstep. It was as if someone had waved a magic wand and delivered the Perfect Man to me—all intense eyes and long lashes. On second thoughts, he was too dangerous-looking for her taste.

"I'm glad I found you," he said with a smooth drawl. I detected a slight accent, but I couldn't quite put my finger on it.

Found me? What did he mean?

He smiled as if he'd read my mind. "The weather is so bad that it's impossible to drive on the roads. It was a stroke of luck that I found Enchantment Pointe. Must be a great place to live." He looked around the foyer, craning his neck to peek into the parlor.

I put on my best business face. I hadn't yet had any guests come to stay at LaVeau Manor and hoped I was coming across as a professional proprietor. "I'll just get some information from you, then show you to your room."

As I walked to my makeshift office in the back of the house, the same thoughts ran over and over on loop in my head. Who was this man and why was he driving through Enchantment Pointe in the middle of the night? I pulled out a clipboard with the information form I'd printed earlier that day, and a set of keys. Annabelle would flip out when she found out I'd had a stranger to stay without telling her.

When I returned to the foyer, the man was standing just where I'd left him. He fixed his gaze on me when I entered the room. Talk about uncomfortable. All I wore was a silk robe—okay, it was some form of satin—and my hair probably looked as if I'd styled it with a hand mixer.

"Please fill this out." I handed him the clipboard, noticing his strong hands as he took it from me. He had an intricate silver ring on his right hand, but no band on the left. I stopped the thought, shocked to realize I was looking for a wedding ring. Had I lost my ever-loving mind?

As he grasped the pen and began writing, I fidgeted with the key. I'd decided to place him on the third floor, so I'd be able to hear him when he moved around. If he came down the stairs during the night, at least I'd be prepared if he really was a nutcase. I studied him as he continued to write on the paper, taking in his lean physique and broad shoulders. I was desperate to know what he was doing around these parts. Where had he been headed?

After a few more seconds, he finished and handed me the clipboard. "All done." He flashed a gorgeous white smile.

I glanced down at the paper to read his name. Nicolas Marcos. *Is he serious?* How exotic and sexy was that? Annabelle would have a heart attack when I told her.

I met his gaze. "Pleased to meet you, Mr. Marcos. My name is Hallo—My name is Hallie LaVeau."

He took my hand and placed it to his lips. My heart rate increased as his mouth lingered there for a moment. His touch was smooth. I definitely didn't trust a man with hands that smooth.

"It's a pleasure to make your acquaintance, Halloween."

I pulled my hand away as if a shark was about to take a chunk out of it. "How did you know my name is Halloween?" I stepped back, putting distance between us.

A small smile curved his delicious lips. "It was on the form you gave me. That's quite an unusual name. I bet you had a tough time growing up."

Heat rushed to my cheeks. Yes, no big surprise, of *course* I'd had a tough time fitting in in school as a witch named Halloween. And of course he'd seen my name on the form. Now I felt like a paranoid nutcase.

"You seem a little tense. I can imagine it's tough for you to allow strangers into your home," he said.

"Mr. Marcos, I have to ask, where are you headed? Not many people are just passing through Enchantment Pointe at this time of night."

"I'm headed to New Haven. I have business in the city." He smiled again.

I supposed asking what type of business would be just plain rude. I bit my tongue and refrained from being too darn nosey.

"Well, the weather is terrible. I don't blame you for stopping," I said, glancing over his shoulder at the rain pounding against the window. "If you don't mind, I have a room for you on the third floor. I think you'll find it very comfortable." I pointed toward the staircase.

He looked me up and down and nodded. "I'm sure I will. Thank you, Mrs. LaVeau."

"Ms. LaVeau," I repeated softly, like some kind of shy schoolgirl.

"You have a beautiful home, Ms. LaVeau." His gaze didn't leave mine.

I fidgeted, shifting from one foot to the other. "Thank you. It was my great-aunt's. Well, it's been in the family for hundreds of years. She was the last owner."

Did he have luggage? And for that matter, where was his car? I hadn't spotted it in the driveway.

"Would you like to get your bags?" I asked.

"I have a small case on the veranda. I wanted to make sure you had a room for me first."

Okay, that made sense, but what about the car? "Is your car out there?" I asked, looking toward the door as if I'd see it.

"Actually, I walked. My car broke down just down the road."

"Do you need to use my phone to call Triple-A?"

He stared for a beat before answering, then finally said, "Thank you, but I already called from the road."

He wasn't exactly being forthcoming.

I hesitated for another moment, not sure what I was waiting for. After an awkward pause, I motioned for him to follow me.

"Let me show you to your room."

Nicolas reached out the door and grabbed his case. I was glad to see that he truly had one.

As I turned to move up the stairs, I felt him behind me. His presence was strong, comforting, and scary at the same time. He was awfully close, but boy did he smell good—vanilla with a touch of sandalwood and spice. It was exhilaratingly masculine. My stomach did a little flip-flop.

When we reached the third-floor landing, I hurried down the hall toward the bedroom without glancing over my shoulder to see if he was following. I shoved the skeleton key into the lock and turned. The old door creaked when I pushed it open. Mr. Mysterious and Sexy was right behind me.

I opened the door and stood back. Nicolas entered the room, but I waited just outside the threshold. Sheer white curtains hung beneath velvet corded drapes on the floor-to-ceiling windows that lined one wall. The room was accented with antiques that Aunt Maddy had collected over the years, each touched by stories that I could only imagine. It had taken forever to clean the layers of dust off everything.

Antique lamp fixtures mounted against each wall lit up the room. On one side of the room rested a softly rounded chaise lounge and on the other was a simple, yet expensive-looking Parsons-type desk. A fireplace in the middle wall had a maple mantelpiece that I'd spent too much time polishing the day before. But the massive hand-carved bed was the most stunning piece in the room.

Nicolas moved across the floor and pushed on the mattress. Checking for lumps, I guess.

That same vibe pulsed through my body telling me to run, run, run, but instead, I stayed, stayed, stayed. This whole experience was nothing short of awkward.

"There are towels in the bathroom." I gestured toward the small bathroom to the right. "Please let me know if you need anything."

He walked over to the desk and picked up the copy of *The Raven* that I'd left for my guest's perusal. Hey, it was an old, dark manor and I figured it would add to the mystique. People who stayed here were probably looking for creepy—I'd try my best to give it to them.

His lips tilted upward at the corners as he placed the book back on the desk. The mischievous smile revealed perfect white teeth, almost blindingly white. Did his gaze move down to my lips or was that my imagination? I thought I glimpsed a hunger in his eyes.

If he continued to smile at me with that perfect mouth there was no telling what kind of stupid comments I would blurt out. It was time for me break off the conversation while I still had an ounce of professionalism as an innkeeper.

"Breakfast is at seven. Do you have any special dietary needs?"

He stared at me before answering, as if I'd asked the strangest question in the world. "No, no special needs. Please don't go to any trouble on my account."

"It's no trouble, really. If you need anything please let me know."

"I'll definitely let you know when I need something."
He flashed another knowing smile.

CHAPTER FOUR

After leaving Nicolas in his room, I hurried back down the stairs to retrieve my phone. I had to call Annabelle. She wouldn't believe it when I told her a dark, mysterious, handsome stranger had shown up at my home in the middle of the night. In a thunderstorm. I felt like I was on an episode of some prank reality show. I kept expecting Ashton Kutcher to leap out holding a video camera.

"I knew you'd call. You heard the ghost again, didn't you?" Annabelle said when she picked up.

I whispered into the phone, "I have a guest." Why was I whispering? The house was so big there was no way he could hear me.

"Hallie, I don't think I'd call a ghost a guest. An *unwanted* guest, maybe."

"No, I have a real person staying here tonight... a paying guest." He would pay me, right? I realized I'd completely forgotten to mention the room rate. I'd hate to have to turn him over to collections.

"What? When did this happen?" Her voice sounded more alert.

"About forty-five minutes ago. I signed him in and took him to the third floor. It was like he just appeared right out of the fog."

"You have a strange man staying at your home? Who showed up in the middle of the night! What are you thinking? What if he wants to kill you? He appeared out of the fog? What does that even mean?"

She sounded hysterical.

"Annabelle, calm down. You know I can't live my life in fear. I'll be fine, but I wanted you to know just in case I do come up missing. Better safe than sorry, right?" I chuckled nervously.

"That's not funny, you know. You shouldn't say things like that. You didn't answer my question. What did you mean by 'he just appeared out of the fog?'"

I let out a deep breath. "There was a knock on the door and when I opened it, he was standing at the front door. He said he walked here."

It sounded crazier when I said it out loud.

"What the hell is going on? He walked there? What kind of serial killer have you allowed in your home?"

"His car broke down. That's all." I was trying to reassure myself more than her. "He was walking and saw that little sign I had out front."

"I knew I should have thrown that sign away," she said under her breath.

"Come over for breakfast in the morning and meet him." I paused. If I treated Nicolas Marcos as some kind of novelty, perhaps I'd stop being afraid of him.

"What's wrong with him?" she asked. "And don't say *nothing* because I can tell by the tone of your voice that something is wrong with him."

"He's gorgeous, that's what's wrong with him. I'll see you at seven."

"That's in three hours!" she protested.

"I don't plan on sleeping anyway," I said. There was too much nervous energy running through me for any rest.

"*I* had planned on sleeping." She sighed. "How gorgeous are we talking?"

"Tall, dark, and yummy. Good enough?"

"Okay. Lock your bedroom door and I'll be over as soon as the sun rises."

After hanging up the phone, I moved back over to the staircase. I paused and gazed up toward the third floor. What was he doing up there? Removing clothing to reveal lean muscles and six-pack abs?

I pushed the thoughts of a shirtless Nicolas to the back of my mind and made my way back to the library. Fidgeting with my hands, I walked the length of the floor, pacing with anxiety. The feeling I'd had all day hadn't left me. If anything, it had grown stronger. And it wasn't only my guest making me feel this way. It was that damn book—I felt its pull. I'd left it tucked securely between a couple old volumes on the shelves. I had to look at it again.

I eased across the old creaky hardwood floor and paused when I reached the book. My hands tingled when I pulled it from the shelf. Holding it securely in my arms, I sat down in the chair and placed it on my lap, flipping the cover open. The same aged pages that had perplexed me earlier stared back at me. I had no idea what I was looking for—but I knew the book was trying to tell me something. If I couldn't even read the words, how would I ever decipher the message?

A wind picked up and the pages began to flip out of my control. Then as suddenly as it had stirred, the wind abated and the pages settled. I looked down at the open book and the spell was now in English. I flipped back a few pages. Everything else was still in the strange language. I turned back to the page marked by my finger and studied the words. It wasn't a coincidence that it had flipped to this page. Had my great-aunt Maddy turned the pages from the great beyond?

I carried the open book into the kitchen and placed it on the large island in the middle of the space. The room was bathed in shades of white. Various apothecary jars covered the spaces around the room. The moon shone brightly through the back door window, casting a ghostly glow across the area.

The page gave no clue about what the spell was for—all it listed was ingredients. Aunt Maddy had almost any item I could possibly ever need for a spell right there in the kitchen. She also had a collection of cauldrons. Not that I needed one. Sure, I owned a cauldron, but with my track record I'd never felt comfortable using it. Except for that time I burned all the pictures and mementos from Tate Monroe. He'd claimed witchcraft wasn't the reason he'd broken up with me, but I knew that was a lie. It was no coincidence we'd split up the day after I cast a spell to help him with his golf game. How was I supposed to know the higher the score the worse the game? And at least *his* eyebrows had grown back.

For my potions, I preferred to use a saucepan on top of the stove. My mother always said, "No wonder the Coven doesn't take you seriously. You use a saucepan, for heaven's sake." But honestly, who wanted to drag out a heavy steel cauldron for a potion that wasn't going to work anyway?

I placed a pan on the stove and poured in spring water. While waiting for it to boil, I retrieved my herbs from the apothecary jars around the room. Vervain, sea salt, frankincense and myrrh were the necessary ingredients. After the water had come to a steady boil, I poured it into a bowl and placed it in the middle of the island.

With more of the sea salt in hand, I sprinkled the crystals around the bowl. Drawing a small circle with the salt, I enclosed the bowl within it. The smell of earth tickled my nostrils and splashes of light—red, green, then blue—covered my vision for a few seconds. A light breeze stirred in the room.

As I placed the herbs in the water, I intoned the words written in the spell book: "Bring the magic to me. Protection from all negativity surrounds me. Harm threefold to thee who sends destruction my way. All hateful actions directed toward me, will be inflicted upon thee."

A few pitiful sputters of smoke puffed up from the pot. The water boiled no more, the breeze stilled, the lightshow in my vision stopped, and the smell of Mother Earth vanished. Using a teaspoon, I placed a small amount of the potion in the amulet I wore around my neck.

Nothing happened.

Disappointed, I took a seat on the counter stool. I was *sure* the book had been trying to tell me something. Unwilling to give up, I shifted on the stool and stared at the pot. I closed my eyelids and took a few deep breaths. I opened my eyes again and my reflection stared back at me. I tried to guide my mind to the psychic light deep inside me—well, it was *supposed* to be deep inside me, I'd never felt much stirring down there. I waited for an image, an impression, for anything to appear. As with every other time in the past, I felt my magic, but instead of a strong vibrating hum, it was more like an annoying mosquito buzzing around my head.

All the water in the bowl had done was allow me to have a glimpse of my own face. Stress, worry and disappointment written all over it. It was the same disappointment I saw on my mother's face every time she asked if my magic had improved.

My cell phone rang, but I ignored it. See, my mother wasn't the only one who got upset when I performed magic. Every time I cast a spell, if there was another witch within twenty miles practicing magic, then my spell would screw her spell up too. And I would inevitably start receiving calls from irate witches claiming that they'd turned their cat into a toad and it was all my fault. I was not a popular witch to say the least.

Frustrated, I dropped my head to the counter. I had to know what this book said and what it all meant. Had it been Aunt Maddy's book? How would I find the answers?

Movement sounded from above me again and I sat straight up, sucking in a deep breath. Footsteps. Either it was the ghost, or my guest was awake and coming toward the kitchen.

I stuffed the book in a drawer and placed the jars back around the room. I didn't want him to know what I'd been doing. *Guilty* was written all over my face in flashing letters. Why should I feel bad? It was my home and I hadn't done anything wrong—right?

I'd placed the last jar on the counter when the footfalls stopped. My heart rate increased as I spun around. The kitchen was empty. Tiptoeing through the library, parlor and into the foyer, I listened for more movement, but heard none. I made my way back to the kitchen and pulled the book back out. Somewhere within the pages there had to be a clue as to what it all meant or who it had belonged to.

I stayed at the kitchen island for what seemed like hours, listening to Nicolas move around the floor above me—at least I assumed it had been him. Why hadn't he gone to bed and what was he doing up there?

CHAPTER FIVE

At some point I must have dozed off, because I woke to find Annabelle gazing down at me with a horrified expression on her face. Morning sun streamed in through the kitchen windows.

"You left the back door open?"

"I did?" I wiped the drool from my chin, then rubbed the crick in my neck.

"Yes, you did. Don't ever do that." She wiggled her index finger at me.

"Yes, ma'am." I saluted.

I wouldn't make a very good night security guard. If not for Annabelle, I probably would have slept all morning.

"This place gives me the creeps. No matter how many times I come over here." She clutched her arms around her chest. "What's going on now? Is he still here?" She peered over my shoulder.

I nodded as I pushed to my feet. "Yes, he's still here. I think I heard him stirring around." Or had I dreamt that?

"Well, I hope he hurries up and gets out of here so I can stop worrying about you. I can't handle this stress." She let out a deep breath. "I don't think I can ever have children. I'd never be able to keep it together. The first time little Bobbie fell on the playground I'd lose my mind."

"I think you'd do just fine." I patted her on the back.

"You look like hell," Annabelle said as she placed her purse on the counter. "Have you been down here all night?"

I attempted to smooth my frazzled hair. "So I took a little nap at the kitchen counter. Big deal."

She clucked her tongue. "Well, I can't say I blame you for wanting to be close to the door in case you needed to make a quick escape."

I shook my head. "Just let me run upstairs and change my clothes. I don't want my guest to think I'm a slob."

Annabelle frowned. "Please don't leave me alone for very long. I'll have nightmares tonight."

"I'll be back before you can say old, creepy manor."

She didn't return my laughter.

Once I'd made the trip back up those ridiculously steep stairs, I hurried to my room, grabbed a shirt and jeans from my closet and jumped into them. My clothing consisted of every color in the rainbow—I'd avoided black since the age of twelve. No need to add fuel to the witchy fire. I brushed on a dab of mascara and ran the comb through my hair.

I wanted to sneak up to the third floor and see if Nicolas's door was shut, but I knew Annabelle would lose it if I left her too long. I rushed down the stairs, across the library and parlor, then back into the kitchen. If I whipped up some pancakes and tossed some flour onto my face to make it look as though I'd been hard at work for hours, he'd never know I had slept in a faceplant on the counter all night like some kind of crazy woman. I wondered if he knew how easy it was to make pancakes? I'd add a few strawberries on top to make them look gourmet.

Annabelle studied me when I returned to the kitchen. "You don't *want* him to go, do you? You've got the hots for a stranger? You *like* this guy, don't you?"

Trust Annabelle to cut to the chase.

"He's not so much a stranger any more. He's been here for several hours and we chatted when I showed him to his room last night. Nicolas was very friendly. Maybe a little strange, but in a good way." I wasn't quite sure why I was defending him. Maybe I was defending myself.

She threw up her hands. "*Nicolas*? Oh well, then he's a friend already, practically family. Nothing to worry about."

I rolled my eyes. "I'm sure he'll be checking out soon. In the meantime, I have to make pancakes for him." I grabbed the ingredients and poured them into a large bowl.

Annabelle coughed. "What are you doing?"

"What does it look like? I'm making pancakes." I waved the spatula through the air.

"Are you sure that's such a good idea? I could run out to the bakery and pick up some pastries."

I threw the towel at her. "You sit down and talk to me while I cook. And we won't discuss my cooking skills."

"Hallie, your pancakes always look more like round cardboard disks than breakfast food. Maybe if you pour on the syrup he won't know the difference."

"That's not being a supportive friend." I glared.

She pulled out a stool and sat down. "So what did you talk about? Did you find out what he does? Why's he in Enchantment Pointe?"

Annabelle had extremely selective hearing.

"He said he's traveling to New Haven on business."

"Sounds suspicious to me." She narrowed her eyes.

"Oh, Annabelle. Why on earth does it sound suspicious? It sounds entirely reasonable." I placed a pancake on her plate.

She shrugged as she poured maple syrup on top. "If you say so."

"I thought you didn't like my pancakes." I pointed with the spatula.

"It's better than having to cook myself," she said, then shoved a forkful in her mouth. She made a face while she chewed.

I swatted her with the towel again.

"Is he coming down for breakfast?" She pointed with her fork.

I shrugged. "I'm not sure, but I figured I should be ready just in case. I guess he didn't get much sleep."

Annabelle stood and pulled a tube of lipstick from her pocket. She marched over to me and popped off the lid. With one sweep, she smudged the soft pink color over my bottom lip.

"Rub your lips together." She mimicked the motion.

"What the heck are you doing?" I stepped back.

"In case he comes down. You're going to scare the man away. I might recommend that as the most sensible course of action, but the way you talk, I don't think you want that to happen." She gestured with the lipstick. "You said he was gorgeous. In case he turns out not to be a freak-psycho-murderer, you'll want to look your best."

"Well, after last night, I've set the bar pretty low."

She clucked her tongue. "First impressions... they're a bitch."

A loud knock echoed, followed by the booming doorbell ringing out. We both froze on the spot. If Annabelle was in my kitchen, then who in the heck was at the front door? My mother would never be out at that time of the morning.

CHAPTER SIX

We exchanged a glance. In my three weeks at the manor, I'd *never* had unexpected guests. Now all of a sudden I was hearing my doorbell twice in less than twenty-four hours. Could a little sign out front bring in business just like that? I wasn't even on Yelp! yet.

"Who's that?" Annabelle stuffed the lipstick back in her pocket, her eyes wide.

"I don't know," I whispered, as if the person would hear me.

I wiped my hands on the towel and made my way through the parlor with Annabelle hot on my heels.

"Make sure to look out the little window before you open the door. Is your guest still here or not? Maybe it's him?"

"Maybe. He could have left while I was sleeping in the kitchen. But I figured he'd say goodbye first." I glanced at the staircase as we moved past. I hadn't heard any movement since the loud bang. Maybe he'd gone out for a walk and was coming back.

I peeked out the window. My pulse quickened. "It's a man," I whispered.

"Not your guest?" Annabelle was practically standing on my back. It was like wearing an Annabelle backpack.

"No, it's a *different* man. What should we do?"

"Call the police?" Annabelle whispered in a panic.

"We can't call the police simply because someone is knocking on the door. I'll open it and see what he wants. He can't do anything to both of us. We can take him down if we have to. I'm not afraid."

Yeah, I had to keep up that façade of confidence for Annabelle's sake. But what I really needed to do was try another protection spell—one from a book that I trusted. Apparently I was going to need it.

"Speak for yourself," she said. "Okay, okay. You're right. We'll kick his ass if he tries any funny business."

"That's the Annabelle I know." I winked and nodded, signaling I was ready to open the door.

"Let's do this," she said.

I took in a deep breath, and grabbed the handle. Annabelle picked up Nicolas' umbrella, which I realized at that moment was still there. With a turn of the knob, I eased the door open.

A tall, dark-haired man stood in front of us. Damn. *He* was gorgeous too. What the heck was going on around here? I hadn't seen one good-looking guy in Enchantment Pointe for at least a year and now there were two at my home in less than twenty-four hours. Did they know each other?

I stared into the face of the rising sun as it peered through breaks in the clouds. The leaves whispered in the wind, sending the smell of fragrant blossoms our way. Moss covered the stone fence that surrounded the manor and trees lined the drive. The man's black sedan was parked in front of the manor. At least he wouldn't claim that he'd walked here.

The fog and the darkness might have moved along, but the air still held a note of creepiness. This new stranger wore a black suit that was tailored perfectly for his frame.

His hair was short and a little curl hung down on his forehead. I wanted to reach up and ease the strand back into place. His blue eyes sparkled in the sunshine.

"Hello. My name is Liam Rankin. I noticed your sign for a bed-and-breakfast. Do you have a vacancy?" He looked over my shoulder into the foyer.

I knew he wasn't looking at Annabelle, but instead, he was looking at the house. Was he looking for something? Someone? Nicolas, maybe? This was in no way a coincidence.

He blessed us with his gorgeous smile.

"Um, yes, I do have a room."

"Wonderful. I just got into town. I'm visiting a friend but I refuse to sleep in that lumpy bed of his for one more night. I've slept in tents that were more comfortable." He flashed that dazzling smile again.

I cast a glance at Annabelle, but she was too focused on Liam. Oh, what the hell. What was one more killer? I'd survived the first night.

I'd halfway expected Annabelle to whack him over the head with the umbrella, but her expression didn't say 'I want to hurt him.' In fact, it said the exact opposite.

"Hello," she said.

Her voice came out as a purr. I knew that look in her eyes. I saw it every time she watched a Johnny Depp movie. I couldn't say that I blamed her. He was an exceedingly handsome man, just like my other unaccounted-for guest.

"Pleased to meet you." He kissed her hand just as Nicolas had kissed mine. "Who do I owe the pleasure?"

"I'm Annabelle Preston and this is Hallie LaVeau. She owns this place." She titled her head in my direction.

At least she'd remembered not to use Halloween.

"What a beautiful name," he said.

I offered a smile and my hand in the hopes that he'd give it a professional shake, but I got the same kiss too. His mouth left a tingling sensation on my skin. There was no way I could allow him to stay without asking a very important question.

"Are you friends with my other guest?"

He quirked an eyebrow. "Your other guest?"

"Yes, his name is Nicolas Marcos. He just checked in last night and I assumed that you know him since my place is a little off the beaten path and neither one of you had reserved a room."

I sounded ruder than I'd intended, but it was a legitimate question. I offered a smile to counteract my bluntness.

He scowled. "No, the name doesn't sound familiar. I'm sorry I didn't make a reservation. It was a last-minute decision, you understand?"

"No reservation is necessary," I said.

"You say this man just showed up in the middle of the night?" He looked from me to Annabelle and back to me.

I crossed my arms in front of my chest. "That's right. His car broke down and he had to walk here."

"That's odd. I didn't pass any stranded vehicles on my way over."

I smiled, trying to hide my suspicion. "You look as if you could be his brother."

He shrugged. "Well, like I said I don't know him."

I didn't believe Liam Rankin. Not one bit.

CHAPTER SEVEN

"Let me get a little information from you and then I'll show you to your room."

Annabelle stood behind Liam making faces and gesturing. To answer her mimed question: I had no idea what I was going to do. I surreptitiously motioned for her to knock it off. Despite all my actions to the contrary, I was attempting to appear somewhat professional. *Attempting* being the key word.

"That sounds great." Liam frowned, then sniffed the air. "Is something burning?"

"Oh no." I dashed through the rooms headed for the kitchen. "The pancakes," I yelled.

The sound of rushed footsteps followed me as I raced to the kitchen and slid toward the stovetop as if I was making it to home plate. Black smoke billowed from the pan. I grabbed the spatula and flipped the burnt pancake off the griddle onto the floor.

Annabelle's mouth hung open and her eyes widened. I knew what she was thinking without her saying a word. First impressions were a bitch, and I'd just made a doozy of an impact on Liam Rankin.

More footsteps echoed through the parlor. When I looked toward the kitchen entrance, Nicolas stood at the threshold, staring down at the black disk that had once been a pancake.

"I'm sorry. Let me whip up a fresh batch." My face must have been blood red.

Nicolas didn't seem interested in breakfast food though. He was glaring at Liam with an expression of extreme agitation. The men stared at each other for a moment, then Nicolas focused his attention my way.

"You really don't have to go to any trouble on my account," he said.

He was taking pity on me. I didn't want my first bed-and-breakfast attempt to be a complete failure.

"It's no trouble at all. I'm making more for me and Annabelle too." I pointed at Annabelle as I scraped the pancake from the floor and dumped it into the trash.

Annabelle's mouth was still wide open. I never thought I'd see the day that I'd officially left her speechless.

She finally came out of her trance and nodded. "Yes, Hallie's pancakes are delicious."

I could always count on my best friend to lie when necessary. Her eyes remained wide as she studied Nicolas, then Liam again.

The smoke had begun to dissipate from the charbroiled pancake, but something else in the air had replaced the smoke. A strange electrifying tension pulled at the air around us.

"I'll serve breakfast in the dining room if you'd like to have a seat. It'll just take a second. It's the first room on the left through that hall." I pointed down in the general direction, giving them a pleading look. "Liam, you'll eat too. You must be tired and hungry."

Liam gestured for Nicolas to go first. I could have sworn Nicolas snarled at him.

Annabelle's jaw had apparently stopped working. "Shut your mouth before it stays that way permanently," I whispered.

She peered down the hallway. When the men were out of sight, she said, "Hallie, what the hell is going on? There's enough electrical tension in this room to light up the house for a year."

I waved the whisk through the air. "Do you feel that too? I thought I was imagining things."

If Annabelle felt it, then I knew something weird was definitely going on. She was one of the most non-magical people I knew. She never picked up on vibes or anything.

"Help me finish breakfast so I can get in there and figure out what is going on." I draped the apron over my head and tied it around my waist.

"Here, why don't you let me do the pancakes and you get some bacon out of the fridge." She eased the whisk from my hand.

I didn't resist.

After hurrying with the food, Annabelle and I rushed down the hallway to the dining room. We stopped short just outside the closed door. The men were talking, but in hushed tones. They clearly didn't want to be overheard.

"What are they saying?" Annabelle whispered.

"I can't make it out." I motioned for her to be quiet as I leaned closer to the door. I picked up one of the OJ glasses off the tray, and placed it to the wood, then put my ear against it.

"You're not fooling anyone, Marcos, least of all me. I know exactly why you're here and if you think I plan on letting you find it before I do, you're sorely mistaken."

That was Liam.

Another voice, I assumed Nicolas, responded in lower tones. I couldn't make out anything besides "Underworld" and "Mara." He sounded furious.

My heart rate increased. Okay, I didn't want to alarm Annabelle, but we were about to walk in on something serious. What were they looking for? Who was Mara? Had I heard him correctly?

I kept my ear pressed against the glass, but nothing. They'd stopped talking, as if they knew we were right outside the door listening.

I'd tell Annabelle what I'd overheard later. Maybe. I motioned with a tilt of my head for her to go in.

She shook her head. "You first," she mouthed.

I let out a deep breath. "Fine," I whispered.

"Breakfast is served," I said in my sweeter-than-honey voice as I pushed through the swinging door.

The men sat on opposite sides of the large mahogany table, as if they were ready for a duel. That same thick tension hung in the air.

I placed the plates in front of each guest, then took a seat at the middle of the table. Annabelle scooted her chair close to mine.

"I had no idea you had another guest," Nicolas said while staring at Liam.

Liam didn't answer. Silence reigned and neither man had even glanced down at their plates. I knew the cooking might be questionable, but they could at least have pretended to take a few bites.

To relieve the awkward silence, I said, "Well, it is a bed-and-breakfast." I smiled and took a bite to show them that the food was perfectly safe.

Apparently it worked, because both men picked up their forks.

"Will you be staying long?" Nicolas asked.

"As long as it takes," Liam replied while attempting to cut his pancakes.

Did they even remember that we were there? They didn't glance at Annabelle or me.

"Tell me... Mr. Rankin, is it?" Nicolas pushed his fork around on the plate.

He wasn't fooling me with that old trick. I had used the same stealthy move to fake eating my mother's pickled beets for years.

Liam scowled. "Yes."

"What is your line of work?" Nicolas asked.

Liam took a bite and chewed as if he was chewing the words. Finally, he said, "I'm a detective."

My jaw fell open. When I glanced at Annabelle, she had the same expression. A detective? Of what? For where?

"That's interesting. What brings you to Enchantment Pointe?" Nicolas tapped his fork against the plate.

Shouldn't I be asking those questions? Nicolas wasn't even going to ask what police department Liam worked for? That was kind of an important question in my book. Annabelle shifted in her seat.

"I was about to ask you the same question of you, Mr. Marcos," Liam retorted.

Nicolas flashed a devilish grin. "I'm traveling to New Haven on business," he said through a fixed smile.

Watching their exchange was like watching a tennis match, only I wasn't able to keep score.

"I heard there's a nice Holiday Inn there. I'm sure you'll enjoy it." Liam stuffed a bite of pancake in his mouth.

Nicolas didn't take his gaze off Liam. They were in a staredown.

"You'd like that, wouldn't you?" Nicolas snapped.

Liam shoved his plate back and pushed to his feet.

I stood. "I'm so sorry, Mr. Rankin. With all the chaos, I forgot to show you to your room. You must want to get settled."

"That would be nice. Thank you. But please, call me Liam. It was a pleasure meeting you, Ms. Preston." Liam reached out and took Annabelle's hand again, lightly placing his lips to her skin. "I'll just get my bags." He nodded a goodbye, then stepped out of the room.

Before I had a chance to speak, Nicolas stood from the table. "If you'll excuse me, I have a few phone calls to make."

"Of course." I smiled.

After he'd cleared the room, Annabelle let out a deep breath, then said, "Well, that was the strangest breakfast I've ever had. And I've been to the all-you-can-eat buffet at Bobby Lee's Steak and Chicken House."

I couldn't tell Annabelle what I'd overheard... not yet. Maybe they'd said something entirely different from what I'd thought I'd heard. After all, I had been listening through glass.

"There is definitely something they're not telling me. But I plan on getting to the bottom of it. They can't come in here and act all weird and not expect me to get involved."

"You tell them, Hallie. Who the heck do they think they are anyway?" Annabelle helped me collect the dishes and we hurried to the kitchen.

"They may be completely off their rockers, but did you see the dimples when Liam smiled at you? That was enough to make me melt right there." Annabelle placed the plates in the sink.

"He is good-looking, huh?" I wiped my hands on the towel.

"Like I said, weird, but good-looking."

"I'll just go show him to his room," I said, walking toward the parlor.

She grabbed the back of my shirt. "Oh, you're not leaving me alone in here. I'm coming too."

"Okay, but let's hurry. I want to hear if they're talking to each other again." I motioned for her to step up the pace.

Liam stood at the front door with his arms folded in front of his muscular chest. Nicolas was nowhere in sight. I'd half expected to find them crossing swords right there in the foyer. Liam grabbed his bag when he saw me.

39

"It's just up on the third floor," I offered.

I was probably asking for trouble by putting them in adjacent rooms.

We made our way up the stairs. I led the way and Annabelle followed behind like the caboose. This guy probably wondered why he needed two women to escort him to his room. A familiar smell circled me as I moved up the steps, but I couldn't put my finger on it. Was the aroma coming from Liam? Spicy and warm, with a hint of something else.

We moved past Nicolas' room. The door was closed, but no noise came from inside. At the end of the hall, we reached the room I'd picked out for Liam. Annabelle stood back as I opened the door. Liam walked through and set his bag down on the hardwood floor.

"Please let me know if you need anything."

"Thank you. You've been a gracious host. I'd like to apologize if things seemed awkward downstairs." He leaned against the tall bed post.

"I wasn't going to say anything, but…" Well, since he'd brought it up first—"Are you sure you've never met Mr. Marcos before? Because it really seems like you have."

"No. I don't know him," he said matter-of-factly. "Some men just feel threatened, I suppose."

Talk about cryptic. I huffed in frustration. Soon enough I'd be rid of both of them and could put this weird encounter behind me for good.

"Like I said, I'm here if you need anything." I stepped out of the room more confused than ever.

After leaving Liam, Annabelle and I passed Nicolas' door. We exchanged a glance. The door was now open.

"It wouldn't hurt to take a peek and see what he's doing in there, would it?" I asked.

I poked my head in and looked around the room. Nothing seemed out of place. But where was Nicolas?

"You can't spy on your guests," Annabelle said as she moved closer. She spoke the words but didn't look as if she meant them.

"He's not in there," I whispered. "Let's just take a little look."

"Are his bags gone?" she asked.

"I don't see them. Do you think he left for good?" Why did my stomach sink with the thought?

Annabelle stepped into the room. "After that breakfast I wouldn't be surprised."

"But he didn't even pay me yet." I peered out the window at the river. Unlike yesterday, the water was perfectly still.

Annabelle shook her head. "People can be so nasty," she said with disgust in her voice. "You should insist Liam give you a straight answer. It's like my mother always says, nagging works. If you nag him long enough maybe he'll cough up the details."

Annabelle's adoptive mother was over-the-top pushy.

"I can't nag my guests. That's a quick way to get a bad review. Do you have any idea how hard it is to recover from a bad review?"

Pluto had appeared next to me, the sight strangely comforting. I hadn't seen him in a couple of days. The cat looped through my legs, then rubbed his face against my pants. Apparently he hadn't heard about my cooking and wanted to be fed.

She nodded. "I guess you have a point."

"And if Nicolas Marcos is gone for good, there's no point in wasting our energy worrying about him, right?"

CHAPTER EIGHT

"I have to get to work," I said as I put the last of the dishes in the washer. "I never thought about leaving strangers alone in the house. It's creepy."

"Well, that's the *only* thing creepy about this whole situation, right?" Annabelle said sarcastically.

I'd always thought I was a good judge of character. I was a little bummed over the way Nicolas had left without saying goodbye.

"You should call the police and report Nicolas for not paying," Annabelle added as she grabbed her purse.

"No, I think I'll just chalk it up as a lesson learned. I'll always remember to collect the money first, or at the very least, get a deposit."

After saying goodbye to Annabelle, I rushed toward Bewitching Bath and Potions. The historic section of town housed all the specialty shops and boutiques. The main road ran along the river, twisting and turning through Enchantment Pointe. A stone wall surrounded the outer edge of town with cobblestone sidewalks and wrought-iron accents sprinkled around.

I knew my mother would be waiting and I wasn't looking forward to telling her about the catastrophe I'd experienced with my first two guests. I'd leave out the parts about the spell and the burnt pancake—and the fact that one of them had skipped out on the bill. No need to give her any more reasons to be disappointed in her one and only daughter.

I pulled up in front of the shop and turned off the ignition. The events of the morning were just now fully sinking in, not to mention that I was starting to feel faint from lack of sleep. Pulling my purse up over my shoulder, I trudged toward the entrance. The bell chimed on the door when I entered. No one was in sight, no customers and no mother.

Annette LaVeau made all the items right there in her shop. Her merchandise included soaps, lotions, scrubs, and bath salts. She had a special knack for mixing scents— magical oils were her specialty. She was a workaholic when it came to her business: sections of the store were specifically designated for specific items, and you'd better not get them out of place either. Fragrances, oils, powders and herbs on the right. Soaps, shower gels, lotions, shampoos and conditioners on the left.

"Mom, are you here?" I walked further into the shop.

She popped up from behind the register where she'd been arranging items under the counter. People could tell immediately that we were mother and daughter. We were the same small size—five-foot-one—but we packed a powerful punch. My mother had recently cut her hair in a fashionable bob with the occasional gray hair showing up in the otherwise dark strands. She wore the store's signature polka-dotted apron over her black T-shirt and black and white Capri pants.

She sighed as soon as she saw me. Must she do that every time I walked into a room?

"Hello, dear." A small swirl of smoke circled behind her.

"Working on another spell?" I asked as I joined her behind the counter.

She held up a light blue bottle. "I'm making a facial lotion for Mrs. Combs." She stirred the pot a few more times, then dipped the bottle into the concoction. "This should help her with the warts."

"I have noticed she's sprouted quite a few more lately." I draped the Bewitching Bath and Potions apron around my neck.

My mother wiped her brow and let out a deep breath. "Whew. I've been swamped all morning. I'm glad you finally decided to show up."

I stared at my mother's forehead.

"What?" She scowled. The color drained from her face. "Not again," she said.

I thought by now she'd be an expert at penciling on those eyebrows and keeping them in place. One brow was still perfectly drawn on, but the other had been smeared all the way across her forehead. To her credit, she'd stopped reminding me of the way I'd destroyed her face. She just let out breathy sighs instead.

She shook her head. "Well, I don't have time to put it back on right now. It'll have to wait a minute. I need to finish these orders for the customers."

"Would you like for me to fix it?" I asked, transfixed by the sight. It was like a car accident; I couldn't look away.

"You don't know how to add the arch that I've perfected over the years." She didn't glance up from her bottles.

Ouch. That hurt.

"Why were you so late anyway?" she asked.

"I was working around the manor." I moved a couple bottles across the counter out of her way.

She snorted, but didn't ask for more of an explanation.

"Can you label those soaps and place them on the shelf?" She pointed.

"Sure." I let out a deep breath, picked up the soap and wrapped it in the paper.

Without warning, that strange vibe took over again. I had to steady myself with a hand on the counter. Was I coming down with something? Why had I been feeling so strangely? If I didn't know better, I'd swear it had something to do with Nicolas Marcos. I hadn't felt this way until he'd shown up. But he was gone now, so shouldn't I be feeling better?

The bell over the door chimed and I looked up. My heart rate increased when I saw who was walking my way.

"Oh my," my mother said.

This was not going to end well. I felt it.

"Hello, Mr. Marcos," I said without looking at my mother.

I knew her mouth must have dropped open. The wheels were turning wildly in her head.

"Nice to see you, Hallie. This is a lovely shop." He looked around the room.

"Thank you," I said.

"I need to talk to you." He leaned in close over the counter.

"How did you find me? And by the way, you left without paying." I frowned. "You owe me for the night."

My mother let out a little gasp, but I refused to look in her direction.

"I asked around town and was told how to find you."

Great. All of Enchantment Pointe would be flapping their gums about me. I could only imagine how those conversations had gone.

My mother was pretending not to listen, but if she leaned in any closer she'd fall right on her face.

"What is it, Mr. Marcos?" I placed my arms across my chest.

He glanced over at my mother again, maybe looking at her one eyebrow.

"Is there some place private where we can talk?"

After the way he'd acted around Liam this morning, I wasn't sure I felt safe being alone with this man.

"We can talk here."

My mother would question me relentlessly after he left anyway. Might as well save myself the time and talk out in the open right in front of her.

He stepped to the side and motioned for me to join him.

I looked him up and down, then slowly moved over to his side. Damn him. He still looked gorgeous and smelled just as enticing.

"Now are you going to tell me what's so important?"

If he dared to complain about my breakfast I'd tell him off right there in front of my mother.

"You need to get rid of Mr. Rankin. Your life is in danger if you don't."

The words had barely left Nicolas' lips when Liam burst through the door. The bell over the door jingled so hard I thought it would fall off.

"Don't listen to a word he says!" Liam pointed at Nicolas with venom in his eyes.

I'd gotten myself into a real pickle this time. My mother wasn't going to let this one go for months.

CHAPTER NINE

"Whatever he says, don't believe a word of it." Nicolas pointed at Liam.

The men stared at each other in a showdown.

I stepped between them. "Nicolas hasn't told me anything yet. But I think it's about time someone tells me what's going on around here."

Nicolas folded his arms in front of his chest and flashed a smug smile at Liam. If he thought I was only talking to Liam, he was dead wrong.

The men continued to stare at each other, neither one budging on giving me an answer. I glanced over at my mother. She looked quite awkward with her mouth gaping open and one eyebrow.

Who was I supposed to believe since both men were warning me about the other? If Nicolas wouldn't tell me why he felt this way, and Liam's lips were sealed too, then what was I supposed to do?

"I won't ask Liam to leave." I glared at Nicolas. "If you can't tell me why he is so dangerous, then I can't ask him to leave."

"You told her I was dangerous?" A look of utter disbelief covered Liam's face.

"For two men who don't know each other, you seem to have quite a few warnings. Let me guess, you have a gut instinct about each other, right?" I asked, exasperated.

This seemed too dangerous. I should have asked both of them to leave, but something made me ignore my logical warning... it was that same strange pull that I couldn't shake. They remained tight-lipped.

I looked at Nicolas. "I'm supposed to take your word for it that Liam is dangerous?"

Who did Nicolas think he was anyway? He showed up in the middle of the night looking like some kind of movie vampire and was now giving me orders? That took a lot of nerve. But was it a legitimate warning? How would I know?

"This guy doesn't know me. He's just spreading rumors. I don't know what his beef is with me." Nicolas gave Liam a brutal, unrelenting glare.

Should I mention that I'd overheard their conversation? What was the woman's name that Nicolas had mentioned? Oh yes, Mara. Who was Mara? And what was the Underworld? Were they involved in something illegal? I decided to see how this scene played out before I mentioned what I'd overheard.

"If anyone shouldn't be trusted, it's him." Liam pointed at Nicolas.

"Is everything all right?" my mother asked. "Do you know these men, Halloween?"

I hesitated, but knew I'd have to tell her the truth. "They are both bed-and-breakfast guests."

Her expression said it all. "Oh, was the breakfast bad?" she asked the men.

I hardly thought they were fighting because of my burnt pancakes. They were bad, but not that bad.

"The breakfast was good," Nicolas offered with a smile.

Apparently, my mother wasn't immune to his good looks because she smiled in return.

Liam, not to be outdone, said, "The food was delicious, ma'am."

My mother blushed and widened her grin. She was enjoying the attention.

"This is my mother, Annette." I gestured toward my mother. She'd stopped blushing, but interest in the men hadn't waned.

"If both of you aren't happy with each other, I can change your rooms so that you're farther apart. Other than that, there's nothing else I can do." I tried to disguise my annoyance.

Nicolas remained quiet. I supposed he wasn't going to give me a straight answer, just vague hints about how he didn't trust the guy.

The same went for Liam. All he could offer was a lame excuse that he thought Nicolas was talking badly about him when he supposedly didn't even know him. I had to get to the bottom of this. There had to be a way to find out who these men were and why they'd popped into my life.

Without saying another word, Liam stormed out of the store. Would he leave LaVeau Manor after this heated exchange? That would probably be for the best, even if I needed the cash. The men had issues that I didn't want to deal with.

I looked at Nicolas. "Maybe it's better if you leave. I can speak with you later. I need to help my mother now."

Nicolas reached out and touched my hand. I sucked in a quick breath. My body tingled, although I tried to will away the feeling. Why did the simple touch of his hand against mine feel so intimate? Why did his spicy scent send shivers across my body? He smelled of rich woods and sweet musk. Years of working at my mother's shop had fine-tuned my sense of smell. Every time Nicolas looked at me it was as if he couldn't take his gaze off me... and as much as I tried to deny it, the feeling was mutual. But maybe I was just imagining things. After all, I hadn't slept much. And that weird sensation from the book was playing tricks on my mind.

"Please be careful," Nicolas said.

"I'm always careful," I said.

"When will you return to the manor?" he asked.

I looked at my mother.

"I'll need your help all morning," she said.

It was completely up to her and how much help she needed today. It was like I was sixteen again and asking my mother if I could date boys all over again. Except this was definitely not romantic. It was strictly business.

I looked at my watch. "I'll be here until at least after lunchtime."

"I'll see you then." He paused and smiled, then walked out the door.

"Well, what was that all about? I've never felt that much tension in the air. There was some kind of magic going on." My mother waved her hands through the air as if trying to shoo the magic away.

"How can you tell?" I asked.

"Didn't you feel it?" she asked with a tint of anxiety in her voice.

"I may have felt something."

She let out a heavy sigh, not hiding her disappointment.

I didn't want to tell her that I'd felt a lot of heaviness since I'd discovered that book. It was almost like I'd unleashed something when I'd opened its cover. Had something happened with the spell last night, bringing these men to LaVeau Manor?

"Where did these men come from?" She stirred her latest concoction.

There was no way I was going to tell her they had just shown up. I'd tell her that they'd booked the nights well in advance.

"They had reservations. I believe they have business in the area." I moved items around, pretending to be busy.

She raised a suspicious eyebrow. "I worry about you. Maybe having a bed-and-breakfast isn't such a good idea."

"I'll be fine," I said as placed the soaps in their designated spots on the shelf. "It's just part of the business."

She should know running your own business wasn't easy. You had to deal with a lot of things that you wouldn't normally want to handle. This just happened to be one of them.

"I don't think they'll stay long," I offered, trying to make her feel better.

It was a lose-lose situation though. My comment showed her that she wouldn't have to worry about the guests for long, but also that I wouldn't have income coming from the bed-and-breakfast for long either.

I found it difficult to concentrate for the rest of the morning. My thoughts were consumed by the men and what was happening at LaVeau Manor. Would Annabelle want to stay over until they left? Who was I kidding? She could barely set foot in the place, much less spend the night. I didn't want to push her. She was doing well to put her phobia aside and come into the place.

Finally the clock hit twelve and I grabbed my purse. "I have a ton of work at the manor. I'd better go." It wasn't a lie. I did have a ton of work. I had to find out what my guests were up to.

"Just be careful," she said as her one painted-on eyebrow slanted into a frown.

"You know I will." I waved cheerfully as I walked out the door. There was no need to let on to my apprehension.

I climbed in my car and headed straight for the manor. My mind was filled with trepidation. Part of me was afraid of what might be going on, but another part of me felt exhilarated and excited.

Pebbles crunched under the weight of my tires as I pulled down the driveway. Every time I saw the manor I felt small and insignificant under its shadow. Liam's car wasn't parked in front and neither was Nicolas'. Was Nicolas really having his car repaired? Maybe that had all been a lie? Maybe they'd both checked out. That would be for the best if they did. I didn't like drama in my life. I had enough to worry about with my substandard witchcraft.

When I stepped into the manor, the only sound came from the faint tick-tock of the grandfather clock. It was like the silence that flooded a church after Sunday service. The cat meowed softly at my feet, voicing his displeasure with me. I had to know if the men were still there. They hadn't left their keys on the table. I placed the roses on the hall table and made my way up the stairs, pausing when I reached the landing. I took in a deep breath, turned the corner and headed for Nicolas' room. I wouldn't look in the room if it was locked of course. If the door was still locked I'd know that he was still there. But if the door was open, I'd take a tiny little peek to see if his bag was still there.

I tiptoed down the hallway, trying to keep the floorboards from announcing my arrival. When I reached Nicholas' door, it was standing open. My heart sank. If he was staying, he probably would have locked the door when he left.

With my foot, I pushed the door open even further. I could say that I'd accidentally kicked it with my foot. That wasn't snooping, right? It was just an accident. The bed had been made... okay, it was made as well as any typical guy would make it. He'd done a fairly decent job though.

My heart beat faster as I stepped into the room. What was I worried about? I owned the place. But I had rented a room to this man. I shouldn't be snooping. I would tell him that I came to straighten up his bed if he happened to show up. If I'd been thinking clearly, I would have brought extra towels for him.

I stepped into the space and looked around. Where was Nicolas' bag? Finally I spotted it to my left, sitting on the floor. My heart did a little dance. Why was I so excited? I needed to get a hold of myself. He was a customer and that was all. My thoughts floated to Liam. Was he still here? And again what did I care? He was just as mysterious as Nicolas. Unfortunately, I was intrigued by both of them.

I stepped over to the bag. Did I dare look inside? No, it wouldn't be right. It was definitely the wrong thing to do. No matter how much I wanted to know about him. Besides, how much would I really learn just by looking in the bag? Whether he was a boxer or briefs fan? Intriguing as that might be, I would have to leave it to my imagination.

When I glanced to my left, I spotted papers on top of the bureau. I guessed if I happened to look down while walking by them that wouldn't be such a bad thing. It wouldn't be my fault if I happened to see something. Maybe the papers would be a clue as to what type of business Mr. Marcos was in town for. I stepped over to the dresser.

"Did you lose something?" the male voice said from very near behind me.

CHAPTER TEN

My heart almost jumped out of my chest and a scream escaped my lips. I spun around and clutched my chest. Nicolas was standing behind me. I had been caught in the act. There was no way to explain why I'd been over there snooping around. I glanced down at the dresser. I had to think fast if there was any chance getting out of this dilemma. The copy of *The Raven* that I'd left for spooky effect was lying there.

I grabbed it and showed it to him. "I came to borrow this book. I hope you don't mind."

The expression on his face let me know that I wasn't a good liar.

"Of course. Please take anything you need out of the room," he said with a knowing grin.

"Thank you. I'm sorry to disturb you. I'll just leave you alone." I moved toward the door.

"Hallie," Nicolas called out.

I stopped and turned around. When he said my name it made my heart do a little flip.

"I had to pick up a few necessities in town," he offered, even though I hadn't asked.

I supposed he was trying to ease into conversation after the incident earlier. Did that mean he planned on staying longer than expected? Well, there was only one way to find out. Why did I feel bad for asking? It was a legitimate question. After all, it was past checkout time and he hadn't even paid me yet.

"Will you be staying an extra night?" I studied my shoes in order to avoid his penetrating gaze. Avoiding the desire to stare into his electric blue eyes was difficult though.

"Actually, I'm not sure how many nights I'll need the room. Apparently, my car needs more serious attention than I'd realized. It may take a few days to repair the vehicle. I hope that's okay. And I apologize that I haven't paid you yet." He pulled out his wallet and handed me a wad of bills. "Please take this and let me know if it isn't enough. I'll give you more as soon as I'm sure of how many nights I'll need to stay."

I glanced down at the bills. "This is more than enough." I tried to hand back some of the cash.

He waved his hand and pushed it back. "Please. Keep it and add it to my bill. Like I said, I'm not sure how many nights I'll be staying."

Wow. Maybe I wasn't so bad at this bed-and-breakfast thing after all. Well, maybe the breakfast part. But that was what they had bakeries for.

I debated on whether I should bring up what had happened at my mother's store. It was beyond weird and he had to know that. I wanted to ask him about the conversation I'd overheard too. But it could be none of my business and perhaps I didn't want to be involved. Should I wait to see if he mentioned it again? I'd let it go and see if he broached the topic again.

The sound of footsteps ascending the stairs caught our attention. Was it Liam? Or the ghost? I looked over my shoulder toward the hallway, then back at Nicolas. His facial expression tensed. I knew he was hoping it wasn't

Liam. But I was hoping it was. Did that make me crazy? I wanted to know as much about them as I could find out.

"I'd better check out my other guest." I pointed over my shoulder.

Nicolas reached for my hand again and my heart skipped a beat. "When can I speak with you privately?"

"If you'd like to come downstairs later I can serve refreshments." I motioned over my shoulder.

I was trying to remain professional, but did I sound too professional? Too aloof and indifferent? After all, I didn't know this man.

He nodded and released my hand. I turned and walked out the door, without looking back. I needed to calm my speeding heartbeat.

I couldn't deny my attraction to Nicolas, so I decided to remain quiet about his earlier warning and disagreement with Liam.

Liam was in the hallway when I came out of Nicolas' room. The strangest look spread across his face when our eyes met. What did he think had happened? Sure, I'd been in a mysterious, handsome stranger's room, but I wasn't a lady of ill repute, as my mother would say.

"Is everything all right?" he asked with worry in his voice.

Why wouldn't everything be okay? "Yes, it's fine. I just came to retrieve a book." I pointed at the hardback.

That sounded incredibly lame. He looked down at the book in my hand.

"*The Raven*. One of my favorites." He flashed his dazzling smile.

How did I end up with two gorgeous men in my home?

"I enjoy Edgar Allan Poe too," I answered softly.

"I'm sorry about earlier. Nicolas and I had words and we shouldn't have involved you, especially at your mother's store." He crossed his arms in front of his muscular chest.

I shrugged. "Testosterone at work, I guess. How did you know it was my mother's place?"

"You look just like her. The same caramel streaks in your golden hair and emerald specks in your green eyes." He reached out and touched a lock of my hair and I sucked in a sharp breath.

How observant of him. "Are you sure you don't know Mr. Marcos?" I asked.

Noise sounded from behind me. Nicolas stood at the threshold of his room's door.

"If you'll excuse me." Liam stepped over to his room, walked inside and closed the door.

When I turned around, Nicolas had retreated into his room as well. I was left standing in the hallway wondering what had happened to my life. They were giving me a headache.

There was work to be done and I had to push thoughts of the men out of my mind. I needed food for my guests, although the thought of going to a bakery at this point was sounding more and more like a good idea. Annabelle had agreed to drive me for more groceries. I knew she didn't want to shop for food, but she wanted more information about what was going on at LaVeau Manor. Having someone to confide in would be about the only thing to keep me sane at the moment. I had to tell her about what I'd overheard. She would freak out when she found out.

When I peeked out the front door, Annabelle was sitting in her blue Honda, motioning for me to come out.

"I see that your guests are still here," she said when I slipped into the car.

"My cooking didn't scare them away after all,' I said around a laugh.

As she pulled onto the road, I studied the scenery out the passenger window, trying to figure out the best way to tell her. I tapped my fingers against the leather seat absentmindedly.

"Is something on your mind?" she asked, glancing over.

Finally, I mustered up enough nerve to explain what had happened.

After describing the whole mystifying scene, Annabelle said, "So he just burst in to the store?"

I nodded. "Yeah, it was straight out of a soap opera. I asked them to leave."

"Your mother must have freaked out." Annabelle said, steering around a curve.

"Surprisingly, she didn't say much." I paused for a moment, measuring my thoughts. "She did mention that there was an odd feeling of magic around."

"What do you think about that?" Annabelle asked.

"I'm not sure what to think." Apprehension gnawed at me.

I knew this was the moment when I had to tell Annabelle about what I'd heard. I had to get someone's opinion.

"There was one thing I didn't mention." I tried to keep my tone casual.

"Oh no. Do I need to pull over? How bad is it?" She glanced at me with wide eyes.

"Well, it's probably nothing." I waved off her concern.

"Tell me. You're scaring me." Her voice raised a level.

"When I listened in on their conversation at breakfast I heard some things," I said.

Her eyes widened. "Like what?"

"Well, Liam told Nicolas that he couldn't believe he was there, which was completely odd," I said.

Annabelle snorted. "Yeah, you could say that."

"Anyway, then Nicolas said something but it was mostly muffled, probably because he was farthest away from the wall. I only made out two words." I paused as their conversation replayed in my mind.

"You're driving me crazy. What were the two words? Please tell me the words weren't murder and women." She motioned for me to hurry with one hand while steering with the other.

I chuckled. "No. He said 'Underworld' and 'Mara.'"

"Underworld? What the heck is that? Is that some kind of sex slavery thing?" Annabelle asked.

"What? Come on. They look like perfectly nice gentleman. They couldn't do that, right?"

She raised an eyebrow. "Anything is possible."

I snorted. "Anyway, maybe that wasn't what he said at all. Like I said, it was muffled."

After a quick trip to the grocery store, we pulled into my driveway and Annabelle cut the engine when we stopped in front of the house. Walls of trees flanked both sides of the property all the way down to the river. Soft moonlight cast an eerie glow over the landscape, making the whole place look like a scene from *Dracula*. I knew even the outside of the place gave Annabelle the creeps. The sensation of being watched was undeniable, so I couldn't say that I blamed her.

"Do you want to stay with me tonight? We could watch old Cary Grant movies and eat popcorn," I said with hope in my voice.

"I have a better idea. Why don't you come back to my place and we'll watch the movies?" Annabelle said.

I contemplated the thought. "No, I can't do that. I have guests."

"You can just let them have the place," she said as she peered up at the manor.

"Don't be silly. I can't do that. Can I? No, no. I can't." I waved off the thought. "Listen, I'll be fine. I promise to call you if anything happens."

"You'll call me if you need anything?" she repeated for reassurance.

"I promise," I said, making an imaginary cross mark over my chest.

The house remained silent when I entered through the front door. I expected guests to make some level of noise.

Their silence was odd. But as I stepped across the living room floor, the sound of footsteps creaked the floorboards above my head. At least I knew they were really still in the house.

Once the groceries were put away, I made my way to my room on the second floor. What were the guys doing up there? I'd heard walking around and Liam's car was in the driveway, so I knew he was there. But I hadn't seen Nicolas, so I wasn't sure what he was doing. Liam could have killed him for all I knew.

My bedroom had a large mahogany bed in the middle of the room placed against the far wall. The walls were covered in a cream color. I'd thought of painting the room in a soft yellow or taupe soon. Aunt Maddy had a gorgeous deep purple velvet chaise in one of the other bedrooms, so I'd dragged it across the hall to use in my room. To the left of the door was a floor-to-ceiling bookshelf where I displayed my small collection of witch figurines along with my large book collection. The white down comforter on the bed called my name.

After soaking in the bath, I slipped into my favorite plaid pajamas and fell onto the bed. The cat curled up at the end of the bed and immediately closed his eyes. Apparently he wasn't worried about my mysterious guests.

I was exhausted from my lack of sleep the night before. My worries would have to wait until tomorrow. Right now I needed to give my mind a break. The house was eerily still and I fell asleep within minutes of my head hitting the pillow. The quiet wouldn't last for long.

CHAPTER ELEVEN

I woke after a few hours to the faint sound of walking around. But this wasn't coming from either man's room. It was coming from the attic. I was sure of it. Had the ghost returned or was it a rat? I'd prefer the ghost. Clearly, the cat wasn't doing his job. Moonlight lit the room with a soft glow. I climbed out of bed, slid into my slippers, and headed toward the attic.

Careful of my footing, I climbed the remaining stairs, then inched across the creaking hardwood floor and down the long dark hallway. When I reached the attic door, I paused. Noise sounded from the other side again. That definitely wasn't my imagination. Something was making a shuffling sound in there. But what? I had no choice but to open the door and find out. I didn't even have anything to fend off the rat if it was in fact a wild creature. Where was the cat when I needed him?

I sucked in a deep breath and eased the door open. My eyes hadn't adjusted to the darkness and I reached out to find the wall to guide me into the room. Why hadn't I brought a flashlight? Was I really that stupid? I felt my way down the wall until I knew I was in the middle of the room. My eyes still hadn't totally adjusted to the dark and I thought I heard movement come from the corner of the room.

There was no sense in being up here. I might as well go downstairs and get a flashlight, then come back. What if someone had broken into the house and I was now in the room with them? But why would they be in the attic? There was certainly nothing valuable up there. Other than Aunt Maddy's old clothes, postcards, and... that was when it hit me. The book! What if someone was looking for the book? But no one knew it had been there. Even I hadn't known until I stumbled upon it.

Just when I'd decided to turn around to leave, someone reached out and grabbed me from behind. I screamed out and fell backward onto the floor.

"Are you all right?" the baritone voice asked.

I recognized Liam's voice right away.

"Let me help you up. Give me your hand." He stretched his hand down.

I reached forward and my hand met his. It was strong and smooth and my heart sped up. He pulled me to my feet.

"What are you doing up here?" I whispered.

Liam didn't answer. I didn't want Nicholas to hear me and come running, although he'd probably already heard my scream.

"What are you doing up here?" I whispered in a harsh tone again.

He still didn't answer right way, then finally he said, "I heard something so I thought I'd check it out."

I supposed that was a plausible explanation, but it was odd for him to be in the attic.

My eyes had adjusted now, allowing me to find my way back to the door. I fumbled for the doorknob, then made my way out into the hallway. Liam followed closely behind me. The soft glow from a nightlight I'd installed in the hallway highlighted Liam's handsome features. I stared at him, waiting for an explanation—although he'd already offered me one, it wasn't good enough. I wasn't ready to accept the story he'd given.

"What kind of noise did you hear?" I asked.

Before he had a chance to answer, a door swung open and heavy footsteps came down the hall. I whipped around to see Nicolas walking toward us.

He frowned. "Is everything okay? I thought I heard a scream."

I pushed a stray strand of hair behind my ear. "Liam scared me is all."

Nicolas glared at Liam. When I looked to Liam, he had a cocky grin on his face.

"What is so funny?" I asked.

My patience was fading quickly. They were messing with my beauty sleep and I didn't appreciate it. Liam shook his head, but didn't answer. I looked back at Nicolas. This macho crap from them had to end.

"I heard a noise and went to check it out. Apparently Liam had heard it too. He was in the attic looking for the source of the noise," I said.

"Is that right?" Nicolas glared at Liam.

"I'm just making sure she is safe." Liam's voice was courteous but patronizing.

"I suggest that everyone go back to their rooms. We can discuss this in the morning over breakfast." Maybe I sounded a little bossy, but someone had to take care of this situation.

The men stared at each other. Their eyes spoke volumes. The only problem was I had no idea what they were saying.

Finally, I pointed down the hallway. "Bed now."

It was like talking to kids. But someone needed to take control of the situation. I pointed down the hall until the grown men finally shuffled toward their rooms. As I watched them walk next to each other, they kept their distance, moving slow and cautious toward their rooms. I was definitely feeling the tension between them, but there was something else. They were fighting like brothers. Not to mention that they looked a lot alike. It was odd. But since they said they didn't know each other, I had no choice but to shrug off my thoughts.

Another question was unanswered too. Had Liam really heard a noise? Was it the same sound I'd heard or was that Liam that I'd heard? What had been the noise Liam had heard? Perhaps he'd heard the ghost.

I followed them down the hallway until both men disappeared into their rooms, shutting their doors with a bit of force. I hoped that was the last disruption I had for the evening.

With one last glance back, I went back down the flight of stairs to the second floor. Lifting the cat out of my spot, I crawled back into bed and stared at the ceiling for what seemed like forever. My thoughts ran wild in my head. The last twenty-four hours had been a whirlwind. Thoughts of the book popped into my mind. If Liam was looking for it, he could easily find it downstairs. Why would he want that book? Where had the mysterious tome come from and how would I find out?

I finally dozed off and didn't wake until the morning sun streamed through the window and splashed across my face. When I finally remembered that I had guests, I glanced over at the clock. It was five minutes after eight. I was the worst innkeeper in the history of hospitality.

I jumped up and didn't even bother to put on my bunny slippers. My feet slipped as I raced down the stairs and I reached out, grabbing the banister to keep from toppling headfirst all the way to the bottom. When I righted myself, I hurried the rest of the way, then raced through the house. Reaching the kitchen door, I stopped short, attempting to catch my breath, but my lack of breath wasn't just from the running.

CHAPTER TWELVE

Nicolas stood in front of the stove with a spatula in one hand and maple syrup in the other. This was beyond embarrassing. I was forcing my own guests to make their breakfast. I could see my mother shaking her head in my mind.

Nicolas hadn't noticed me watching him. How he hadn't heard me run through the house like a crazy woman was beyond me. The smell of cinnamon and syrup whirled through the air. He looked sexy with my polka dot apron tied around his waist. Underneath it he wore jeans and a black T-shirt. The casual look was good on him. But the dress pants and shirt he'd worn last night looked good too. As a matter of fact, I thought he'd look hot in just about anything.

As I was opening my mouth to announce my presence, he must have sensed me and turned around. "I saw your recipe book was open to the French toast. I hope you don't mind that I started to cook without you." He pointed at the sizzling pan.

Nicolas eyed me up and down. That was when I realized what I must have looked like. I eased my hand up to my hair and attempted to smooth it down. I probably looked like a peacock. I adjusted my shirt from where it had become twisted while sleeping.

"I'm sorry I overslept. You must think I'm a terrible hostess," I said.

My stomach fluttered at the sound of his laughter. "It's okay. You had a late night."

I stepped into the kitchen and stood beside him. He smelled so good, like fresh soap and maple syrup. My knees went weak standing next to him and I thought that I'd collapse into a pile on the floor any second.

"Please let me finish." I motioned for him to hand me the spatula.

He hesitated and studied me with his gorgeous blue eyes. Was he pausing because he knew my cooking sucked?

Finally, he handed me the spatula. "I really don't mind. If you'd like to get dressed, then I can finish."

Hmm. He had a point. I hadn't even brushed my teeth or my hair. Did I really want to sit across the breakfast table from this gorgeous man looking like a zombie? He smiled again and held his hand out for the spatula.

"Okay. I'll just go get dressed. If you're sure you don't mind?"

He shook his head. "I'd be honored to make breakfast for you."

That reminded me. Where was Liam? Was he still asleep? I hated to bring up the subject, but I decided to ask anything.

"Where is Mr. Rankin?" I asked.

Nicolas turned his attention back to the food and scooped the toast from the skillet. "He went out. I don't know where he went. I didn't ask."

Hmm. I guessed that was more of an answer than I'd expected.

"I'll just go change," I said, motioning over my shoulder.

He flashed a huge smile. For a split moment, something looked different about his appearance, but I couldn't place it. Whatever I'd thought I'd seen must have been my imagination because as I searched his features again, nothing seemed different. My mind was playing tricks on me.

I rushed back upstairs and slipped into jeans and my favorite cream-colored sweater. It was tight enough to accentuate my curves but not so tight that it looked as if I was trying to impress Nicolas or Liam. I pulled my hair back into a ponytail and brushed my teeth.

As I neared my bedroom door, the floorboard in the hallway squeaked. Was it that ghost again? I had to admit I was on edge thinking that there was possibly a ghost in the house. I tried to be tough, but it was a little creepy. Did I dare call Annabelle and tell her what I'd heard? No, it was best if I didn't tell her. She'd never set foot in the house again. But I had to talk with someone about what was happening.

I eased out the door expecting to see a ghost, but instead came face to face with Liam. He looked dashing in his dark pants and dark blue shirt. His compelling blue eyes, his firm features and the confident set of his shoulders didn't go unnoticed by me.

"Is everything all right?" I asked.

He looked into my room as I was closing the door. "I just wanted to apologize again for last night."

"Think nothing of it. It was no big deal, really." I shrugged dismissively. "Would you like breakfast? We're having French toast."

Would he figure out my plan to lure him into more conversation over breakfast?

I wouldn't dare tell him that Nicolas was preparing the meal. He'd find out soon enough though.

"I could go for French toast. Thanks." He flashed his perfect smile.

"Great. We can walk down together," I said breezily. Was my nonchalant act working? Probably not.

"I'd like that." The smile in his eyes contained a sensuous flame.

His infectious grin had set the tone and I couldn't help but reciprocate. "So where are you from, Mr. Rankin?"

"Please call me Liam."

"All right. Where are you from, Liam?"

A melancholy frown flitted across his features. "I'm from New Orleans."

"And you're here on business?" I asked.

"Yes, I'm investigating a case. But I'm afraid that I can't discuss it," he said.

How did he know I was going to ask what the case was about?

"I understand," I said as we moved down the steps.

What was so top secret that he couldn't discuss it?

"So this house is all yours now?" he asked.

Had I told him about inheriting it? I didn't remember having that conversation with him. I hadn't spoken to either of them about it. Even if I had, I doubted that Liam would talk to Nicolas about it. They didn't seem to discuss anything other than arguing.

I glanced over at him. "Yes, it is mine now. How did you know?"

"You told me, don't you remember?" He looked at me enigmatically.

I couldn't accuse him of being a liar. That would be rude. But I knew I hadn't told him. This was very weird.

"My family once had a place like this," he said softly.

I studied his clean-cut profile. The tenderness of his voice made him seem almost vulnerable at the moment. "Really? What happened to it?"

His expression stilled and grew serious. "It just got into the wrong hands, I suppose."

"That's unfortunate," I said.

"Yes, it most certainly is." Liam reached the bottom of the stairs first.

He held out his hand to help me down the bottom step. Without warning he flashed that gorgeous smile again and my stomach danced. He was a charmer.

"Thank you," I said softly, trying to hide a huge smile.

As we made our way through the library, Liam asked. "Have you noticed anything strange since you've moved in?"

I whipped a glance at him. "What makes you ask that?"

Had he seen the ghost?

He hesitated. Was he trying to think of what to say? Or was he afraid to tell me about what he'd seen?

"It's a big house. I figured maybe you'd heard the creaks and groans that come with them."

"Are you trying to scare me?" I asked.

He chuckled. "Of course not. Have you had many other guests?" he asked.

This was an answer that I didn't want to give. Should I lie or be truthful?

"As a matter of fact..." I paused. "You and Mr. Marcos are my first guests. But I hope you don't hold that against me," I said.

"Of course not. You're doing a wonderful job." A dimple appeared on each cheek.

"Even with the burnt pancakes?" I asked.

"Hey, the next batch was good." His eyes grew openly amused.

Nicolas must have heard us talking because he popped out from the kitchen. He was still wearing the red and white polka dot apron. Liam's face turned from pleasant to frustrated in a nanosecond.

"I thought I heard you talking. Breakfast is served." He wiped his hands on the apron.

"Are you working for Ms. LaVeau now?" Liam asked sharply.

"I made her breakfast," Nicolas said with a slight smile of defiance.

"You know, I'm not hungry after all," Liam said with a steely glare.

Nicolas shrugged. "Suit yourself."

"I have business to attend to. I'll see you later, Hallie." Liam reached for my hand and placed a delicate kiss against my skin.

After his lips lingered for a second, I watched as he moved across the library and out of sight.

When I turned to Nicolas, I said, "When are you going to tell me what is going on between the two of you? I'm not stupid and I know something is going on. You know each other and I don't believe you're being honest with me."

"Please, let's have breakfast and we'll talk." He stretched his hand out to me.

That statement made me wonder if I'd want to eat after I heard what he had to say.

As soon as my fingers touched the warmth of his outstretched hand my whole body tingled. His gaze looked with mine and I found it hard to look away, as if I was being hypnotized.

"Why do I feel as if I am about to receive bad news?" I tried to keep the banter relaxed.

He squeezed my hand and smiled. "Come on, I put a lot of effort into breakfast."

I sighed and allowed Nicolas to escort me into the dining room. He'd even set the table with my pretty white napkins and the special crystal glasses that I liked to use. In spite of the knot in my stomach my mouth watered. Nicolas had outdone himself with breakfast. Strawberries and powdered sugar decorated the French toast on the plates. He'd even cleaned up the kitchen.

Nicolas pulled out the chair for me and said, "Please have a seat."

"I'm pretty sure I'm the one who is supposed to be doing all this for my guest," I said as I sat in the chair.

"You can make breakfast any time. I don't get a chance to make breakfast that often. I'm usually on the go too much."

I studied his every move as I took a sip of my orange juice. "So tell me what is going on. How do you know Mr. Rankin and why did you tell me I was in danger simply by being around him?"

Nicolas looked down at his plate for a moment and finally met my gaze. "I'm just passing through on business."

What? Okay, he was crazy. That's not what I'd asked. They were just playing games with me.

"I don't believe you. There has to be more to your visit. Do you work with Mr. Rankin?"

Just when he was about to answer, Nicolas' cell phone rang.

"Will you excuse me for just a moment?" he said while pulling the phone from his pocket.

I nodded as he stood and moved out of the room. After a couple more minutes, Nicolas hadn't returned and I went back to the library to check on his call status. When I reached the library, I found Nicolas not on the phone, but standing close to the shelves studying the titles on the bindings. I got the feeling that he was looking for something. Did he want a book to read? Would he notice the spell book to his left? I didn't want him reading that. I'd have to explain what it was and I wasn't sure he'd understand the whole witchcraft thing.

As if he sensed my presence, he turned around. The expression on his face was odd, as if he'd been caught doing something he shouldn't be doing.

"I didn't hear you enter. I was just looking at the wonderful collection of books you have." He pulled one of the books from the shelf.

"They were my Great-Aunt Maddy's. She left me this manor recently," I said.

Nicolas flashed a knowing smile. "Is that right? Is that why you decided to run it as a bed-and-breakfast?" He placed the book back in its spot.

I nodded. "What else was I going to do with all the rooms, right?"

He nodded, then walked over to the desk in the middle of the room. I was just glad that he'd moved further away from the mysterious book. Why did I have such an overwhelming desire to hide it? Out of all the books on the shelves, it was unlikely that he'd pick up that one book. Regardless, I didn't want to chance it. They first opportunity I got, I'd hide the book.

"How long have you been in the manor?" he asked while running a finger along the intricate detail of the wooden desk.

I couldn't help but imagine that I was that desk and his finger was tracing the curves of my body. I shook off the thought and met his gaze.

"Just a few weeks," I said.

"You've certainly been busy then." Nicolas fixed his gaze on my face and looked away as quickly as possible.

Finally, I glanced back at him. "Yes, I have. There was a lot of cleaning and prep for the bed-and-breakfast."

He turned to look at the books again. "So your aunt collected books?"

Again I was nervous that he'd find the spell book. I needed to get him away from here.

"She collected a lot of things," I said. "So how about your breakfast? You worked so hard to prepare it. Would you care for refreshments?"

"Refreshments?" He quirked a brow.

I'd instantly regretted the question. What was wrong with me? This wasn't 1875 and he wasn't my gentleman caller. "There's more orange juice and coffee in the kitchen."

The kitchen far away from the book, I thought. When he didn't take the hint, I moved a little closer to the door, hoping he would follow like a little puppy. He didn't budge as he fixed his gaze on me. I wasn't about to leave him alone in this room with the book.

Nicolas must have realized this, because he finally said, "Yes, I'd like that."

He moved toward me with ease and my heart skipped a beat. As soon as he was munching on breakfast, I'd slip back into the room and grab the book. But where would I hide it? I could put it back in the attic where I'd found it. Why had it been there in the first place? Had Aunt Maddy hidden it?

No, there had to be a safer place... a place closer to me. A spot where I could keep my eye on it. But other than carrying it around on my body at all times, where would that be? I certainly spent a lot of time in the kitchen, but that was a place my guests would go too, considering I'd discovered Nicolas there this morning. Heck, they could go anywhere in the house... except for one room. My bedroom. That was off limits. A flash of one of the men in my room crossed my mind. They were certainly both sexy, but they were off limits too.

"You know, I just remembered something that I need to take care of. I hope you'll forgive me."

What could I say? No? I hadn't gotten the answers I wanted from him yet and it looked as if he was trying not to answer them. What could have been so important that he had to take off in such a hurry?

CHAPTER THIRTEEN

That night I woke again for no apparent reason. What had woken me this time? I couldn't say for sure that it had been a noise. I lay perfectly still and listened, but the only sound was the cat purring in my ear. The house was silent... eerily silent. A strange feeling settled over me, as if eyes watched me. It was like a presence was right there beside me. I was almost afraid to look around the room to see if anyone was there. But the curiosity would get the better of me, so I knew I had to look.

I slowly rolled over in the bed and looked to my side. When I saw a woman standing near my bed, I sucked in a deep breath. My mouth wouldn't work though. Screaming or even speaking wasn't an option. My eyes widened and my heart thumped wildly as I stared at this woman. Her gaze was fixed on me.

The woman wore a long, light blue dress. She had long flowing blonde hair and her eyes glowed a brilliant blue. There was one thing definitely strange about her though. I could see right through her body. I lay there paralyzed. Neither one of us made a move.

Finally, I managed to squeak out, "Who are you?"

She didn't answer, but instead just continued to stare at me.

"What do you want?" I demanded.

Still no answer.

Why wasn't she speaking? Slowly she began to move. She didn't walk, she glided. Her arms and legs flowed like water. Was I finally seeing the ghost? This was definitely not my great-great-great-grandfather. Who was she and where had she come from?

When she reached the door, she paused. Then she turned around and looked at me again. She had a haunted look in her eyes. That was fitting, right? What did she want with me? After a couple seconds, she turned and floated right out the bedroom door. Definitely a ghost. Annabelle would have had a heart attack.

I lay there with the covers pulled up close to my face and shivered. The room was freezing. Watching the door for what seemed like forever, I waited for her to return. I listened for more noise but heard nothing. Maybe Liam really had heard a noise in the attic. I'd told Annabelle that dealing with a ghost was just part of living in a big old manor house, but now that I was faced with the true reality of it, I wasn't sure it was as easy as I'd thought it would be.

The book was calling to me again. Since I couldn't sleep after what had happened, I allowed it to lure me from bed. I pulled it out from its hiding place and slipped downstairs to the kitchen. The men should be fast asleep in their rooms and I shouldn't be disturbed. Placing the book down on the table, I sat on the stool in front of it. I stared for a minute, wondering if I should really open the book. Was there another spell that I could read? Even so, I still didn't know what the spell was for. And look what happened the last time I performed a spell.

But I supposed it wouldn't hurt to have one more peek inside the book. Maybe I'd stumble on a clue as to what it all meant. My fingers paused on the cover. Releasing a deep breath, I finally opened the cover. There were several pages that seemed to be introduction pages, but I still couldn't read them. Had I thought they'd magically change? Had I thought I'd be able to somehow read them now? Nothing had changed to make that possible. Was there a spell that I could perform that would allow me to read the foreign language? Who was I kidding? I couldn't even perform a spell to make my cooking better, much less translate an unknown language.

I flipped through the pages again and nothing made sense. I wasn't able to read one single word. If only there was a way to search for the language online. Maybe I'd take the book to the library. Would they have something with this language? I let out a sigh and closed the book. Now what?

Just as I was about to pick the book up and go back upstairs, that same strong wind began to blow—a slight breeze at first, then a wild gust. The air blew the hair on my head around wildly and moved dishes with ease. Thank goodness they hadn't fallen to the floor. Would the noise wake Nicolas and Liam? The book cover flipped open and the pages flicked until they finally came to rest. The wind subsided and I looked down at the open page. To my surprise, it was written in English. I could actually read the page.

It was another spell, but it still didn't say what the outcome would be. Should I risk doing the spell? An unseen force was pulling me to it though, making me what to give it a try. How much worse could it be than the spells that I was already trying?

After studying the list of ingredients, I rushed around the kitchen checking to see if I had all that was needed. Luckily, Aunt Maddy had an abundant supply of almost anything that I would need to work magic. Again, I plucked the ingredients for the spell from the shelves— basil, bay leaves, frankincense, just to name a few. I'd have to hurry in case Liam or Nicolas came downstairs. Being caught in the middle of pouring something into my cauldron would be hard to explain. Once all the ingredients were added, I waited for something to happen. A spark, a poof of smoke, a flash of light... something... anything. But still nothing was different. Apparently, I'd make a mistake, yet again.

I did receive a call from Abigail Smith saying that I'd messed up her beauty potion and she now had warts on her face. That was what she got for not going to my mother for those types of things. I cleaned up my mess, grabbed the book and hurried back upstairs. No noise came from either of my guests' rooms. Thank goodness they hadn't heard me. I placed the book back securely under the floor into its hiding place and slipped into bed.

As I tried to drift off to sleep, my thoughts went back to the ghost. Was she around all the time? Listening and watching everything that happened in the house? I wasn't quite sure how long I'd lain there watching the door before I finally drifted off back to sleep. I did know that for a second night running I didn't sleep much. That would make for another difficult day.

I woke to that strange sensation of not being alone in the room again. The ghost of the mysterious woman stood by the door this time, staring me. She wasn't surrounded by a bluish glow. How long had she been watching me sleep? I tried to ask her what she wanted again, but I received the same blank stare. Once again, she turned after a minute and vanished out the door. I'd expected some remnants of the apparition, a trail of mist or a puff of smoke, but she had disappeared as if she'd never even existed. I wondered if my mind was just playing tricks on me.

This time I jumped up and slipped out the door after her. I didn't find the ghost, but Liam was standing in the hallway with his back facing me. Was he sleepwalking? He wore blue and white striped pajama bottoms, but no shirt. His broad shoulders tapered down to a trim waist. He turned around and looked at me. The way he soaked in my full appearance, I knew he was fully awake. At that moment I wished I was wearing more than a short satin nightgown. I tried not to stare at his hard chest and tight abs, but that was virtually impossible.

"Did you hear something?" I whispered.

He gave me a knowing look. Had he seen her too?

"It must have been the wind," he said.

He knew it wasn't the wind just as much as I knew it wasn't the wind.

We watched each other for a few seconds longer until I said, "I'd better go back to bed."

I turned around and hurried back into my room before he had a chance to answer. After securing the lock on my door, I climbed back into bed and pulled the covers up close. I'd have to ask my mother if she knew who this spirit could be. Maybe Aunt Maddy had mentioned a ghost in the past. I knew one thing for sure, this spirit wanted something from me and I wasn't sure I wanted to give it whatever that something was.

***

Liam and Nicolas had both declined breakfast by leaving a note on my door the next morning. Where had they gone so early? Was it their so-called business in town? Maybe I should follow them sometime just to see exactly where they went. That kind of move wouldn't win me the innkeeper of the year award, but I needed answers.

When I arrived at Bewitching Bath and Potions Shop, I pulled up in front, but hesitated before climbing out of the car. I knew my mother would have a million questions for me as soon as I walked through the door.

Fat bars of sunlight streamed through the windows and brightened the already white space. My mother was standing behind the counter. This time she had both eyebrows still on her face. A large pot with her ingredients surrounding it covered the space in front of her. She was hard at work.

She smiled and tapped her finger against a box next to her. "We have a bunch of new orders to fill."

I quirked a brow. Why wasn't she demanding to know everything?

"It's been busy already this morning," she said as she continued wrapping soaps in their packages.

I grabbed my apron and looped it over my head. Pulling out items from the box, I continued to stare at her.

Finally she looked up at me. "What?" she asked.

"Don't act all innocent with me. What's going on?" I asked.

"What do you mean?" she asked sweetly.

"Why aren't you asking me what happened?" I stared at her.

She continued her work, pouring an unknown concoction into a pot. "I figure if you want me to know you'll tell me."

Oh, now I got it. "You're upset because I didn't return your call last night."

"I still feel magic all around you. And it's not the normal feeling. Are you going to tell me what's going on?" she asked with a suspicious glare.

I continued taking things out of the box without looking over at her. I knew she was glaring at me. The staring was getting to me too. She had always had a way of making me talk. I knew she would win this battle.

Finally I gave in. "Okay. I found this book the other day and I performed a couple spells out of it. It seems like there's been this strange energy around me since it showed up. Or maybe it has been since Nicolas and Liam showed up."

"Oh. You're on a first-name basis with them?" She raised an eyebrow.

"Mother! Out of everything I just said, that is the one thing you decided to focus on?" I looked at her incredulously.

79

She shrugged. "No, it's not the one thing, but it was just the first thing."

"Well, using their last names seems so formal." I sniffed one of the soaps. "I want them to think of my place as a cozy, friendly spot."

Uh-huh. Yeah, my mother wasn't buying it and I knew that wasn't the reason either. But I'd never admit it out loud.

"So tell me about this book," my mother said. "Where did you find it?"

"It was in the attic," I said nonchalantly

She brushed her hands on her apron "Well, your great aunt had a lot of old books."

My voice lowered. "This one was different from the others."

"How so?" she asked.

"Well, for starters, it wasn't on the shelf with the rest of them. I found it upstairs in the attic. Or more like it found me." I stirred the pot then met her stare.

"Honey, what are you talking about?"

Just then the phone rang and she held up her finger, making me pause. It was just as well though. I was having second thoughts about telling her about the book. Maybe I could think of something else to say. I could start talking about Nicolas and Liam. That would distract her from the situation.

My mother cast a glance at me as she apologized to the person on the other end of the line. What had I done this time?

She hung up the phone and looked at me. "Been doing spells in the middle of the night, have you?"

"I knew that witch Abigail would rat me out. I can't help it if I messed up her spell. Besides, I can't exactly do spells in front of my guests. Well, unless it was an emergency."

"Can't you wait until they leave?" The amused look suddenly left her eyes. "It wasn't an emergency was it?"

"Not exactly. Well, I don't know if it was an emergency." I bit my bottom lip.

"You're not making any sense, sweetie. Why don't you tell me the whole story?" She patted the stool next to her and motioned for me to sit down.

"There's not much to tell really. Like I said, I found the spell book in the attic. It was hidden behind the beams. I don't know who hid it there, but I'm assuming it was Aunt Maddy."

"That sounds like something she'd do. She probably forgot about it. What kind of spells are in the book?" my mother asked.

This was the tricky part, telling her the story had been easy up until now.

"I'm not sure what kind of spells are in the book." I plopped down on the stool behind the counter.

"What do you mean you don't know what kind of spells? Aren't they labeled?" Her eyes widened.

"I don't know if they are labeled," I said.

"You're still not making any sense. Did you hit your head again?" She touched my forehead.

I let out a deep breath. "What I'm trying to say is the book is in a different language."

She froze with her hand midair. "What language is it written in?" she asked with wide eyes.

I picked at a piece of paper on the counter, trying to find the right words. "I don't know. I've never seen it before."

"Then how did you do a spell out of the book?" she asked.

I shook my head. "This is the really strange part. A big wind came through and opened the book precisely to a page that was written in English."

Her face blanched. "Then why the heck did you do the spell? Did it say what it was for?"

I shrugged. "I was compelled to. I don't know what came over me."

81

"This is not good." She wiped her forehead and narrowly missed the eyebrow.

She looked at me as if to say 'look at what you've done.'

"I need to call the Coven," my mother said with alarm in her voice.

I stopped her from reaching for her phone. "No! You can't do that."

"Halloween, you don't know what this book is or what it could do. You have to seek advice from people who are experienced in this sort of thing," she pleaded.

She did have a point. But I didn't want them involved. Not yet anyway.

"Just give me a little time to figure it out on my own, okay? I promise if I don't figure it out I will tell the Coven. Do you promise not to tell them yet?" I asked.

She hesitated, then finally nodded.

"Thank you," I said, giving her a warning glare.

The bell on the door jangled and we both looked up. I was thankful for the momentary distraction. A man carrying a beautiful bouquet of roses approached us.

"Oh, how beautiful," my mother cooed.

If I'd known that roses could have captured her attention so much I would have sent flowers a long time ago. I'd have to remember her reaction.

"I have a delivery for…" He paused and looked down at his clipboard.

My mother held out her hands but stopped short.

The man finished his sentence. "Halloween LaVeau?" He quirked a brow and looked down at the paper to make sure he'd read it correctly.

"That's me," I said with shock in my voice.

CHAPTER FOURTEEN

I'd never received roses before. Well, unless you counted the time my date cut roses from the bush outside my front door. I took the vase from the man's outstretched hand, then placed it on the counter for closer inspection. There was a note attached.

"Who are they from?" my mother asked with excitement.

I pulled the card out and read it while my mother loomed over my shoulder.

Dear Ms. LaVeau,

I'm sorry for the way I've acted since arriving at your beautiful home. Please allow me to take you to dinner to make up for my actions.

The note attached was signed from Nicolas. My mother had a huge grin spread across her face. He had some nerve. Did he think I could be persuaded to trust him with a few flowers? They would die in a few days anyway. Then what? If he couldn't tell me why Liam must leave, if he couldn't be truthful with me, then why would I want to spend any time with him? Except, I did want to spend time with him. I wanted to know more about him. I wanted to taste his lips...

The bell announced another visitor and snapped me out of my daydream.

"Oh, dear," my mother said.

Oh dear, was right. Liam was walking toward me. A strange, eager look flashed in his eyes.

Liam looked especially handsome in his casual black slacks and olive green shirt. He had a smile on his face that looked devilish and sweet at the same time.

"Good morning," he said softly.

His voice would make any girl's heart flutter. What was he doing here? He looked at the roses and a slight look of disappointment fell over his handsome features.

"Is everything okay?" I asked.

"Yes, everything is fine." He looked at my mother and smiled. "Hello, Mrs. LaVeau. You look especially beautiful today."

She blushed. "Thank you."

Liam stepped close. "I wanted to ask you a question, if that's okay?"

I glanced to my mother. She picked up a few items and pretended to go back to work, but I knew she was really eavesdropping.

"You look stunning today," he said.

"Thank you," I said, hoping that I didn't blush.

He paused. He was making me nervous. What could he possibly have to say? Was it about the ghost that I knew he'd seen last night?

"I'm listening," I continued, pulling items out of the box. Things needed to appear as normal as possible, although I didn't know what normal was anymore.

"I know things have been strange since my arrival. I hope you'll let me treat you to dinner to make up for my behavior." His lips curved at the corners.

My mother giggled. This was unbelievable. What would I do? Although it was just dinner. I supposed I could let the men treat me to a meal, as long as it was separately of course. They'd kill each other if we all went to dinner together.

Liam stared at me expectantly.

Finally, I answered. "When did you have in mind?"

"How about tonight?" Liam's voice was smooth and sexy.

Nicolas might be upset if I went out with Liam before him, so maybe I'd better make it tomorrow night.

"How about tomorrow night?" I asked.

He nodded. "Okay. Tomorrow night it is. " His gaze was fixed on me as he reached out and grabbed my hand, placing his lips softly against my skin. "I'll see you later," he said, releasing my hand.

My mother and I watched as he disappeared out the door and down the sidewalk. When he'd turned the corner and was no longer in sight, I turned to my mother.

"Now what are you going to do?" my mother asked.

I shrugged. "I guess I have two dates."

"You have dates with men who are staying in your home and who also seem to hate each other. You'd better figure out what is going on between them."

"I intend to."

My mother shook her head. So I'd gotten myself into another pickle. She shouldn't be surprised. Nothing new.

"Well, you'd better find out about the book. Because you need to before I'm forced to tell the Coven about it."

"I promise to look into it today. If you'd let me leave this shop, I could do some research right now."

"You always manage to leave just when the work is getting fun."

I snorted. "I thought the work was always fun?"

***

After finding a parking spot, I grabbed the book and made my way down the sidewalk toward the tall Gothic-style building that housed the public library. The more I walked the more I felt as if someone followed me. It felt as if a dark and dangerous presence trailed my every movement, like a penetrating shadow hovering over me. Out of the corner of my eye I caught a flash of the silhouette of a man. My imagination was in overdrive because for a moment I thought it looked a lot like Nicolas, or was that Liam?

Ignoring my uneasiness, I carried the book into the library as if it was a fragile egg. A few patrons sat at tables on the right, but otherwise the inside of the building was empty. The librarian behind the reference desk looked up at me, so I took the book over to her, hoping she would have answers to my many questions. When I opened the book, she looked at me like I was crazy when I showed her the language.

"Do you recognize the writing on these pages?" I asked with hope in my voice.

She pushed the glasses up on the bridge of her nose and peered down at the book. "I've never seen anything like that before." She pushed the book back toward me as if she wanted me to get it the heck out of there. "Sorry."

I let out a deep breath. "Thanks, anyway."

She went back to her computer screen, letting me know that I'd get no more help from her.

That strange presence had invaded my space in the library too, so I decided to hurry up and get the heck out of there. Of course I didn't see anyone following me, but I felt them. I was officially losing it. After some searching up and down the stacks, I picked up a couple books on obscure languages, but I didn't hold out much hope that I'd find the information I was looking for.

After hurrying out of the library and jumping into my car, I knew I couldn't avoid it any longer and I'd have to head to the manor. Before I arrived though, I wanted to call Nicolas. Somehow it seemed easier if I didn't have to look him in the eyes. The way his gaze penetrated right through me made me feel slightly out of control, although I'd have to deal with looking at him when I went to dinner with the man.

Nicolas had left his cell phone number on the card attached to the flowers. Yes, giving him an answer over the phone would be much easier than doing it in person. How would I avoid telling him about my dinner plans with Liam? I wouldn't mention it, and I hoped he didn't bring up his name either. But then again, I wanted to get to the bottom of why they were fighting. As much as I didn't want to, it looked as if I'd have to tell him about our plans.

After a quick phone call, I'd thanked Nicolas for the flowers and agreed to dinner with him. I couldn't believe I'd done it... I'd agreed to go out with him too. Of course I hadn't had the nerve to ask if he'd been following me into the library. I would have appeared crazy if I had. He hadn't followed me, right? I'd read too many mystery novels. My imagination was out of control.

Nicolas had said he had the perfect place picked out for us. That seemed terrifying and exhilarating all at once. I had to confess what I'd done to Annabelle—that I'd agreed to go out with both men.

When she picked up the phone, I said, "I have something to tell you and you're probably going to be shocked."

I still hadn't told her about seeing the ghost and I wasn't going to either. Not unless I absolutely had to.

"If this has anything to do with finding old bones in your attic, I don't want to know."

I chuckled. "No, it's nothing like that."

"One of your guests killed the other one?" she quipped.

"No. Well, not yet anyway." As if she could see me through the phone, I studied my fingernails, trying to play it cool. "In fact, I received roses from Nicolas and an invitation for dinner, then Liam asked me out for dinner too."

"Get out. What do they want?" Her voice shot up in surprise.

I laughed. "My thoughts exactly."

"You said yes to both of them, right? You have to find out what all of this is about."

"Don't worry, I intend to. I'm going out with Nicolas tonight."

"Good luck. Do you need me to come for backup?" she asked.

"I'll call you if I do," I said with a chuckle.

The massive structure towered over me as I pulled up in front of LaVeau Manor. Branches on the old oak trees swayed in the wind, as if waving a warning. There was an undeniable essence about the house. Liam's car was there along with Nicolas' rental car. I hoped I could slip upstairs without seeing either of them. I had a few hours before my date with Nicolas and I wanted to look through the library books I'd checked out. With the library and the spell books clutched in one arm and roses in the other, I hurried up the steps, not looking over my shoulder to see if anyone followed me. The presence from the library still haunted me.

When I stepped into the foyer, I paused and listened for noise. The place seemed bigger each time I came home.

The cat meowed loudly and rubbed against my leg. "Sorry, Pluto, I don't have a treat right now," I whispered.

I placed the flowers on the hall table and soaked in another big whiff of their fragrant aroma. Movement sounded above me grabbing my attention. My heart rate increased when I realized it sounded as if someone was walking around in my room. I'd locked the door, so who could possibly be in there? That was when it hit me. With the books in my arms, I rushed up the stairs. What was I going to say if it actually was a ghost? Shoo, ghost, shoo?

I panted for breath as I reached the landing, then ran to my bedroom door. It was still closed. I pulled the key from my pocket and shoved it in the lock. The sound of someone walking around continued from the other side of the door. Whoever was there didn't care that I was about to walk in on them. I pushed the door open and let out a gasp.

CHAPTER FIFTEEN

A woman stood beside my bed.

She smiled wide, and then said with a sweet Southern drawl, "I'm glad you're home."

"Who the hell are you?" I asked.

I asked, but I knew who she was. Well, I didn't know exactly, but I'd seen her before. This was the ghost who'd been in my room for the past two nights. She looked different now though. She had been see-through before, but now she looked like any other living person. She was a beautiful woman with long blonde hair and big blue eyes. When I'd first seen her she wore a blue gown, but now she wore a tight green dress that hugged her voluptuous curves.

"Who are you and what are you doing in my house?" I demanded, trying to hide the shakiness in my voice.

"You called me here, so why are you asking me?" she replied with slight disdain.

I placed the books on the table next to the door.

"What do you mean? I called you here. How could I call you here when I don't even know who you are?"

She raised her arm up and pointed at the table where I'd just set the books.

"What?" I asked. "What are you trying to tell me? Why don't you just come out with it already?"

"You don't pick up on clues, do you?" she asked as she stared at me.

"No, I don't suppose I do. I'm having a hard time wrapping my mind around the fact that I'm talking to a ghost. You are a ghost, right? I saw you for the past two nights. Did I not?"

"Yes, that was me," she said smugly.

Her cool demeanor irked me.

"So how did you get here?" I asked.

She pointed again. "I got here with the book. You called me here with the spell book."

I glanced over at the book. The spells that I'd performed. How was that possible? Why had it happened?

"Was that you who made the pages turn?"

She shook her head. "I don't control that book. You control that book. It's your spell book. You're the one who has all the power."

"Power? What kind of power? I don't know what you're talking about. The book is not mine," I said.

Annoyance hovered in her eyes. I was getting on her last nerve.

An expression of satisfaction showed across her face. "I was just a ghost in this manor, now you have released me."

"Released you from what?"

"From the dead. I am alive again thanks to you." She looked very much alive.

"How is that possible? I am a terrible spell caster. There is no way I could have done this. This doesn't make any sense."

She shrugged and sat on my bed. "Don't ask me. All I know is I watched you when you performed the spell. Then little by little I came back from the dead."

I rubbed my temples. Who would I call? I needed answers. How would I find out what was going on? I didn't want to believe that I could bring the dead back with one little spell. But I couldn't deny that it was a big coincidence that I'd performed the spells and then this woman showed up claiming to be a former ghost. What would I do to get rid of her? The last thing I needed was for anyone to find out what I'd done.

"I do hope you have a room for me? Although I could stay with one of the fine men who are currently occupying your other rooms." She twisted a strand of her golden locks around her finger and batted her eyelashes.

Uh-oh, this could be a huge problem. She looked like trouble.

"You can't stay here," I said in a panic.

"Well, you can't kick me out on the street," she snapped. "You're the reason I'm here. You have to let me stay until I can make other arrangements. I've been dead for a number of years and I don't exactly have the resources to do anything else right now."

I let out a deep breath. She did have a valid point. I couldn't just kick her out. Well, I guessed I could kick her out, but I didn't have the heart to do that to her.

"You have to tell me who you are at least." I crossed my arms in front of my chest. I wanted to put together all the pieces, but she wasn't helping.

She flashed her million-watt smile. "My name is Isabeau Scarrett. Pleased to meet you, Halloween."

"It is very disturbing to know that you know everything about me."

"Yes, I do know most things. Although I refrained from popping in the bathroom when you were in there." She shivered.

"Thank you," I said drily.

"I was a witch like you once. Well, let me rephrase that. I was a witch, but I was quite a bit better at it than you." She grimaced in with mocking humor.

I rolled my eyes. "Thank you for insulting me."

"It's not insulting. It's just stating the facts. I watched you try magic since you moved in. And it was not very good." She shook her head.

"Where are you from?" I asked.

"Far away," she said as she stood, then walked over to my closet. "I hope you don't mind if I borrow some of your clothing. Just until I can buy a new wardrobe." She opened my closet door.

"I'm kind of particular about my clothing," I said as I moved closer to the ghost, er, woman.

She looked at me incredulously, then shook her head. "Oh, dear. You really need to go on a shopping trip. There is nothing good in here."

I placed my hand on my hip. "So now you're insulting my clothing?"

The sound of footsteps caught our attention and we both looked at the door.

"It sounds like one of your guests is in the hallway." She brushed around me and I hurried after her.

How would I explain her presence?

This couldn't be happening, could it? I had to be dreaming. I reached out and poked the woman's side with my index finger.

"Ouch. What did you do that for?" she asked with a scowl.

I pasted on a smile of nonchalance. "I wanted to make sure you were real. I figured I was dreaming."

"I can assure you I am one hundred percent real." Her coolness was evidence that she was not amused.

When I made it out into the hallway, Liam was turning the corner to go up the next flight of stairs.

"Hello there," the former ghost called out.

Liam turned around to look at us. Why had he been on the second floor? Was he coming to my room? He froze when he spotted Isabeau. She sashayed over to him with a devilish smile on her face. She walked a complete circle around him, looking him up and down. Liam remained frozen, as if he didn't know what to do or say. I'd never seen him this flustered.

"Hello, and what might your name be?" she asked with a devilish tone.

He stiffened as though she'd struck him. "Liam Rankin."

She knew who he was. If she'd been hanging around the manor as a ghost, then she had to know him. She was just playing games. Did Liam recognize her as the ghost? Perhaps that was why he looked so confused. I couldn't tell him that I'd brought her back from the grave.

"Are you a guest here at the manor?" Liam asked.

She looked at me, then back at him. "That depends. I will be if Halloween will be so kind as to find me a room."

I'd put her in the worst room for using my full name. That was totally unnecessary. Plus, I didn't like the way she was acting around Liam. A little subtlety went a long way, but obviously that was something she knew nothing about. She'd put me on the spot. I couldn't say no now.

Liam stepped back from Isabeau as she moved closer. Isabeau was sexy and alluring and apparently wanted to make up for the years she'd spent in the grave.

"Come on, Isabeau. Let me show you to your room. You must be exhausted from your long travels." I grabbed her arm.

Liam quirked a suspicious eyebrow, but didn't say anything about my comment. I motioned for her to follow me and she reluctantly obeyed. I'd put her in the room across from mine so that I could keep my eye on her. There was no way I'd let her stay on the third floor.

"You call me Hallie, got it?" I whispered.

"Sure thing, Halloween. I mean, Hallie."

I glared at her and she flashed an innocent smile. Kicking her out was sounding more and more like the better plan.

Isabeau followed me into the spacious room. I stood by the door as she walked into the middle of the space.

Another large wood bed like the one in my room sat in the middle of the far wall. It was covered with rich burgundy comforter and many plush pillows. A velvet-covered chair was by the window with a small table, a perfect spot for reading. Enjoying a good book seemed to be the last thing on Isabeau's mind though.

"Um, there are towels in the bathroom. And the bed has fresh linens." I pointed at the bed.

This whole thing was so incredibly creepy.

"Are you going to tell me who you are and where you're from?" I didn't hide my impatience.

"I told you my name is Isabeau," she said curtly

"I know that, but other than your name, that is all I know about you. It would be nice to have a few more facts," I said.

"I'm from Enchantment Pointe and I died a number of years ago. Happy?" She smirked and crossed her arms in front of her chest.

"That's it?" I stared, speechless.

Was that all I could get from her? That wouldn't cut it.

"What is a number of years ago? What are we talking here? Two, four, sixteen, one hundred?" I retorted tartly.

"A woman never reveals her age, does she?" Her mouth curved into an innocent smile.

Hmm. She had me there.

"Do you have family in the area?" I regarded her with curiosity, then noticed the change on her face.

I had her now. If she didn't have family in the area then that meant she was probably so old that they had all died too.

She weighed the question, then answered, "My family wasn't originally from Enchantment Pointe."

I wouldn't let her win this little game. She might have the high score at the moment, but I was at the top of my game. We stared at each other, wondering who would make the next move. Silence hung in the air until the doorbell chimed, echoing throughout the house. She'd been saved by the bell. I wouldn't let her off the hook though.

"If you'll excuse me. I'll be right back." I offered the sweetest smile I could muster.

She smiled. "Of course take your time."

I stared for a second, then the bell rang again. I didn't trust her alone, but I had to answer the door. I just hoped that Liam had locked his door. Isabeau was going to be nothing but trouble for me. I sensed it already.

I hurried down the hallway and made my way down the steps to the front door. Who could it be at my door? I prayed it wasn't another strange guest. I wanted a successful business, but so far my guests had all been trouble, even Nicolas. I peeked out the little hole in the door, but didn't recognize the man standing on the veranda. There was something strange about him. Maybe it was the smudged glass in the door, but he looked blurry.

CHAPTER SIXTEEN

I eased the door open just enough to poke my head out. The man studied my face but remained expressionless. However, he was tapping his foot. Had I taken too long to answer the door? I glanced over his shoulder. Liam's car was still there, but apparently Nicolas had left. I hadn't heard him leave.

"May I help you?" I asked.

The man looked to be in his early eighties. Was he lost? He wore a tweed suit and a fedora hat. His expression soured as his lips pinched into a thin line.

"I heard you can bring me back?" His mouth pulled into an unpleasant grin.

My stomach dropped. Surely he wasn't talking about bringing him back from the dead? Was he dead? He wasn't see-through like Isabeau had been, but his features had a strange blurred quality.

"I'm sorry. Are you lost?"

"You can bring back the dead? I found you and I'd like for you to bring me back."

Oh no. My mouth dried and stomach turned. This couldn't be happening. What had I done now? The Coven was *so* not going to like this.

"I don't know what you are talking about." I tried to retain my composure and not freak out.

I'd try to play dumb and maybe this ghost would go away. How in the heck had he found me? When I performed the magic had it sent out some kind of message to the otherworld?

His face suddenly went grim. "No, no, no. You know what I'm talking about. I'm recently passed and I figure if you can bring me back that would be great. I got good tips to bet on the ponies in the upcoming races."

"You want to be brought back from the dead so you can gamble?" I stared at him in disbelief.

"We all have our vices," he said, as a flash of humor crossed his face.

I shook my head. "I'm sorry. I can't help you."

As I began to close the door, he placed his foot over the threshold. It was too late for me to stop the door from being shut. My reflexes weren't that good. I glanced down, but half of his foot was on the inside of the door and the other half remained on his body.

Why had he rang the doorbell to begin with? I was surprised he hadn't just come on in. I hurried away from the door. I needed to get the spell book to see if there was a spell to reverse what I'd done. Maybe if I ignored him he would just go away. Forgetting about something made it go away permanently, right? I ran up the stairs, but when I reached the landing, I remembered that I'd left my bedroom door open, and the spell book right out in the open for anyone to see. Well, the only people who were in the house at the moment whom I worried about seeing it was Liam and Nicolas. I didn't think Isabeau would have any interest in it. I hoped Liam wouldn't go into my room without me being in there. After all, I'd caught him on the second floor.

I hurried over to my room and slid through the door. When I glanced to my right, my stomach sank. The library books were there, but the spell book was missing. I glanced at the floor and on my bed, but there was no sign of it. I turned around and looked across the hallway. Isabeau's door was closed. Liam was up on the next floor. Would he really come down and sneak into my room while I was downstairs? That left only one place where the book could be: in the hands of my least favorite guest, Isabeau.

I ran over to her door and knocked.

"Who is it?" she asked in a sweet voice.

Isabeau wasn't fooling me with that act.

"Let me in," I demanded.

"What do you want?" Her words were as cool as ice water.

I lowered my voice. "I want the book back."

"What book?" she said with an even more unconvincing sweet tone.

"You know damn well what book I'm talking about. I want the spell book back. Now open the door before I open it for you." I pounded on the door again but she didn't respond.

I knew as an innkeeper that I probably shouldn't open the door and go into her room, but she wasn't a typical guest, so why should I act like a typical innkeeper? I pulled the key from my pocket and shoved it into the keyhole. I twisted the key, then grabbed the knob. Just as I had my hand on the knob, Isabeau opened the door. I almost fell flat on my face.

She chuckled. "You're not very patient are you?"

"Where is it?" I snapped.

"Where is what?"

I rushed over to the bed and looked around. "My spell book."

I pulled the covers down and yanked the pillow away. There on the bed was my spell book. I grabbed it and stomped toward the door.

I squared my shoulders and pointed at her. "Don't ever touch my things again or go into my room. I'll toss you out on your butt if you ever do it again."

"Just so you know, I have my eye on Nicolas and Liam." She plopped down on the bed and ran her hand across the silky comforter. "I sure wouldn't kick either of them out of my bed for eating crackers."

I refused to allow her to get under my skin. If Nicolas or Liam wanted Isabeau... well there was nothing I could do about that. It was their problem if they fell for Isabeau's fake laugh and annoying constant hair-flipping.

She smirked, but didn't offer another snarky comment. Good thing for her too because I was in no mood for it right now. Isabeau sure hadn't wasted any time before causing mischief.

After stomping back to my room, I closed my door and locked it. Isabeau would never get her hands on the book again. I carried the library books over to the bed and sat down, placing the spell book on my lap. First, I'd see if there was any information on what language the book was written. If I could figure that out, then maybe I'd find someone who knew how to read it.

The book looked the same. Had I really expected something to change? The spell appearing in English had been a fluke. Grabbing the other books, I flipped through the pages until my eyes blurred. It was no use. There was no match for the language in any of the books. Not even close. I opened the spell book again. It looked the same. I'd waited for another wind to pop up, but it never happened. When I needed the magic the most...

I shuffled through the pages again, but they were still all in the same mysterious language. I couldn't even find the pages with the spell I'd performed. I knew I'd seen it. I hadn't imagined it. How had this happened? It was looking more and more like I'd have to ask the Coven for advice, as much as I didn't want to. Who else did I have to ask? They were my only connection to the magic world.

The search for the book and a reversal spell had so consumed me that I'd forgotten about the man at my front door. Was he still out there? I opened my closet door and pulled up the loose floorboard and slipped the book back under it. Now that Isabeau was alive she wouldn't be able to slip into my room anytime she wanted. I'd keep my door locked at all times. There was no way anyone was getting their hands on that book. I'd made a mistake once, but I'd never let that happen again.

Moving over to the window, I peered down, expecting to see the ghost. The man had seemingly vanished. Maybe he'd gone for good. He hadn't been a dream.

As if he'd read my mind, the echo of the doorbell rang out through the house again, jarring me from my thoughts. Uh-oh. I should have known it wouldn't be that easy. It looked as if he wasn't going away anytime soon. Soon I'd run out of rooms. And the bad part was that the once-dead guests didn't even have money to pay me for their visits. But I guessed I had been responsible for bringing them back. The least I could do was to offer them a place to stay.

Apparently, the spell book really had given me the power to reanimate the dead. It took a day for the magic to work, but now that it had, I knew that I was in trouble.

When I reached the door, I peeked out again. To my relief, the man wasn't there. Annabelle stood in front of the door, but she seemed distracted. She was looking over her shoulder. What had she seen? Was the man still hanging around? How was I going to tell her about what had happened?

I opened the door and she motioned for me to step outside.

"I thought you may need help picking out something to wear for your date. Of course you'll have to bring the contents of your closet downstairs. I need to be close to the door in case I have to run out." She looked around suspiciously.

Annabelle had long legs and could run fast if she needed to. It wouldn't surprise me if she took off in a sprint.

A whisper of a breeze floated across my skin as I stepped out onto the veranda and looked around. The treetops stirred, but other than that, all was quiet and the elderly man was nowhere in sight. I didn't trust him and waited for him to reappear. He wouldn't leave that easily. If I told Annabelle that there really were ghosts she'd never come in the house again. But I had to tell her. There was no way around it. She'd just have to get over her fear.

"What are you looking for?" Annabelle asked.

I ran my hand through my hair and let out a deep breath. "Did you see a man standing out here when you pulled up?"

She glanced around. "No, why? Did you have another potential guest?"

I stared for a beat. "I'm not sure."

"You don't look so well. Your face is a little white. Why don't you sit down?" She grabbed my arm.

"I'm fine. It's just that there's something I have to tell you." A knot formed in my stomach.

"Oh no. This can't be good. Are you all right? Is your mother all right?" she asked with panic in her voice.

I nodded. "She's fine. And I'm okay."

"You don't sound confident. Hurry and tell me what's wrong before I hyperventilate."

I opened my mouth to answer, but was cut off by Isabeau's voice. Annabelle's eyes widened and I turned to see Isabeau standing in the doorway. She slipped through the house like a cat so it was no surprise that I hadn't heard her sneak up. She had that look a cat got when it ate the canary.

"Hello," she purred.

CHAPTER SEVENTEEN

Annabelle looked at me as if to say, *Aren't you going to introduce us?*

I reluctantly said, "Annabelle, this is my new guest, Isabeau."

"Nice to meet you," Annabelle said.

"Likewise." Isabeau smiled.

I couldn't break the news to Annabelle with Isabeau standing right there.

"Are you a guest of the manor too?" Isabeau asked Annabelle.

"No, I'm Hallie's best friend."

Isabeau narrowed her eyes. "Oh, well, isn't that sweet."

"Are you a guest?" Annabelle asked.

"Yes, I guess you could call me that. But I think it's just a little more than that."

"I'm confused." Annabelle looked from me to Isabeau.

I reached for the doorknob. "Isabeau, if you'll please excuse me and my friend. We have a few things to talk about."

Isabeau frowned but I didn't let that stop me from closing the door in her face. She mumbled something from the other side. Annabelle stood with her mouth wide open.

Finally, she said, "What the heck is going on, Hallie?"

"Let's sit down."

I knew I'd scared Annabelle to death at this point. We sat on the veranda steps and she looked at me expectantly. The sun inched toward the horizon. It would be dark soon.

"Did she show up like Liam and Nicolas?" Annabelle asked.

"Not exactly." I fidgeted with my hands.

"Will you just spit it out and stop being so cryptic?" She wiped her forehead. "You're giving me a panic attack."

I let out a deep breath. "Do you remember the spell book that I showed you? It was written in a strange language?" She nodded. "Well, somehow a couple of the spells appeared in English and I did the spells."

"Why would you do something like that?" she shrieked. Annabelle fanned her face. "Sorry, I panicked."

I shook my head. "I don't know. It was as if I wasn't myself. I was compelled to do it. Something strange came over me."

She stared wide-eyed at me for a second. "So what happened after the spell?"

"Well, nothing right away." I looked over my shoulder to see if Isabeau had slipped up on us again. She wasn't back there and there was no sign of the elderly man either. I continued, "But I just found out what happened because of the spell."

She stared with her mouth open, then she said. "What happened?"

"It appears that…" I twisted my hands again.

She motioned for me to continue.

"It appears that I turned a ghost back into a living person again." I rushed my words.

Annabelle opened her mouth to speak, but nothing would come out.

I stared for a second, then said, "Are you okay?"

Finally, she managed to speak. "I'm trying to figure out what you're telling me. How is that even possible?"

"It's magic, I guess." I shrugged.

"So let me get this straight, you turned a ghost into a living person?" Her eyes widened even more with the realization. "You mean to tell me that woman was a ghost?" She pointed toward the front door.

I nodded. "Yes, I'm afraid so."

"Who is she?" Annabelle looked back toward the door.

"Well, all she'll really tell me is that her name is Isabeau and she claims to be from Enchantment Pointe." Movement came from my left and I jumped. A bird fluttered from the shrub next to us and flew off into the distance.

"Are you okay?" Annabelle asked, grabbing my arm.

I nodded. "Just a little jumpy, I guess."

She shivered. "It's understandable considering our surroundings. So, do you know when and how she died?"

"No, she won't tell me anything. But she did steal my spell book. You know, the one I showed you earlier." I tucked a strand of hair behind my ear and peered out across the property toward the tree line.

"What? Why don't you kick her out of your home?" She sat up a little straighter.

"I can't do that. Where would she go? She has no money or anything. I'm the reason why she's here so I feel somewhat responsible. Plus, I don't want the Coven to find out what I've done. Not until I can reverse it at least." I rubbed my temples.

"How are you going to do that? Does she know you want to take away her born-again status?" Annabelle searched my eyes for an answer.

I glanced over my shoulder again. "No, and I don't intend to tell her either. She's not very nice."

"Apparently. Are Nicolas and Liam real?" Her eyes widened with the thought.

"What? Oh yeah." I waved off her concerns. "Well, I didn't do any spells from the book until after they'd already showed up, so I'm pretty sure they are real."

"Whew. That's good to hear. So what can we do to find out how to send her back?" She exhaled a deep breath.

"I don't know. I looked through the book again but none of it was in English again. Poof. It was gone again." I snapped my fingers.

"That doesn't make any sense," Annabelle said.

"None of this makes any sense. The men showing up, then Isabeau, and then..." I bit my lip, wondering if I should continue.

She whipped a look at me. "And then what? Do you have other guests??"

"There was a man who came to the door right before you got here. He said that he wanted me to bring him back." I glanced around for my ghostly visitor.

Annabelle stiffened. "You mean there are more ghosts roaming around? I told you this place was creepy as hell. But you wouldn't listen." She rubbed her arms.

"Okay. I'm listening now. But there's nothing I can do about it now other than try to get rid of them." I shook my head.

"Good luck with that. Now that you can bring back the dead, they'll all hear about it soon enough. This place will be crawling with ghosts." Annabelle stood, then grabbed my arm. "We need to get out of here."

"I can't leave. This is my home." I waved my arm through the air to showcase the place.

I knew what she really meant was she needed to get out of there. If I went with her, great, but if she had to leave me behind that was just an unfortunate fact of life.

Nicolas' car inched down the driveway, the pebbles crunching under the weight of the tires.

"I'll have to worry about fixing this after my dinner with Nicolas. I can't tell him I have to cancel because I have to cast a spell to get rid of a woman I brought back from the dead." My stomach was still clenched tight.

"Yes, I can see where that would be a bit awkward. What are you going to do with her in the meantime?" she asked.

I shrugged. "I don't know. Do you want to entertain her?"

Her eyebrows rose. "A ghost? No way."

"She's not a ghost anymore." I smiled despite the uncertainty.

"I don't know who she is, so unless you force me, I'll pass." She adjusted the purse strap on her shoulder.

"You know I'd never force you." I grinned.

"You forced me to go on that roller coaster one time." She grimaced, remembering the plummeting to earth, no doubt.

"I did not. I merely suggested that you were a chicken if you didn't do it."

Nicolas approached and cut off our conversation. I hadn't thought it possible, but Nicolas looked even better in the natural light. His charcoal-black hair was tousled in all the right places. He flashed his perfect white smile showing off his high cheekbones. It was next to impossible not to stare with a gaping mouth at this man.

"Not a word of this to him, okay?" I whispered.

"I promise," she said.

Nicolas smiled broadly. "Hello again," he said to Annabelle.

She smiled in return and I thought she blushed a little too. He had that effect on women.

"Are we still on for seven?" Nicolas asked.

There was unintentional seduction in his eyes. He couldn't stop his sex appeal no matter how hard he tried. Not that he was even trying.

I smiled. "Yes, I'll be ready."

"I'd better go," Annabelle said with a wink.

"I'll call you," I said.

I wanted her to stay. But what could she do? There was no way she could help me out of this pickle. I threw up my hand to her as she climbed back in her car. I tried to keep the sad look off my face.

Nicolas opened the door and I stepped into the foyer. The cat jumped out and made me scream out.

"Oh, he scared me," I said, clutching my chest.

Surreptitiously I looked around. Where was she? I had to tell Nicolas about my new guest before she got to him. Hoping that Nicolas wouldn't pick up on my strange behavior, I hurried over and peeked into the library. Isabeau wasn't there. I moved over to the parlor door and looked in. Nope. She wasn't in there either.

I took a deep breath, then released it slowly. Nicolas stared at me, so I knew I had to tell him now.

"Someone else is staying with me here at the manor. She just checked in this afternoon." I rushed my words.

"Oh, that's great." His smile was as intimate as a kiss.

Yeah, that was what he thought.

I searched for the right words. "She's a bit... well, she's not shy. So let me know if she bothers you."

Would she bother him? I mean, what guy wouldn't love a beautiful woman flirting with him?

Nicolas froze. His body stiffened and I could have sworn his eyes changed colors for a split second. The stress really was getting the better of me.

"What's wrong?" I asked. Nicolas' behavior had taken a complete turn.

He gazed toward the staircase for a moment, then met my stare. Each time he looked at me with his piercing blue eyes I had to use every ounce of strength I had to look away.

"Nothing. Nothing at all. Everything is fine. So I'll see you downstairs at seven?"

I nodded. "Yeah, see you then."

Nicolas climbed the staircase and I decided to find Isabeau. It was real torture having to watch Nicolas' butt as he took each step. I made my way up the stairs after him, but stopped at the second floor as he continued on toward the third. As soon as my feet touched the landing, I headed straight for her door. It was closed, so I rapped against the solid wood.

After a couple seconds, she answered with a sweet smile on her face. "May I help you?" she asked.

I tried to place a forced smile on my face. "Do you need anything else? Are you comfortable?"

"Well, I am famished. Do you have any food?" She tapped her foot impatiently.

"Oh, there's plenty in the kitchen. Please help yourself to anything you'd like… in the kitchen," I added after I realized what I'd said. "I'll be gone for part of the evening." I internally slapped myself for that. Why had I told her?

"Oh, do you have a hot date with the other guest? What was his name, Liam?" She wiggled her eyebrows.

No, I didn't have a date with that hot guest until tomorrow night. Tonight, I had a date with another hot guest. What the heck? How had I gotten myself into this crazy situation? I should cancel with both men. But if I cancelled I might never know what really brought them here. So I had a legitimate reason, right?

"Actually, there is another guest here tonight. I'm going to dinner with him. It's his way of thanking me for allowing him to stay here." I smiled to myself as I spoke.

"Is he a paying guest?" she asked with her hands placed on her hips.

"Well, yes," I said defensively.

"Then you're not doing him any favors and he doesn't have to take you out to thank you." She smirked.

Why was I even telling her any of this?

"He's being polite. That's something you might consider trying," I said as I turned around and walked over to my room.

She scoffed. We'd definitely gotten off to the wrong start.

After making sure that the book was still in the spot where I'd hidden it, I pulled a red dress from my closet. I only had a few dresses, so it wasn't hard to pick which one to wear. Since I never went anywhere nice enough to dress up, there was no reason to spend money on clothing I could never wear. This one had a scooped neckline, a fitted bodice and a Fifties-style full-circle skirt in a stunning red jacquard fabric with pretty gold paisley print.

Even though my anxiety increased at the thought of being alone with Nicolas, I jumped in the shower, slipped into my dress and heels, then attempted to do hair and makeup. It would have been easier to say no to him and forget all about dinner. But I couldn't be rude, right? I looked at my reflection in the mirror. Well, this was as good as it got. I hoped Nicolas approved. I spritzed on perfume, then stepped out into the hallway and locked the door behind me.

Isabeau was standing in her doorway staring at me. As she leaned against the doorframe, she studied her fingernails, then looked up at me again.

"Have a nice time," she said with a fake smile.

I knew I wouldn't have a nice time. Because I'd worry about what she was up to the entire time. She'd managed to ruin any chance of me having a nice time.

"I will," I said through an equally fake smile.

As I was making my way down the stairs to meet Nicolas the doorbell rang again. Things were quickly spiraling out of control. Was it the elderly ghost again? If Nicolas was already waiting for me down there, how would I explain that to him?

When I reached the bottom of the stairs, I let out a sigh of relief to see that Nicolas wasn't there yet. The only sound was the ticking of that darn grandfather clock. Even the cat was nowhere in sight. It was just as well that he hid after scaring the life out of me earlier. I glanced at the time. It was exactly seven. What if Nicolas decided not to show up? My heart sank a little at the thought. It was probably for the best though. After all, I didn't even know him.

I reached the door and eased it open, fearing the worst.

CHAPTER EIGHTEEN

My fear soon turned to relief, then happiness. Nicolas stood in front of the door, looking more handsome and dashing than ever. Okay, I'd said that about him earlier in the light, but now he was wearing a dark suit with a red tie and that made him look exceptionally debonair.

"What are you doing?" I asked with a laugh.

"I'm picking you up for our date." He stretched his hand out and I took it in mine.

Technically, I'd never called it a date. I thought it was more like a thank-you dinner. Was it a date? I supposed people would consider it a date. His skin was tan against the contrast of his white shirt. He flashed his white smile and my stomach did a flip.

Nicolas held out his hand to me. "Are you ready?"

I nodded. "Um, sure. Where are we going?"

"A place where we'll have the best seat in the house." There was excitement in his voice.

The evening was unseasonably warm and the sun had just disappeared. I stepped off the veranda and walked toward Nicolas' car. He took my elbow and guided me in the opposite direction.

"Where are we going?" I asked.

"I told you it would be the best seat in the house."

I quirked an eyebrow. "Yes, but technically it's not *in* the house."

Nicolas directed me around the house. The soft night air was quiet except for the occasional rustle from tree branches. When we made it to the back, I noticed a table and chairs near the river.

I looked at him. "How did you do that?"

He shrugged. "It wasn't easy. I thought for sure you'd notice me going out there and setting everything up."

I had been a little distracted with my new guest and the ghost at my front door, so it was no surprise that I hadn't seen him. A white tablecloth topped the table and flowed in the breeze. Dishes sat atop the table. When we reached the chairs, Nicolas pulled one out and helped me sit. The bright full moon smiled its approval over the intimate setting. Moonlight cascaded down, highlighting Nicolas' handsome features. The soothing sound of the water lapping against the river shore lulled me into a trance.

"I couldn't find a better view at any restaurant in town." He pointed at the river, then at the sky. "So I decided why not a picnic under the stars?"

I smiled. "That's a great idea."

Wait until Liam found out about this. How would he top this? I knew he'd have to try.

"What are we having for dinner?" I asked.

"Well, unfortunately I couldn't cook. Although you know I'm an excellent chef by my French toast." He winked.

I nodded with a smile.

"So I ordered food from the Italian restaurant. I hope you like pasta."

"I love pasta," I said.

My mind was a bit distracted though. How would I eat with so many thoughts on my mind?

"Thank you for doing all of this." I pointed at the dishes.

Nicolas poured the blood-red wine into my glass. "It was nothing. It's the least I can do since you allowed me to come into your home." He held up his glass for a toast. "To you," he said.

"To me?" I lightly touched his glass against mine, but had no idea why we were toasting to me.

"For being beautiful," he offered as if he'd read my thoughts.

I looked down as I felt the heat rush to my cheeks. Okay. He was definitely trying to charm me. What did he want? I was suspicious.

I sat my glass down and stared out at the water. "I should do this more often. Thanks for reminding me how beautiful it is out here."

"You're welcome." He took a bite of his food, then asked. "How long has the manor been a part of your family?"

"For as long as I've known. It's never left family's hands." I spun pasta around my fork.

He took a drink, then asked, "Who was the original builder?"

"My great-great-great-grandfather." I looked away, hoping he wouldn't ask for more information.

And what did he do? I should have known he'd ask that question. What would I tell him? That he was esteemed in the witchcraft world? That gene surely hadn't been passed down to me. I had to get more answers from Nicolas. I couldn't allow him to direct the conversation. I didn't want to talk about me. I wanted to find out everything about him.

"He was a... a pharmacist." That wasn't entirely a lie, right? I changed the subject before he had a chance to ask more questions. "You still haven't told me what brings you through Enchantment Pointe. I know you have business in New Haven. But what is that business? Tell me about Nicolas Marcos," I said, then took a sip of my wine and waited for him to answer.

"I am a consultant for people." He focused on his plate of food.

"A consultant? What do you consult on?" I asked, not taking my eyes off his face.

Okay, now I sounded like my mother. But apparently this was the only way I'd get answers.

"Let's just say I help them save things." He took a bite.

That was a weird answer, but before I could ask for more information, a bird flew from a treetop, cawing and capturing our attention.

"The surroundings are great here," Nicolas said, pointing toward the trees.

I nodded. "Yes, they are, I'm glad you're enjoying them. You seem to be getting along better with Mr. Rankin."

"I wouldn't say we are getting along, but I am tolerating him. If he won't leave, then I don't have a choice. He just rubbed me the wrong way on that first day."

"I guess that's understandable. Some people just don't click, I suppose. Is that all you can tell me about yourself?" I pushed.

"There's not much to tell really." He took another drink.

"Where are you from?"

"I live in New Orleans."

"Were you born there?" I asked.

"No, I was born in Bayou L'Ourse. I left for college and never went back," he said, looking down at his plate.

"What do you do for fun?

This was like twenty questions. He seemed uncomfortable with my questions. But he couldn't retain his mystery man status forever.

"I don't have a lot of free time, but I enjoy reading and golf." His expression eased.

Uh-oh. I was staying out of his golf game. I'd learned my lesson.

"How old are you? If you don't mind me asking." I hoped I didn't sound too rude.

He chuckled. "I don't mind. What do you think my age is?"

"I'm not very good at guessing things like that." I grinned.

He fixed his gaze on my face. "Why don't you give it a shot?"

I looked down to avoid his stare. "Well, if you won't be offended if I guess incorrectly."

"Not at all." He smiled.

"Okay. Are you thirty-two?" I asked.

"You got it." He stared for a second.

Was he just telling me that? He didn't have any reason to lie. I didn't care how old he was though. I had other things on my mind. I hated to ask such personal questions, but it needed to be done. Surely he wouldn't ask me out if he had a girlfriend, right? That was something I should have asked before I even agreed to have dinner with him.

"Do you have a significant other?" I asked.

He smiled. "No."

"You're not married, are you?"

"Of course not. You're not married, are you?" he asked around a smile.

"Of course not. Don't you think you would have seen my husband in the house?"

He flashed his perfect teeth again. "Yes, I think I would have. Would you care to dance?" Nicolas reached out his hand to me.

"But there's no music," I said.

Nicolas pulled out his iPhone and touched the screen. Music spilled out from the little speaker. It wasn't loud, but it was just enough for me. I took his hand and we stepped away from the table. Nicolas pulled me close and my heart sped up. He smelled so good. His gaze traveled over my body and searched my eyes. The smoldering flame in his eyes startled me and excited me at the same time. His nearness made my senses spin.

The song was talking about yearning arms and being lonely. Did he have to pick such a sensuous song?

A lonely rustle of the night wind carried across the air. The stars twinkled overhead and I knew this might be the most romantic evening I'd ever spend in my whole life. And with a stranger. There was no way Liam could top this, right? The grass was hard to dance on, but I didn't care. I was having fun and that was something that hadn't happened since... well, I couldn't remember when I'd felt like this.

When I was in Nicolas' arms, I was able to forget about everything. I wasn't worried about pleasing the coven, or not disappointing my mother. For once life was carefree. But all good things must come to an end and my happiness lasted a nanosecond.

CHAPTER NINETEEN

There was a constant whispering in the woods. I had figured it was the farewell of the leaves as they fell to the ground, but now I knew better. The elderly man was hiding behind the big oak tree, watching us. I'd seen his little head peek out. How was I going to get rid of him? Nicolas must have recognized my tension because he pulled away slightly.

"Is everything okay?" He caught me looking over his shoulder.

"I'm fine." I plastered a smile on my face. Would he see through my charade?

He looked over his shoulder, but fortunately, the man had retreated behind the tree again. Nicolas frowned, but didn't say anything about what he'd seen. We continued dancing, but after a couple seconds, the man popped out again. Movement on the right caught my attention and I looked over to discover a woman hiding behind another tree. She looked to be younger than the man, maybe in her fifties. She had the same blurry appearance though. Her dark hair was cut in a chin-length bob and she wore a green sweater and black pants. Was he bringing his dead friends now?

An eerie white glow surrounded the ghosts, shining brightly in the darkness of night. I swallowed hard, fighting off the panic that was about to set in. What was the worst that could happen if I told Nicolas that there were ghosts hiding behind the trees? I could never again share a dance with him? That was the worst that could happen. I was afraid that my date with Nicolas was now officially over.

The man ghost stepped forward and a tree branch popped. I hadn't thought a ghost could make that kind of noise. The ghost zipped behind a tree. I didn't know that an elderly ghost could move that fast either. Nicolas whipped around.

"What was that?" he asked.

"I'm not sure. It was probably just an animal. My cat is probably chasing a mouse. Or it could be a bird," I said casually.

Just then the old man peeked out. It didn't go without Nicolas noticing this time.

"Who was that?" he asked. Before I answered, he called out, "Who's there?"

Of course the man didn't answer.

"I didn't see anyone," I said.

Like that would keep Nicolas from looking for the ghost. Would the female ghost come out too? Nicolas walked toward the tree.

"I saw you. There's no reason to hide now," he called out.

Silence filled the night air and the distant cloudscapes shifted slowly across the sky. Maybe Nicolas had scared the ghost away. I might as well tell Nicolas the whole story. Isabeau would probably tell him everything the first chance she got anyway. She'd probably embellish the story too. I'd stand a better chance if I told him first before he heard her skewed version. Nicolas made his way around the tree and I followed along, preparing my story in my mind. The man had vanished and was no longer hiding behind the tree.

Where had he disappeared to? I glanced to my right and spotted the female ghost. She watched us, but Nicolas hadn't noticed her yet. I tried to avoid making eye contact but it didn't work. Nicolas walked all the way around the tree, the branches popped and crunched under each step. The man was still nowhere in sight.

"Where did he go?" he asked. "I know I saw someone. You didn't see him?"

I shook my head. "No. Maybe it was a shadow that looked like a real person," I offered.

It was bad of me to lie to him.

"No, I definitely saw his face. He looked like he was around eighty years old and he wore a suit with a Fedora hat." Nicolas spoke with his hands, showing his anxiety.

Yeah, that was the man. Another noise sounded from the right where the woman stood. She had disappeared this time too. Were they playing a game of cat-and-mouse with us? Maybe this was payback since I wouldn't bring him back to life.

"I know I heard something that time." Nicolas moved over to the tree where the woman had been.

How long would he search for them before he gave up?

"Come on. I don't think it's safe out here anymore. We should go inside." Nicolas packed the dishes into the basket quickly, then grabbed my hand. "I'll get the rest in the morning."

I grabbed Nicolas' hand. As we neared the house, I felt eyes on me. I looked up at the upstairs window and saw Liam looking down at us. He had a look of determination in his eyes. He turned around and walked away. Where was Isabeau? I was surprised she hadn't been spying on us too.

Nicolas held my hand as we walked across the grass and around the house. The touch of his skin against mine set shivers through my body.

Nicolas opened the front door and gestured for me to go first. "After you, gorgeous."

120

My cheeks probably turned bright red as I flashed a shy grin his way.

Once we'd entered the foyer, I asked Nicolas, "Would you like some coffee?"

"Sure, I'd like that," he said as he sat the picnic basket down.

The house was quiet, which made me suspicious. No footsteps sounded from upstairs. Nicolas followed me into the kitchen, but I stopped on the spot when I crossed the threshold. Water dripping from the faucet played out a steady rhythm against the sink basin. Broken eggs and their shells covered the tabletop. Empty wrappers were strewn about. Flour covered the floor with footprints tracked through it. Dishes were tossed everywhere with food containers.

"It looks like someone was hungry." Amusement flickered in his eyes.

"Oh, no. I didn't do this." I waved my hands.

"Liam made this mess? I'll straighten this out," Nicolas said as he spun around.

I grabbed his muscular arm. "No, Liam didn't do it either."

His expression eased. "Oh, well, who did it then?"

"I guess I made a mess, huh?" the sweet voice said from over Nicolas' shoulder.

Isabeau even looked stunning in my old T-shirt and sweats. Her blonde hair glistened and her skin looked flawless under the soft glow from the light.

"Aren't you going to introduce us?" Isabeau wiggled her eyebrows at Nicolas.

I tried to focus on what Isabeau was saying, but I felt the pull from that darn book again. The book was the giant piece of metal and I was the tiny magnet. It felt as if I had no control over my body. I had to go to the book soon. What did it want this time?

Nicolas looked at me. "This is your new guest?"

"This is Isabeau. She'll be staying with me for a while. Isabeau, this is Nicolas." I half-heartedly gestured toward Isabeau.

"Well, well, well, you're just as handsome as the other one." She drank in every inch of him with her eyes.

Nicolas frowned. I knew he didn't like being compared to Liam.

"Did you find what you were looking for?" I asked, pointing around the kitchen.

Isabeau stared straight at Nicolas with a devilish grin on her face. "I sure did."

CHAPTER TWENTY

"I guess I'll clean up my mess now," Isabeau said as she moved forward.

I blocked her. "No, you're a guest. It's not necessary."

She smiled as if she was proud of what she'd done. The sly look on her face let me know that she was aware of my desire to keep her away from Nicolas.

"I'll help you clean up," Nicolas said, avoiding Isabeau's stare.

"Oh no, I wouldn't think of it. I'm real particular about cleaning," I said as I directed Nicolas out of the room.

He looked confused, but allowed me to guide him away from the kitchen. Isabeau wasn't complaining about not having to clean. I knew she didn't want to clean it or she wouldn't have left the mess in the first place. Isabeau looped her arm through Nicolas' as he walked across the library toward the staircase. Nicolas looked back at me as if to say he was sorry. It wasn't his fault that I'd brought back a slutty ghost.

Isabeau glanced back at me. If she thought her flirting would make me jealous... well, she was right. I had to get rid of her. I turned around and looked at the mess. If only I could wave my hand and do the cleaning spell that my grandmother used to do. I'd tried it before, but it always had the opposite effect. It created more of a mess. What was that spell? What were the words? I tapped my finger against my chin, trying to remember.

Oh yeah, now I remembered.

With one sweep, carry the unwanted away. Make it sparkle, make it gleam, it is now clean. So mote it be.

With a wave of my arms, a whirl of wind whipped around the room. I blinked several times, unable to believe my eyes. Items were moving through the air on their own. Spills were disappearing as if they'd never been there and trash was finding its way into the garbage can. How was this happening? I'd never been able to perform magic like that before. My mother wouldn't believe me. She'd also be so excited that she'd pee her pants. I stared around in awe at my sparkling clean kitchen.

"Wow. That was quite impressive." I spun around to find Liam standing behind me.

How long had he been there? Had he seen the magic? Of course he had. I could tell by the look on his face. How would I explain this? I stared, unable to say a word.

"You're a witch. I know," he said.

"How did you know?" I managed to sputter out.

"You don't hide it well," he said.

I'd admit to the truth gracefully, but only if forced.

Silence filled the air for a moment before I finally said, "I didn't want to scare you. Some people are funny about being around witches."

"I'm okay with it." He waved his hand and moved a plate around the kitchen until it finally came to rest again on the table.

"You're a witch too." I stared in disbelief.

"Yes, I'm surprised you didn't know before now," he said with humor in his eyes.

"How would I know?" I shrugged and busied myself picking up around the kitchen.

Liam stepped further into the kitchen. "Didn't you feel the magic around me?" His eyebrows rose inquiringly.

I had felt something, but I didn't want him to know that my feeling had come from the book. But there was no way for me to know if it was the book for sure.

"No, I didn't. Am I supposed to?" I asked.

"Most witches sense other witches." His mouth curved into an unconscious smile.

"Is that why you're here?" I asked with a hint of anxiety in my voice.

He stared at me. "I needed a place to stay."

Something told me he wasn't being truthful with me.

"Are you part of a coven?" I asked.

"Yes, in New Orleans," he said.

I nodded. That seemed legitimate enough. I'd have to ask my mother about them. I tucked that thought away.

"Your powers are quite impressive." Liam leaned against the counter.

His statement surprised me. Hadn't he seen my mother's missing eyebrow?

He wouldn't think that if he'd seen me a few days ago.

"Not really. I'm nothing special," I said.

"I think you're very special." Tenderness flickered in his bright clear blue eyes.

"You don't even know me," I said.

"I'd like to get to know you." His smile was so warm and his voice was so sincere it would be hard to say no.

It was hard not to melt on the spot. But I had to resist his charms.

I had to pull my thoughts together. "I'm sorry. Did you need something?"

A subject change was definitely in order. Perhaps we should discuss the weather.

"I just came down for a drink of water." He pointed at the faucet.

"Oh, I have bottled water in the refrigerator. Let me get you one." I reached in and grabbed a bottle.

When I turned around Liam was right behind me. Dangerously close. I sucked in a deep breath, almost hypnotized by his warm touch. Liam's breath was minty and a whiff of spice tickled my nostrils. There was an inherent strength in his face.

"Oh, you scared me," I said, clutching my chest.

"Did I startle you again?" His voice was barely above a whisper.

"Yes, you're becoming very good at it." My heart thumped wildly. I tried to ignore the pulsing knot that had formed in my stomach.

"I'm sorry." A secretive smile curved his lips.

When he took the water from my hand, his fingers lingered for a moment too long. Unfortunately, his hand against mine felt good. How could I possibly have feelings for two strangers? I needed to get out of the house more often.

He stared at my lips. My gaze moved to his as his handsome face moved closer to my mouth. Was he really going to kiss me? I had to stop him. Why I had to stop him I wasn't sure. I just knew my mind was telling me not to let him kiss me. Of course my body was saying an entirely different thing.

His lips were nearly touching mine when I pressed my hands against his hard chest and pushed him away. I stepped around him, leaving Liam standing there wondering what had just happened.

"I should go to bed. It's been a long day," I said when I reached the doorway and turned around to look at him.

He ran his hand through his thick dark hair. "I understand. Thank you for the water."

"You're welcome," I said softly.

For a moment there was an awkward silence, then I turned around and walked away. When I reached the staircase, I hurried up to the second floor landing, then peered up toward the third floor. Was Nicolas already sleeping? I glanced down the hallway. What was Isabeau doing?

Once I made my way down the hallway, I stopped at her door. I raised my hand to knock, but stopped midair. If she was sleeping, did I really want to wake her? Let sleeping demons lie, right? At least if she was sleeping I wouldn't have any problems out of her. I pressed my ear against the door. No noise came from the other side, so I assumed she'd finally gone to bed. Although since she'd been a ghost, I wondered if she was good on sleep for a while.

My thoughts drifted to the ghosts we'd seen outside. I knew they wouldn't go away. If I turned them back into the living would they leave me alone? Next thing I knew I'd have an endless stream of ghosts wanting me to turn them back. I definitely didn't need that.

After locking my bedroom door behind me, I stepped over to the window. I had a full view of the backyard from my vantage point. The moon cast a white ghostly glow over the yard. I scanned the area for the ghosts, but saw nothing out of the ordinary. They'd be back. I knew they would. The only question was how many would they bring back with them?

I climbed into bed and pulled the covers up tight, relishing the feel of the soft sheets against my skin. Who knew when I'd discover another ghost lurking around in my room. My thoughts ran a million miles a minute. The last thing I remembered thinking about before drifting off to sleep was Nicolas. How had he persuaded me to join him for dinner? I couldn't deny that we'd had an amazing night together dancing under the stars by the river. It had been a perfect date, except for the fact that he still wouldn't answer any of my questions. Oh, and the ghosts. But what was I going to do with Liam?

CHAPTER TWENTY-ONE

I woke the next morning with a start. My heart was racing. Had I been dreaming? Maybe it was the stress of everything that was going on around me. I lay there for a minute staring at the ceiling until my heart rate had returned to normal. Once I'd calmed down enough, I jumped up and hurried into the shower, then slipped into my jeans and a warm yellow sweater. I had to make it to the kitchen before Nicolas. I especially had to make it down there before Isabeau. She'd only make another mess.

How had I been able to perform the cleaning spell so well last night? It had to be a fluke, right? When I stepped out into the hall, Isabeau's door was still closed. Maybe she'd decided to leave? Could I get that lucky? Probably not, but a girl could dream. The house seemed eerily silent as I made my way downstairs. It was like the calm before the storm. Why did I feel as if I was waiting for the bomb to drop?

Trying to keep quiet while I rushed through the rooms toward the kitchen was no easy task. When I reached the kitchen door, I let out a deep breath. The kitchen was still clean and no one was up yet. Of course it was six a.m. so I wasn't surprised that they were sleeping in. I wished I was still in bed too. But I'd signed on to run this place as a bed-and-breakfast. I doubted my guests would appreciate eating breakfast at twelve just because I wanted to sleep in.

I flipped the switch on the coffee brewer, then filled the cat's food and water dish. The coffee couldn't brew fast enough because I needed it now more than ever to help me get through the morning. I intended to serve breakfast in the sunroom this morning. It was a bright and beautiful fall day and the leaves were starting to turn. The view of green, orange, red and yellow leaves was spectacular. Although with all the windows, I worried that if the ghosts were out there, Nicolas or Liam would spot them right away.

I needed to find out if Isabeau knew anything else about the spell that had brought her back. Not that she'd tell me if she did. Why was she being so difficult? I decided to try my hand at an omelet this time, along with waffles and bacon. I'd just assembled all of my ingredients when noise sounded from the parlor. Lately any little noise made me jump. I was completely on edge.

I wiped my hands on my apron and moved toward the library. When I saw Nicolas standing in the room, I stopped in my tracks. His gaze locked with mine. The hungry look in his eyes suggested that he didn't want waffles to satisfy his craving. Nicolas rushed toward me. I didn't protest when he pulled me close to his hard chest. His fingers burned into my tingling skin as he caressed my cheeks. Without saying a word, his warm lips met mine with an urgency that I'd never experienced before. His mouth covered mine hungrily as his lips moved over mine with ease. His tongue traced my lips, then he explored my mouth. My own eager response to his touch shocked me.

When I thought I might collapse to the floor, Nicolas gently eased his mouth from mine. I finally caught my breath.

He wrapped his arms around me. "I'm sorry. I just couldn't help myself. I've been thinking about you since last night."

Did I admit that I'd been thinking of him too? Did I admit that Liam had almost kissed me last night and that I'd come close to allowing him?

Nicolas touched my cheek again. "There's something special about you, Halloween. I've been drawn to you since I first laid eyes on you."

Wow, I hadn't expected that. Before I could answer he placed his lips on me again. Every time he kissed me it knocked all the air right out of my lungs. I'd never been kissed this way before. Nicolas moved from my lips to my neck as he placed feathery kisses against my skin. My heart thumped harder.

Suddenly Nicolas pulled away. "I'm sorry," he said. "I shouldn't have kissed you."

He looked confused as I searched his eyes.

"What's wrong?" I asked as I touched his arm.

"There's something I need to tell you." His tone was apologetic.

My heart rate spiked again. What was he going to say? It couldn't be good news, right? Not with that kind of expression.

Nicolas turned away. Leaning over, I looked at his face. I let out a loud gasp and stumbled back, bumping into the bookshelf.

"I'm sorry," he said, finally turning to look at me.

"Your mouth." Those two words were all I managed to get out.

He just stared at me with his sharp white fangs poking out over his bottom lip.

"What are those?" I asked pointing at his mouth. "Why do you have fangs?" I moved around the bookcase and backed further away from him.

Nicolas' eyes shone the brightest blue I'd ever seen.

"Hallie, I'm a vampire." His voice was soft but alarming.

His words didn't register on my dizzied senses. I shook my head. "And you're just now telling me this? Did you think this was something you can hide from me? Did you think this is something you should hide from me?"

He shook his head. "No, I didn't think I should hide it from you and I wanted to tell you from the moment we met."

"Then why didn't you tell me?" I stood there blank, alarmed and shaken.

"There was never a right time." He ran his hand through his thick hair.

"How about when we had breakfast? Or how about at dinner when I asked questions about you? Heck, you could have written it on the note with the flowers. P.S. I'm a vampire."

"It wasn't that simple," he said.

"I think it was," I said in disapproval.

"I'm sorry," he said with sincerity in his eyes.

"If you're a vampire then why can you go out into the sun?"

"That's all a myth. Obviously, we can go out into the sun." Nicolas radiated an energy that drew me to him like a magnet.

"But you drink human blood?" I shivered at the thought.

"I'm not going to lie to you, Hallie, we do need it. We crave it."

My neck felt barer by the second.

"I've never met a real vampire before," I said.

"I didn't want to have feelings for you, but I can't stop them. I have strong feelings for you. I've tried to deny them... we shouldn't be together."

His admission made my insides tingle with excitement.

"None of this makes any sense. Why do you say such things?" I paced restlessly across the room.

He inched closer and I moved back a couple steps more.

"It's frowned upon for you to date me." There was a spark of some indefinable emotion in his eyes. A war of emotions raged through me.

"Why? It's frowned upon by whom?" I asked in frustration.

"The Underworld doesn't want it. You could have your right to perform magic taken away permanently."

My eyes widened. "How do you know?"

"It's not a coincidence that I came here."

I felt as if I might faint. So he was an axe murderer after all. I should have listened to Annabelle.

"Your magic was putting off a strange vibe. I had to find you before someone else did. Unfortunately I was not fast enough because Liam showed up too."

"It's not a coincidence that he's here either, is it?" I asked.

He shook his head. "No, it's not."

"When did you become a vampire?" I had to know.

He shook his head. "That's not important."

"It is important to me," I said.

"It was a long time ago." He looked away.

"What are we talking here? A hundred years, two hundred years?" I focused on his face.

"It was around the Civil War. I just got caught up with the wrong crowd. We don't need to discuss me right now. Like I said, you are in danger."

Nice way to change the subject. "Why am I in danger? Did one of you come here to kill me?" I asked.

His eyes widened. "Of course not. Well, I can't speak for that witch Liam, but I did not. I came here to help you."

Liam stepped into the room. His jaw was tense, mouth clamped, and eyes fixed on Nicolas. "Thanks for the introduction, Nicolas. But if anyone is here to hurt Hallie, it's you."

CHAPTER TWENTY-TWO

I didn't know what to think. My head was spinning. I grabbed the table next to me to steady myself.

Nicolas exposed his fangs to Liam as some kind of warning, I guessed. "You're walking on thin ice," Nicolas said.

Liam ignored Nicolas' threat. "I came here to get rid of the book," Liam said.

"You know about the book?" My mouth dropped open.

The room spun even more and the last thing I remembered was hitting the floor hard. I woke with Liam and Nicolas standing next to me arguing.

"You'll never get your hands on the book," Nicolas said.

"It's the only way to get rid of her," Liam said.

I blinked, trying to focus my vision. Not wanting to hear another word, I jumped up from the sofa.

"Whoa. I think both of you need to leave now." I pointed at the door.

"Look what you've done. You've scared her." Liam's eyes glowed with anger.

"Do you blame me?" I asked.

"Hallie, you're in danger because there's another witch looking for you. It's only a matter of time until she tracks you down. She'll want to eliminate you." Nicolas spoke in an urgent tone.

"What do you mean, eliminate me?" My voice raised a couple levels.

Liam looked at Nicolas and they both frowned. It was the first time they'd looked civil to one another.

"She'll want to kill you," Nicolas said bluntly.

My legs wobbled again. I had to get a hold of myself. "Why would anyone want to kill me?" I asked. "I've done nothing wrong, other than a few botched spells. I've never harmed anyway too badly with them."

"Mara Abney is an evil and powerful witch. She's desperate to take charge of the Underworld. She'll be coming for you soon," Liam explained in a calm tone.

"What is this Underworld I keep hearing about?" I folded my arms in front of my chest.

I was convinced that both men were crazy. I should have known it was too good to be true. Two crazy men were after me. One was a vampire, one was a witch and to top it off I had a crazy ex-ghost in my house and other ghosts wanting in. My life had gone from wacky to full-on insane.

"I've never heard of Mara Abney and there is no reason for her to want me dead. If she is after me, then I'm sure it's just a misunderstanding."

I looked at both men but their expressions didn't change. Apparently, they were convinced that this woman really wanted to cause me harm.

"Why do you want my spell book? Is that why you were upstairs in the attic?" I stared at him accusingly.

"Never mind that," Liam said. "Where is the book?"

I snorted. "Wouldn't you like to know? There is no way I'm telling you that. And there's no way you're getting your hands on it."

Liam blew out a deep breath. Apparently I had frustrated him. But what did I care? He was talking nonsense.

"Let me try to explain this to you."

"Oh, please do." I waved my hand through the air.

"The Underworld has been without a leader for some time now." Nicolas sat on the edge of the desk.

Liam paced across the room.

Liam continued Nicolas' sentence. "Because of that, things have quickly turned chaotic. Vampires are violently turning people again. They're drinking witches' blood."

I whipped around to look at Nicolas. Was that why he was here? To drink my blood? He must have realized what I was thinking because a hurt look flashed in his eyes. But was he being sincere or was that all part of his act?

"Not all vampires are drinking witches' blood," he said defensively, then glared at Liam.

Liam shrugged, then continued. "Anyway, the witches are performing black magic too."

"I'm not performing black magic," I said in my defense.

Or was I? I had brought back someone from the dead. That sounded a lot like black magic. But it wasn't as if I'd done it on purpose.

"Can someone please tell me what the hell the Underworld is? I keep hearing the phrase repeated over and over yet I know nothing about it. Is it really underground?" My lack of knowledge was embarrassing.

Nicolas smiled. "No, it's not literally underground."

Okay, now I felt like an idiot. I should have known that detail.

"The Underworld is the overseer of all things paranormal. Vampires, witches, fairies." Liam sat on the edge of the sofa.

"Why haven't I heard of this before? I'm a witch."

Nicolas shrugged. "If you haven't done anything wrong, it's not surprising that you've never been aware of it."

"What about all my botched magic spells?" I asked.

"Minor offenses," Nicolas said.

"Yeah well, tell that to my mother and her eyebrows." I smirked.

The men looked at me as if I'd lost it.

"Never mind," I said. "So it's kind of like a court and law enforcement?"

Liam nodded. "You got it."

"What has this got to do with me? The spell book is linked to the Underworld somehow?" I blew out a deep breath.

"Do you have the spell book now?" He searched my eyes.

"Yes," I answered reluctantly.

"Then Mara wants it because she will be the leader of the Underworld once it's in her possession."

A chill ran down my spine. That was a pretty high-stakes reason to want the book. I had so many unanswered questions. Did my mother know anything about this Underworld? How did the book get in Aunt Maddy's attic? Most importantly, how the heck would I ever find the answers to those questions?

"Are you okay? Maybe you should sit back down?" Nicolas touched my arm.

I backed away and walked clear across the room, putting distance between us. I wanted to be near the door in case I needed to make a fast getaway. Nicolas looked nothing short of hurt by my actions.

Liam cleared his throat. "Anyway, like I said when I first arrived, I am a detective with the Underworld."

"You failed to mention you weren't a normal detective though. And that one..." I pointed at Nicolas. "He never told me anything about what he does." A sense of controlled power coiled through my body, waiting to burst out.

Liam stood. "I'm a detective with the Underworld and I took an oath to uphold the law."

Nicolas stepped toward Liam. "You have no law here," he snapped.

I frowned. What was that all about?

"I do have law here and the law says that Halloween is now the leader of the Underworld. She must take the position," he said forcefully.

The dizziness overcame me again. My stomach turned and the room spun out of control. This was craziness. Had he really just said that I was the leader of the Underworld now?

"I'm sorry, what did you just say?" I held my head in my hands.

Maybe this was all one big dream. I'd wake up soon and this mess would all be behind me.

CHAPTER TWENTY-THREE

"You are in possession of the book. This means you are now the leader of the Underworld," Nicolas said matter-of-factly.

"I don't want to be the leader. I tried to lead an aerobics class in college one time and I had everyone bumping into each other. I'm not good at leading. I think I'm better at blending in with the background," I said with anxiety evident in my voice.

"You are far from blending in with the background."

"Well, maybe I do perform spells poorly but that doesn't mean I stand out in a crowd. Furthermore, that is even more reason why I shouldn't be the leader of anything."

"You're upsetting her." Nicolas gestured at Liam.

"She has to know the truth," Liam said, fixing his stare on Nicolas.

The air around us seemed electrified.

"You don't know that to be the truth," he said, challenging Liam's words.

I had to get out of there. I didn't know what to think any more or who to believe. I didn't want to believe either one. I wanted it to be the way it was from the beginning when I first inherited the manor. This was all too complex and confusing.

"The fact of the matter is, Hallie, if you don't join the Underworld I will lose my job."

"Oh, no pressure there," I quipped.

Liam looked at Nicolas. "Besides, now that Halloween has performed a spell from the book, Mara will be able to track her down. You know that."

Nicolas was silent for a moment. The tension rippled off him in waves.

"Is this true?" I asked him.

He looked down at his shoes for a moment, then back up to me.

"So I take it by your silence that you refuse to corroborate or refute Liam's story." I didn't take my eyes off Nicolas.

"I'm sorry, Hallie. I am not behind Liam's plan." He looked down, avoiding my stare.

"What exactly is the plan? For me to be the leader of the Underworld. I can't say that I'm on board with that plan either." I shook my head.

"Nicolas knows Mara is evil. Why he'd want you to have any interaction with her is beyond me."

"Are you saying that I don't care if Hallie is harmed?" He stepped closer to Liam.

I hoped they didn't fight. I was in no mood to deal with that.

"I think that's what I'm saying." Liam puffed out his chest.

Denying this craziness was no longer an option.

Nicolas flashed his fangs. Liam jumped up, waving his hand and causing a wind to whip wildly through the room. Nicolas threw back his head and released a loud peal of laughter. Liam didn't find the situation nearly as humorous. The men stood in front of each other, their gazes fixed on one another. Liam's eyes glowed.

"Enough!" I yelled.

Both men whipped around and looked at me with shocked expressions.

"I don't need to put up with you two fighting right now. I have enough to worry about with this ridiculous Underworld story that you've thrown at me." I backed away.

"I'm sorry, Hallie," Nicolas said. "Please let me help you."

"There's nothing you can do." I shook my head. "There's absolutely nothing you can do to make this better." I turned away, not wanting to hear another word of their story.

Without giving the men a chance to respond, I stormed out of the house and jumped into my car. I had to go to my mother's shop. As much as I hated to tell her about my mistakes, I knew I had to confide in her.

As I drove down the driveway, I spotted the man and woman ghost from last night, peeking out from a couple trees on my right. Ugh. I knew they were still lurking around. They were the least of my problems right now though and I never thought I'd say that.

Nearing the gate to pull out onto the road, I looked in my rear-view mirror. Isabeau was running after my car, flailing her arms through the air like she was trying to wave down a plane. She was wearing my favorite red sweater and a pair of my jeans. So glad she could just help herself to my closet.

As much as I wanted to leave her, I had to find out what she wanted. I still felt guilty for putting her in this predicament. I stopped the car and waited as she ran toward me. I was probably going to regret this later.

She pulled open the passenger seat door and climbed in. "Where are we going?" she asked breathlessly.

I closed my eyes for a moment, willing her away. I hoped when I opened my lids this would all be a dream. Slowly I opened my eyes and looked over at her. No such luck. She was still sitting there smiling at me.

"What are you doing?" I asked.

"You can't leave me in that big old house all day. I'm hungry and you didn't even make breakfast. I thought this was a bed-and-breakfast. Emphasis on the breakfast part. It's that time of the day, you know?" She tapped the clock on the dashboard of my car.

"It's breakfast for paying guests. You're not a paying guest." I smirked.

"Did you make breakfast for your paying guests?" she asked with an innocent smile.

"It's complicated," I said as I pulled out onto the road.

"How was your date?" she asked mockingly.

I glanced over at her and she looked as if she already knew the answer to that.

"Were you eavesdropping this morning?"

She batted her eyelashes. "Of course not. I would never do such a thing."

I snorted. "Yeah, right."

Had she heard the whole Underworld discussion? I hoped not. I didn't want anyone to know.

We drove in silence for a few minutes. Isabeau looked out at the trees and occasional houses lining the road. The thoughts in my head weren't silent though. Leader of the Underworld? That was the craziest thing I'd ever heard of. Complete and utter nonsense. And I was still wondering how in the heck I'd been able to perform that magic spell so well. I was itching to give another one a try. Would it work again or was it just a fluke? Heck, if I took one step forward with the magic, I'd probably end up taking two steps backwards and my magic would be worse than ever. Was it even possible to get any worse? They'd ban me from performing magic ever again if that happened.

"So where are we going?" Isabeau asked, breaking the silence.

"We're going to my mother's shop. She has bath and beauty products."

"Oh good. I really need some of those."

How was I going to explain this to my mother? She'd freak out.

"What are you going to do about the other ghosts?" Isabeau asked.

"You saw them too?" I glanced over at her.

She nodded. "Yeah, and they won't go away. I mean, they're trapped here, where else do they have to go? They have nothing better to do. Trust me when I say it gets very boring."

I wanted to ask more about being a ghost, but we'd pulled up in front of the Bewitched Bath and Beauty. That discussion would have to wait until another time. My mother had a prime location for her store in the middle of the historic downtown. A few people strolled up and down the cobblestone sidewalks, but for the most part, the town was quiet.

It was no wonder I received strange looks when I pulled up in front of the store as if there was a fire and I was the only one who could put it out. I usually took my time and drove slowly, but not today. I wanted to be somewhere that I could get some sense of normalcy, although I'd brought part of the problem with me.

"Whoa. What is going on with all the magic around you?" my mother said as soon as I walked into her shop.

I looked around me. Did I have a sign over my head announcing that I'd been up to magical no good?

My mother eyed Isabeau suspiciously. "You're early," she said. "You're never early. What's wrong?"

I couldn't lie to her and say nothing was wrong. I wasn't a good actress. She'd know I was lying in an instant.

"Mama, this is Isabeau. She's staying at the manor." I gestured toward my guest.

That wasn't a lie, right? I'd just omitted the important parts.

"Do you bring all of your guests here?" She shook her head, but her blonde curls didn't budge.

"Hello," Isabeau said, gliding toward my mother with her delicate hand stuck out. "You have a lovely store. I can't wait to try your products."

My mother glanced from me to Isabeau. "Um, nice to meet you."

"Yes, I brought her here to try your products." My smiled faded a little when I saw my mother's doubtful glare.

That made perfectly good sense and my mother couldn't question that. After all, I was bringing her business, even if I would be paying for the items.

My mother shook Isabeau's hand, but I still saw the suspicion in her eyes.

"What type of products are you looking for? You have lovely skin," my mother added as she eyed Isabeau up and down. "Would you like to see the bath products?"

"I'd love to." Her voice was saccharin-sweet.

My mother took Isabeau to the other side of the store while I waited on another customer who had just entered. Once I finished with the customer I hurried over to where they stood. There was no telling what Isabeau had told my mother. Had she told her the truth? I needed to get rid of Isabeau so that I could talk to my mother alone about the book and this so-called Underworld.

"Did you find what you need, Isabeau?" I asked.

"Yes, I found a bunch of things that I need." She gave me that look. The look that said she was going to make my life a living hell.

She knew I felt guilty and that I was stuck paying for whatever she wanted. Did she know I was broke? It had taken every penny I had to get the bed-and-breakfast up and running.

"Um, I'll pay for all the stuff. Just put it on the counter." I gestured with a wave of my hand.

My mother set the items on the counter, but didn't take her eyes off me. She knew I wouldn't pay unless there was a really good reason. Last week I'd invited her over for dinner and served peanut butter and jelly sandwiches. She knew I didn't have much money.

"Isabeau, you must be starving. There's a little café next door." I took a few bills from my wallet and handed them to her. "Why don't you get us breakfast? My treat."

She smiled. "I'd be happy to. What would you like?"

"Surprise me," I said.

On second thought, maybe that hadn't been the best thing to say to her. I watched as she sashayed out the door, waving the cash I'd given her as a farewell. I felt my mother's gaze boring a hole through the side of my head. I moved things around on the counter and pretended to work. Finally, I couldn't stand her stare any longer.

"Okay. Just spit it out," I said, turning to look at her.

"Who is that woman? Why are you buying things for her when she is a paying guest at your bed-and-breakfast? And why is there such strong magic around you? What kind of mess have you gotten yourself into?" She gestured toward the door with a tilt of her head.

"What makes you think I've gotten myself into a mess?" I picked an imaginary piece of lint off my sweater.

"For the reasons I just listed," she said, putting her hands on her hips. "There's never been magic that strong around you in the past. Something has changed and I want to know what right this minute. I'm your mother and I deserve to know the truth."

"I may or may not have performed magic from the spell book I told you about and allowed Isabeau who was a ghost to become living again because of me." I rushed my words.

The bell on the door jingled and saved me for having to explain more at the moment.

My mother clutched her chest. "You're going to be the death of me, Halloween. The only spell you can do correctly is bringing a corpse back to life."

I looked at Isabeau. She didn't act as if she'd heard my mother's comment.

"I'm back," Isabeau said, waving the bag of food in the air as she approached.

My stomach was too upset to eat.

"You can have mine. I've lost my appetite," I said as I stared at my mother.

My mother still clutched her chest. "Halloween, we need to discuss this."

"Come on, Isabeau. We'd better get back to the manor." I grabbed her big bag of bath products and wrangled her toward the door.

"I'm not done talking to you, Halloween."

My mother had always called me Halloween. She refused to use the nickname I'd picked out for myself.

"Your mother wasn't happy with you. Is everything okay?" Isabeau asked innocently.

She knew part of the reason for the tension was her. I wasn't falling for the innocent act.

"Look, we need to have a discussion about what you're going to do." I said, slipping behind the wheel of the car.

"What do you mean?" she mumbled as she stuffed a bite of bagel in her mouth.

"What are you going to do now that you are living again? I mean you can't continue to live with me. Don't you have family you can stay with?"

"Oh yeah." She pointed the half-eaten bagel at me. "I'm working on that. I'll be out of your hair in no time."

I glanced at her. "You're sure?"

"Oh yeah, positive. I'm just thankful that you allowed me this journey back to the living world. I'm forever grateful to you and I'll repay the favor." The tone of her voice didn't sound sincere, but I'd give her the benefit of the doubt.

That offer didn't sound appealing to me. I'd been around a lot of backstabbing women in the past and I could tell when someone wasn't being sincere... and Isabeau definitely had her own agenda. Did I have time to figure it out or should I just kick her out on the spot? Who was I kidding? I knew I couldn't kick her out. I'd gone over this a million times in my head. I was a pushover in this type of situation.

As much as I didn't want to go back to the manor to deal with Nicolas and Liam, I had no choice. What else would I do? I had nowhere else to go. I'd almost killed my mother with the news about Isabeau. What would she say about the whole Underworld business?

The first thing I wanted to do when I got back to the manor was snatch up the book and find a way to get rid of it. Liam had said he would take it, but I didn't trust him. I'd get rid of the thing and all my problems would be over. But was the book the reason that I'd been able to do the spell last night? I wouldn't lie, that had been cool. I wished I could do magic like that all the time. Maybe before getting rid of the book I needed to try out another spell or two and see if my powers really had improved or if last night was a fluke.

Regardless about last night, the spell to turn Isabeau had worked. I had the proof sitting right next to me stuffing a pastry into her mouth.

"You do know all that stuff has calories, right?" I asked as I navigated a turn.

She studied her fingernails. "I haven't eaten in fifty years. I think I'm entitled to a few cheat days on my diet."

"So you've been dead for fifty years!" I exclaimed. "Finally, I have a little detail about your life."

That was when it hit me. Why hadn't I tried to research her while I was in town? Duh. There had to be a death certificate. I'd have to put that on my to-do list. Or better yet, maybe Annabelle could research it for me. She could do it without Isabeau even knowing what we were up to.

Isabeau frowned at her slip-up. Why didn't she want to divulge any information about herself? Why was she so secretive?

"Whatever. It doesn't matter how long I've been dead." She licked her fingers.

"No," I said with a sly smile. "It doesn't matter."

With any luck, Annabelle would soon find out all there was to know about Isabeau, whether she liked it or not.

CHAPTER TWENTY-FOUR

When I steered onto the driveway, I let out a deep breath and steadied myself for what was ahead.

Neither man's car was there. I knew they wouldn't be too far away though—after all, they were after the book. It was just as well that they weren't there. It would give me time to try out a few spells though. If only I had something to keep Isabeau occupied.

When I was looking for a spell to test in the rest of Aunt Maddy's stash of books, I'd look for a spell to get rid of Isabeau. If there was a spell in the mysterious book to bring her alive again maybe there was another book with a counter-spell to send her packing for the rest of eternity. Heck, I didn't care where she went. I just wanted her to get out of my house.

When we reached the front door, I said, "You go on in, Isabeau, I'll be just a second."

She shrugged, but eyed me suspiciously before entering the house.

I reached in my purse and pulled out my phone. After dialing Annabelle's number, I stepped over to the side of the veranda where Isabeau couldn't eavesdrop.

"Are you okay?" Annabelle asked when she picked up.

How did I even begin to tell her? The story of the Underworld was definitely something that she needed to hear in person. I'd have to share that delightful news later.

"How would you like to do some research for me today?" I asked with hope in my voice.

"Sure, what am I researching?" she asked.

I glanced over my shoulder. "You're researching Isabeau Scarrett. There has to be a death certificate on file for her if she lived in Enchantment Pointe."

"I'm on it," Annabelle said.

I could always count on her. After a couple more minutes of assuring her I was fine, I slipped the phone into my purse and headed for the front door. I spotted the man and woman out of the corner of my eye. They were hiding just behind the trees in the distance again. I was pretty sure I saw another ghost with them this time, but I couldn't say for sure that it hadn't just been a shadow.

When I opened the door, I let out a scream and clutched my chest.

"What the hell are you doing?" I asked.

Isabeau was standing right in front of the door. She obviously had been trying to eavesdrop on my conversation with Annabelle. I had to get rid of this woman.

"I'm hungry," she said.

"You just ate!" I said.

She shrugged. "It wasn't enough. Do you have cupcakes? I like chocolate cupcakes with white icing and sprinkles too."

I glared at her. "If I find you cupcakes will you leave me alone?"

"Of course." A sly smile slid across her face.

"It'll be a bit while I make them, okay? Why don't you watch TV or something? You'll probably be fascinated by the reality shows." I waved her off.

"What's a reality show?" She scrunched her brow.

"You'll figure it out," I said over my shoulder.

"Why don't you just use your magic to make cupcakes? They'll be done in a second." She snapped her fingers.

I turned around. "I've tried that in the past and it didn't work out so well."

She shrugged and walked off. Her statement put a thought in my head though. Maybe I really could whip up a batch of cupcakes with magic this time. After all, I'd cleaned up the kitchen until it sparkled. Then I remembered. I'd forgotten about the food I'd left out in the kitchen. I'd left it in a mess this morning when Nicolas and Liam had dropped the bomb on me.

Now was a chance for me to test the magic out again. Would I be able to do the cleaning spell again? I stepped into the kitchen and stood in the middle of the room. I waved my hands through the air and recited the words.

Again the wind whipped and moved the objects around the room with ease. Nothing exploded and nothing broke. Thank goodness no fires started either. I giggled on the inside. My new skills were pretty darn awesome. Maybe I really could make those cupcakes.

I reached for one of Aunt Maddy's magical cookbooks and picked out a recipe for the cupcakes. After pulling a few ingredients from the shelves, I recited the words listed on the page.

Make me a perfect white cake confection with fluffy buttercream frosting and sprinkles adding to the perfection. So mote it be.

The next thing I knew, there was a giant puff of smoke and when the smoke settled, a gorgeous tray of cupcakes was on the counter in front of me. Sure, they looked great with creamy swirls of frosting and delicate sugar adornments on top, but what would happen when someone ate one? The good thing was I had someone to be my guinea pig. If one exploded when bitten into, it wouldn't be me with the singed eyebrows. That was mean of me, right? Hey, she was the one who'd wanted cupcakes. I would definitely get a bad review if this cupcake thing went badly.

Since Isabeau wasn't expecting cupcakes for a while, I decided to use the time to search the books for a spell to get rid of her. I didn't care if it was just a spell that would banish her from my house. I'd get rid of the other ghosts lingering outside too. Books lined the shelves in a sea of hardback bindings. I got dizzy just looking at all the titles. How would I ever find the spells I was looking for? If they were even there.

I pulled off a couple of books and curled up on the velvet chair in front of the stone fireplace. Page after page and there was nothing that even resembled a spell to banish a ghost who had been turned back to the living. I did find a spell that would keep the ghosts out of the house. I'd have to try it because I knew the ghosts would finally enter the manor. Once they came in, I knew I'd never get rid of them. I didn't want my place to turn into a ghost motel.

I placed a piece of paper between the pages to mark my spot and continued looking. After an hour of searching, I hadn't found anything useful and the sound of footsteps made me slap the books closed and slip them back onto the crowded shelves. Isabeau must be restless and wanted her cupcakes.

When she appeared from around the corner, I said, "I made you cupcakes." I forced a smile on my face.

She frowned and eyed me suspiciously. "What did you do to them?"

I frowned. "I'm offended. What makes you think I'd do something to them?"

"Because you don't like me." She walked past and toward the kitchen. My jeans fit her better. The hem didn't drag the ground like when I wore them.

"I never said I didn't like you," I mumbled.

She scoffed. "You don't have to."

"Well, I get the feeling you don't like me much either." I folded my arms across my chest and leaned against the counter.

"So you do admit you don't like me?" Her eyes widened when she spotted the tray of cupcakes.

"No," I said defensively. "I just said I had the feeling you don't like me. Just like you have a feeling. Your feeling is wrong though."

"Oh, so you do like me?" She smiled and snatched a cupcake like she hadn't eaten in years. "I have a feeling we'll be the best of friends." She took a big bite out of a cupcake.

I held my breath, but nothing happened, other than Isabeau making mild noises of enjoyment.

"I'm glad you like them," I said with an innocent smile.

She shook her head as she grabbed another one. I had a feeling the tray wouldn't last long.

The doorbell rang and I froze. It was not the sound I wanted to hear. Unless it was Annabelle, I knew it couldn't be good news. Annabelle was supposed to be going to town to research, so I doubted it was her.

Isabeau continued stuffing her mouth full of the sugary confection while I hurried to the door and peeked out. It was a woman who'd I'd never seen before. I would have thought she was selling something if not for her blurry appearance. She wore a cotton candy pink dress and had long black hair that reached all the way past her waist. Her grainy appearance looked like the man and woman in the woods. No need for her to tell me what she wanted. I knew she was a ghost and I knew what she wanted. The thought of not opening the door crossed my mind, but I knew she'd just keep trying and eventually make it into the house. I opened the door just a crack. I wanted to tell her to go away, but I couldn't bring myself to be that rude.

"May I help you?" I asked in my sweetest voice.

Like I didn't know what she wanted.

"We're waiting for you to turn us back into living beings." She gestured over her shoulder.

The man and woman were standing in my driveway. They waved. Oh dear. This was really putting me in a pickle.

"I told them that I can't do that. I'm sorry." I started to close the door.

"Please," she said.

I glanced at her face and she looked so sad. Way to lay the guilt trip on me.

I let out a sigh. "Look, even if I wanted to do this for you, I can't. The spell isn't in English now."

"What do you mean?" she asked with a frown.

"The spell only appeared to me in English the one time. Before and after that it's written in a language that I don't understand. I don't even know what the language is."

The scowl on her face remained. "I don't understand."

"It's complicated," I said. "To make a long story short, I just don't have the means to do it."

Isabeau stood behind me, chewing on what I assumed was remnants of a cupcake. "You haven't looked at the book when they were around, how do you know that it isn't in English now? Maybe it's just up there waiting for you to work the magic."

I turned to look at her. "How did you know the book was upstairs?"

She looked at me blankly. "I don't know it's up there. I just assumed you were keeping it in your room like before."

"Because you can't find it anywhere else?" I glared at her.

And she wondered why I didn't like her? She was sneaky and I didn't trust her. Why was she here really? Maybe she was after the book too? After all, she'd already stolen it once. I wasn't going to let her or the ghosts pressure me into doing anything. I wasn't so sure I should be bringing anyone back with a spell. It was one thing to do it on accident and an entirely different thing to do it on purpose.

"I'm sorry." I looked at the woman's sad face. "I just can't do it."

I closed the door without meeting her gaze again. If I looked at her again I might invite her in and that wouldn't be a good thing.

When I'd closed the door and locked it, I glared at Isabeau. "I think you need to mind your own business. Now if you'll please excuse me."

"I didn't do anything wrong," she huffed. "I was merely trying to help. You're just a bully."

"A bully?" I looked at her with wide eyes. "Are you kidding me? I turned you back into a living person and I'm the bully? You're staying in my house and I'm giving you food and my clothing. I think that's nice. It's far from rude. Rude would be if I kicked you out."

"You'd love that, wouldn't you?" she asked.

"You're being unreasonable," I said.

"Then why don't you help those poor people out?" She placed her hands on her hips.

"That's not something I think I'm supposed to do." A vision of the Coven members wagging their pointy fingers flashed through my mind.

"Why? What harm can it do?" she asked sweetly.

"I'm pretty sure there's something in the Coven Rulebook that says we're not supposed to do that. Technically, I think I performed black magic when I turned you," I said.

"That's not black magic. Don't you know anything? If it was black magic something bad would have happened to someone." She shook her head in disgust.

I glared at her. "My point exactly."

"Very funny. You're a clever one." She wiggled her finger at me.

I wanted to find a spell that would shut her up so badly. I hurried up the stairs. I wasn't going to talk with her about this any longer. I didn't owe her an explanation. I had to lock myself in my bedroom for a moment's reprieve. She was giving me a headache. This would give me a chance to look at the spell book anyway. I knew that it wouldn't be in English this time, but Isabeau had had a point. I'd never looked after the ghosts had appeared to see if the words had changed. What would I do even if they had? I wasn't going to turn the ghosts.

With each step up the stairs, I moved faster. Was it a coincidence that the magic was pulling at me? I felt it again the same way I'd felt it when it pulled me to do the first spell. I wanted to fight it, but I wasn't sure there was any way to fight the feeling. How could I fight something I knew nothing about?

CHAPTER TWENTY-FIVE

The power wasn't pulling me to my room though. It was drawing me toward the attic. I moved up the rest of the stairs and found myself at the attic door. Was the magic messing up now? The book was in my room. Why did I feel compelled to go into the attic?

I hoped Isabeau didn't hear me in the attic. I'd hate to have to kick her out. Her insistent talking was getting on my last nerve. Maybe if I just kept her with an endless supply of cupcakes she'd leave me alone. Why had she wanted the book anyway? It seemed everyone wanted the book. Did she want to be the leader of the Underworld too?

I eased the door open and poked my head in as if I was expecting someone to be in there waiting for me. And to think I'd been worried about finding bones in the attic. That was the least of my worries now.

No one was in the room. That was unless I had another ghost I didn't know about. There was a strange vibe in the room though, pulsating around me. It lured me toward the middle of the room. I stepped inside and stood right in the middle of the room, as if saying, *Here I am, now what?* I scanned the space, but nothing looked out of place or different from when I'd been in there just a few days ago. Had it only been a few days? It seemed like months.

A odd tug was coming from the corner of the room. I stepped into the shadowy corner and instinctively reached behind another beam behind a hidden cranny. Something was back there. I wrapped my hand around the object and pulled it out. It was a piece of paper that had been rolled up and tied with a ribbon.

This was like some kind of weird magical scavenger hunt. I blew the dust off the paper and turned it over in my hands. I contemplated shoving it back where I'd found it. I'd forget about it, tell Isabeau to leave, get rid of Liam and Nicolas and try to forget any of this had ever happened. I knew that was fantasy though. There was no way I would do any of that. My curiosity would get the better of me and I'd have to know what the paper said, what any of this meant. It was crazy, but I had to know. I'd never been one to live dangerously, but suddenly I felt like I was living on the edge.

Finally, with shaky hands, I untied the ribbon around the scroll. My breathing came in short gasps as I unrolled it. It was a small map of the house. My aunt Maddy really was a strange woman. She had a tendency to forget things though, so it was understandable why she'd sketched a map of her little treasures. The attic had two spots marked, the location where I'd found the book and another spot in the middle of the room.

I walked over to the area where I'd found the book and stuck my hand behind the beam. The space was empty. I had to make sure there wasn't something else there. I studied the map again. It had a spot marked right in the middle of the room. What could be there?

Walking over to the marked spot, I looked down. Nothing was there. I knelt down and ran my hand across the floor. It was smooth except for the imperfections in the wood. When I ran my hand across it again though, I noticed the board moved ever so slightly. I ran my fingernail under the edge, but couldn't get it to come up. I needed something to pry the board up with.

I scanned around the room, then spotted a box in the corner marked dishes. I rooted through the box and found a few random utensils. A butter knife was one of the items. I was thankful that my aunt was so eccentric now. I never knew what I'd find in her stuff.

I rushed back to the spot in the floor and used the knife to pry up the loose board. It was hard to see if there was anything under there. I didn't really want to stick my hand down there where I couldn't see any possible rodents. I poked the knife down there and hit the subfloor. When I moved the knife back and forth, it didn't catch on anything. Just when I thought I wouldn't find anything, the knife hit something and a small clang sound rang out. Something was down there, but now I had to decide if I was sticking my hand down there to retrieve the item.

It didn't look as I had any other options, so I closed my eyes and inched my arm down there. As if closing my eyes would protect me from something. I moved my hand around and reached, but still couldn't find the source of the noise. Stretching into the far corners of the space, I finally felt it. It was a small, cold object.

I pulled my hand out of the space to see what I'd found. It was a key. I sit on the floor and stared at it. It was a long brass skeleton key. What was it for and why was it hidden? I flipped it around in my hand. There was nothing written on it, just a wispy swirl pattern on both sides.

The map was on the floor where I'd dropped it. I reached over and grabbed it. There were two more spots marked around the house. What was in those locations? There were two problems though. One location was in Nicolas' room and the other was in Liam's room. That could get tricky. And what was hidden there? Did it have anything to do with the key that I'd just found?

There was only one way to find out. I had to look quickly before they returned and I was caught. If they wanted the book, did that mean they'd want whatever else was hidden in the house? This just kept getting more complicated. What was Aunt Maddy's involvement in the Underworld? There had to be a connection. I'd run out of options and knew that I had to break down and tell my mother about this, as much as I didn't want to. She was my only connection to Aunt Maddy. She'd be the only one who could answer questions about her.

Pushing the board back into its spot, I grabbed the map and the key, then slipped out of the attic. I paused for a moment and listened. Isabeau wasn't making noise, which was probably a bad thing. At least she was on the second floor and wouldn't see me slip into Liam or Nicolas' room, although I'd have to walk lightly or she might hear my footsteps.

What was I worried about anyway? I had a right to be on the third floor. It was my place. I could do whatever I wanted. She could just mind her own business. If she happened to see me I'd tell her I was cleaning the rooms, which technically I needed to do. But I'd have to look for the secret hiding spots before I did any bed-making or dusting.

I tiptoed down the hall, trying to avoid the spots in the floor that I knew squeaked. I eased into Liam's room first because it was the first room on the right. He'd made his bed and everything looked relatively tidy. Discarded clothing lay across the chair in the corner of the room. Was it creepy that I wanted to pick up his shirt and give it a whiff? He just smelled so darn good that I couldn't help myself.

I unrolled the map again and looked down. Apparently, something was hidden in the closet. Or had been hidden there at one time. Whether or not it was still there was the big question. I glanced over my shoulder. Liam and Nicolas were both still out, so what was I worried about?

Sucking in a deep breath, I made my way over to the closet. When I opened the door, I peered in the dark space. Liam had a few pieces of clothing hanging up, but other than that the closet was empty. I reached up and felt along the shelf, but couldn't see because I was too short. When I didn't feel anything, I gave up.

The only other place to look was in the floor again. Why hadn't I brought that knife with me? I knelt down and waved my hand across the floor. If Liam walked in and caught me, he'd think I was crazy. Just when I thought I was wasting my time, I felt another loose board at the very back of the closet. I pushed on it and tried to use my fingers, but it was no use. The thing wasn't coming up.

I needed to hurry up. I still had to check Nicolas' room. I jumped up and looked around the room. Did Liam have anything that I could use? I prayed I didn't find a knife in his room. That would make my overactive imagination go into overdrive with visions of him as a serial killer. I mean, I'd found out he was a witch and Nicolas was a vampire. I just didn't know if they really were being sincere or if they wanted to harm me just to get to the book.

Liam claimed this Mara woman wanted the book. He'd wanted me to give him the book. Maybe that was just a ploy to get the book from me. I stepped over to the dresser and spotted his bag. I hated doing this, but I had a good reason, right? I'd take just a peek.

The only thing in Liam's bag was boxers and socks. I guessed that answered my question of boxers or briefs. If Liam caught me looking at his underwear, well, I'd never get over the embarrassment. There was no way to explain that one away. I'd be forced to tell him the truth. Even then, I doubted he'd believe me.

Just then I remembered that there was a letter opener in the desk drawer. I hurried over and yanked the drawer open. Thank goodness it was still there. I grabbed it and hurried back to the loose board. I poked the letter opener beside the board and pried it up. Most of my body was now in the closet. I reached my hand in. Again it was dark, even darker in that closet than in the attic. Seeing a thing was almost impossible, but I felt something right away this time. It was metal and quite large. It had a handle too, so it was easy to lift it out of the space.

I pulled it out into the light. It was a box and right there on the front was a hole for a key. Bingo. I pulled the key from my pocket and slipped in right into the hole. I should have taken the box to my room, but I just had to know what was in it first. My heart rate increased as I turned the key. When it clicked, I let out a deep breath. I lifted the lid on the box, not knowing what to expect. Inside the velvet-lined box was another book. Another spell book? What would this one do if the other reanimated the dead?

My hands wrapped around the book and I pulled it out. It looked just like the spell book that I'd found in the attic. Apprehension coursed through me as I studied the intricate cover and the leather binding. I was almost afraid to open the cover. What would I find this time? I inhaled and blew the air out of my lungs slowly, then flipped the leather cover. Staring back at me were words that I understood. This time the pages were filled with English and I knew every word.

I scanned the first page. I hadn't been prepared for what I read though. According to this book, the witch who unlocked the power of the Book of Mystic Magic would be the leader of the Underworld. It was just as Liam had said. The witch was destined to oversee the laws and rules set forth. My head was spinning. Was I the witch who had unlocked the powers of the book? No, it couldn't be.

I flipped through more pages. The text went on to list my duties as the leader. Basically, I would be the one everyone turned to for answers. That was a joke. They surely didn't want my advice. Movement sounded from downstairs so I shoved the book back into the box, grabbed the key and bolted from the room.

I hurried down the flight of stairs toward my bedroom before I was caught so that I could to hide this book with the other one. I wasn't sure if the footsteps coming up the stairs belonged to Liam or Nicolas, but either way I didn't want them to see the book.

Forget making fantastic cupcakes. I just wanted things back the way they were. I enjoyed my substandard spells. I'd always wanted to be better at magic, now I was regretting that wish. Be careful what you wish for… or was it be careful what you witch for?

CHAPTER TWENTY-SIX

I rushed into my room and closed the door, locking it behind me. There was one curious thing mentioned in the book. It claimed that I could change my appearance. Of course that caused an idea to cross my mind—but it could be a very risky endeavor. That was if in fact it actually worked. The book said I had all these special powers now, but would I perform the magic any better than my lackluster attempts in the past? I had spell books that my mother had given me in the hopes that I'd someday need them, but they didn't have spells like the ones listed in the Book of Mystic Magic.

The spells I really needed would be in the mysterious spell book hidden in my closet. Or the Book of Mystics Spell Book as it was apparently called. I retrieved the heavy tome from its hiding place, then sat on the bed with the book on my lap. When I flipped open the cover, I couldn't believe my eyes.

The book was now all in English. I understood the spells and ingredients. There was even a table of contents. I scanned the list with my index finger stopped when I found the spell I needed. Could I really pull this off? Could

I change my appearance and trick Liam into giving me the information that I knew he was withholding?

Aunt Maddy hadn't led the Underworld, so why had she had the book? The book might have said that my magical powers were now needed in the Underworld, but I didn't want that much power. I just wanted life to go back to the way it was before I cleaned out that darn attic.

But I couldn't dismiss the fact that the book seemed to have had an effect on my magic skills. My witchcraft had improved beyond my wildest dreams. Baking delicious cupcakes was no longer a problem—would they come out perfect every time? My mother would be so proud. I could reanimate the dead, for heaven's sake.

The book listed all my newly acquired powers now that I'd unlocked the magic of the book. It said that I could change an object's appearance or even my own appearance if I wanted. That was a scary thought. Using magic for vanity would never work out in the end. At least that was my philosophy.

I hadn't believed it, but the spell to change my appearance was actually listed on page fifty-two. Did I really have the nerve to try it? What if I was stuck that way forever? Try explaining to Nicolas why I had changed my appearance to look like him and then couldn't switch back. I'd have to slip down to the kitchen to collect the ingredients for the spell. I hoped Isabeau wasn't still down there stuffing her face with cupcakes.

There was no sign of Liam when I slipped out the door. The fact that he wanted the book made me nervous. I wouldn't put it past him to be lurking outside my door at any given moment. Isabeau's door was closed, so I tiptoed over and pressed my ear against the wood. I'd broken every code in the bed-and-breakfast proprietor rule book. I'd looked at one of my guests' underwear, for heaven's sake. Not on purpose, but I doubted that would be any excuse.

Noise sounded from the other side of the door. Thank goodness she was in her room. I rushed down the stairs, trying to keep from slipping and killing myself. I doubted Isabeau would use magic to bring me back if I died.

Once I reached the kitchen, I hurried and gathered my items—cinnamon, basil, cloves, and frankincense. I dumped the ingredients into the cauldron that was already in the big stone fireplace. It was about time that I tried using Aunt Maddy's things. Someone once told me that anything could be performed easily with the right tools. Maybe I'd always assumed my magic was atrocious, but if I'd used the right tools, my magic wouldn't have been half bad.

After adding water to the cauldron, I swiped a long match against the stone then lit the fire underneath. While I waited for the water to boil, I eased back to the kitchen door and peeked around the corner. No one was there. I hoped Nicolas didn't catch me doing this. I hadn't prepared an excuse in my mind if he did. There wouldn't be one. If he caught me, I'd just tell him the truth.

Once the water came to a boil, I recited the words.

"For a brief time, make my appearance not mine. Alter my look to that of Nicolas Marcos and no one's beliefs will falter."

Nothing felt different. No wind whirled or brilliant light show appeared like with the spells I'd worked earlier. Maybe I'd been over-confident in my new found skills. After all, I'd only cleaned a kitchen and made cupcakes. What made me think I could change my entire appearance to look like someone else? Furthermore, what was I even going to say to Liam if it had worked? What made me think that he would fall for it in the first place?

As the thoughts whirled in my head, the wind began to stir in the kitchen. Pots and pans and dishes clanked. Blue and red and white lights pulsed and flickered around the room. The water bubbled like a sea churning in a hurricane. When the concoction finally settled down, the wind stopped and the lights settled down, I glanced down at my body. Everything looked the same to me. My hands looked the same, my body was the same. Nothing had happened.

I'd messed up the magic once again. There was no telling what this spell had actually done. I just prayed that it hadn't reanimated more ghosts. I was running out of rooms. I hurried and cleaned up my mess, then grabbed the book and headed back upstairs.

I'd hide the book once again, but I was finished with this Underworld business. It was all a ruse. Probably some weird story made up by some wackos. Unfortunately, the wackos were the good-looking men staying in my home. Good-looking or not, they had to go. Why did they have to be crazy? Why couldn't I just for once meet a sane guy? Of course if I did meet a sane guy, I always managed to do something to chase him away.

Once I made it back upstairs, I locked the door behind me and hid the book again. This was becoming my new normal and I hated it. I couldn't deny that I was a little disappointed that the spell hadn't worked. Not that I wanted to be the leader, because I didn't, but I wanted to try to get answers from Liam. That would have been majorly deceitful though, so it was probably best that it hadn't worked. Anyway, I was going to confront him right now about this fake Underworld business. If he wanted to continue to stay at LaVeau Manor, then he'd have to stop with that nonsense.

As I walked toward the door to have a confrontation with Liam, I caught my reflection in the dresser mirror. Only the problem was that it wasn't my reflection at all. Staring back at me from the mirror was Nicolas' face. I glanced down at my hands. They were still my hands. I looked down at my body and it was still the same. But when I looked in the mirror again, Nicolas' reflection looked back at me.

Incredible. The spell had actually worked. I stared at Nicolas' reflection. He really was gorgeous with his strong jaw and chiseled features. His long lashes rimmed his sexy cobalt blue eyes.

No matter how gorgeous he was, what I had just done was freaking me out. I reached up to touch my cheek. It still felt like my cheek, but in the mirror I was touching Nicolas. As I stared into the mirror, my heart pounded and I shivered at the realization of what I'd done. I had to talk with Liam and get rid of this spell before Nicolas came back. What if the counter spell didn't work? It was too late for what-ifs though. The deed had already been done.

Would I be able to convince Liam that I was Nicolas? How did Nicolas walk? I watched in the mirror as I walked forward. I had way too much swing in my hips. Nicolas didn't walk like that. I spread my feet apart a little and attempted my best guy walk. It looked more like I was approaching someone to kill them than to have a normal conversation. This being a guy stuff was a lot harder than it looked. What did guys do? Should I scratch my genitals? Burp? No, Nicolas was way too suave for that, right? Oh, who was I kidding? All guys did that stuff sooner or later.

Okay, my guy walk would have to do for now. But what about talking? Did I have Nicolas' voice?

"Hello, I'm Nicolas Marcos," I said out loud.

I gasped. It actually sounded exactly like Nicolas' voice.

Well, it was now or never. I'd get to the bottom of this Underworld nonsense and find out if this whole story was real or not. Attempting to master my manly swagger, I marched out my bedroom door and down the hall, but before I could make it to the head up the third flight of stairs, Isabeau approached me with a come-hither look on her face. Oh dear, I hadn't thought about this scenario. Would I be able to fool her?

"Where have you been hiding, gorgeous?" she purred.

Isabeau stepped closer and ran her hand down my chest.

I stepped back. "Hey, you're invading my personal space," I said.

The words came out in Nicolas' voice.

Isabeau scowled. "Don't you like me?" she asked, then stuck her bottom lip down in a giant pout.

"I'm sure you're a very nice person. I'm just very funny about people invading my personal space." I stepped back, pushing my arms out to fend her off.

"I bet I could change your mind." Isabeau lunged toward me with her arms stretched out to grab me.

I jumped to my side, avoiding her embrace. She fell to the ground with a thud. Oops.

"What is wrong with you?" she snapped.

If she only knew. She looked up at me expectantly. I sighed. Apparently, I was supposed to be a gentleman and help her up.

After a couple seconds, I stuck my hand out and said, "Let me help you up."

The words came out way less enthusiastically than I'd hoped. She scowled, but reached up and took my hand. As I pulled her to her feet, she pressed her lips together in anger. Did she know my secret? My stomach turned. What if the spell had worn off? No, if it had she would have said something by now. She probably sensed something though.

Isabeau continued to look at me. "There's something different about you," she said.

"Nope. Nothing different. Now if you'll please excuse me. I need to speak with Mr. Rankin."

I hurried toward the landing and started up the stairs. When I glanced down at Isabeau, she still stood in the second floor hallway with her hands on her hips, glaring at me. She was suspicious and if given enough time she might figure me out. But it didn't matter. If I could talk to Liam and reverse the spell quickly, she'd never know the truth.

CHAPTER TWENTY-SEVEN

My heart pounded in my chest as I knocked on Liam's door. Every nerve in my body pulsated with anxiety. If I pulled this off, it would be a miracle.

Liam opened the door and glared. "What do you want?"

He'd knocked me off guard by answering the door shirtless, only wearing jeans. It was like staring at a hypnosis wheel. My eyes were fixed on his hard chest.

"Wow, you must work out a lot?" I blurted out.

Heat rose to my cheeks. I didn't just say that, right? What a stupid comment.

Liam's eyebrows drew together in a scowl. Was he wondering why Nicolas was ogling his chest?

Finally, I snapped out of the trance and said, "I need to talk to you."

"There's nothing to talk about," he responded sharply, not budging from in front of the door.

Liam wasn't about to let Nicolas into his room.

"Can I come in?" I asked.

He frowned and stared at me a second. Was he on to me? What made me think I could pull this off? Just when I thought I couldn't stand it any longer, he stepped to the side and opened the door further. I did my best Nicolas walk and entered the room. Lucky for my act, he grabbed a T-shirt and slipped it over his head. I leaned against the dresser and propped my arm against the top. That was the way a guy stood, right?

"So what do you want?" Liam asked in an icy tone.

I wondered why there was such animosity between them. That would be hard to find out though since Nicolas should already know the answer.

"I want to talk about the book." I stood with my feet apart in my best attempt at a guy stance.

"There's nothing left to say about the book." Liam plopped down in the chair. "If I can get rid of it, then maybe Halloween will be safe."

"Do you really think getting rid of it will help?" I shoved my hands in my pocket.

"You know damn well it will. Why are you fighting me on this?" A shadow of annoyance crossed his face.

"How do I know you don't want the book for yourself?" I held my breath waiting for the answer.

Liam scoffed. "I expected that from you. What happened was a long time ago. Why don't you let it go?"

Hmm. Let what go? What had Liam done? There really was something to the hostility between them.

"Halloween as the leader of the Underworld? Don't you think that's a bit drastic?" I added sarcasm to my tone.

"Hey, it's not my decision. I don't make the rules." He gave me an unfriendly stare.

"No, that's why you should leave Hallie alone," I said in the most commanding voice I could find.

Ha! I thought that sounded good. That was something Nicolas would say, right?

"It's only a matter of time before Mara arrives." Liam ran his hand through his hair.

"Right, Mara," I said.

Liam looked at me. I avoided his stare.

"When was the last time you spoke with Mara?" he asked.

There was too much hesitation. He'd be on to me. But what should I say? Had Nicolas really talked with Mara? Was this a trick question? I pondered the question for a moment, but Liam's stare was fixed on me. There was no way out of answering his question.

"I haven't talked with Mara," I answered.

I sounded less than confident though. I even heard it in my own voice.

"Right, you didn't talk to her." Liam stood, shoving his hands into his pockets. "So you don't agree with what she said the last time you spoke with her?"

Whoa, I didn't have the answer for that one. It was time to abort this situation. I wished I'd never even tried this stupid scheme. What had I been thinking? It had seemed like such a great idea at the time. How many bad ideas started out that way though? He waited for my answer. I might as well confess my guilt right now. I stood up straighter. This was my one last try to convince him I was really Nicolas.

"No, I don't agree with her."

Liam narrowed his eyes and nodded. I couldn't read his expression. Had my answer been right or wrong? Tension hung in the air. I needed to say something, but I had no idea what to say. I'd already made a mess of the situation. Did I really want to make matters worse by opening my mouth again?

Finally, when I didn't think I could stand the silence any longer, Liam said, "Nice try, Halloween." He flashed a sly smile.

"What do you mean?" I asked, avoiding his unrelenting stare.

"I know what you've done," he said with amusement in his tone.

Should I continue with the charade or admit to what I'd done?

"Your powers are much better than you ever let on."

This whole situation was so disturbing.

"What powers?" I asked. My voice even faltered.

He chuckled. "Wait until Nicolas sees another version of himself."

My stomach dropped. He really did know it was me. Had it been the walk? Yeah, that had to be it. Maybe I had missed some kind of guy movements. I should have had more of a swagger or something.

Movement caught my attention and I whipped around to find Nicolas standing in the doorway. His eyes widened and his mouth hung open. I'd never been more embarrassed in my whole life. This was even worse than the time I'd turned my date into a donkey. In my defense, he had been an ass. How would I explain this? There was no explanation... only the truth. I'd said I wouldn't lie if I was caught. It was time for me to admit what I'd done. I wished I could crawl under the bed and stay there until they both went away. No, I'd gotten myself into this mess and it was time I owned up to it.

I cleared my throat, then pushed forward with my words. "I'm sorry," I said softly.

Nicolas laughed. "It's strange to hear myself talking."

I looked down. "Yeah, well, I have to go figure out how to get rid of this spell."

Nicolas had a strange look in his eyes. "You didn't check the spell before you did this? Are you sure there's a spell in the book you have?"

I looked from Nicolas to Liam. "There's another book of spells, isn't there?"

Finally, Liam nodded. "Why aren't you trying to find all of the books? The other two are useless without the first one. Whoever owns the first one possesses the power."

"Lucky me," I said drily.

"Don't worry about it," Nicolas said. "I'm sure there is a spell in the first book."

There was only one problem that I didn't want to tell them about yet—I hadn't found the book that must have the counter-spell in it. I'd been so eager to try the appearance spell that I hadn't looked for the counter-spell. Now I had to find the map and look for the book's location. If that book wasn't there then I was screwed. I'd made yet another stupid mistake.

"Hallie, let me help you," Nicolas pleaded.

Not looking back at the men, I ran out of the room. I didn't want them to know just how incompetent I really was. And they thought I was capable of running the Underworld? They seriously didn't know me at all. Heck, I'd been voted most likely to cause a disaster in my high school yearbook. I ran down the stairs and bolted for my bedroom before Isabeau the human leech found me.

Taking the map from its hiding spot, I unrolled it again, I laid it out on the bed. There was a big problem though. The last place marked on the map was outside. Oh, for heaven's sake. Did Aunt Maddy really expect me to go outside and find something hidden when I had ghosts roaming around looking for me?

I rolled the paper back up and hid it in the waistband of my pants. I locked my bedroom door and started down the hallway. The door to Isabeau's room was open slightly. She must have thought I wasn't home otherwise she would have been lurking around the house trying to follow me. I eased over to the door and peeked in. She was standing in the middle of the room, but she didn't see me. Her arms were stretched up as she reached toward the sky.

Isabeau was reciting words to a spell—at least that was what it sounded like she was doing. What kind of spell was she trying? Something told me it couldn't be good. The words were mumbled, but Isabeau performing magic was probably one of the worst things possible. I decided to get out of there before she realized I was watching her—although technically she'd think that Nicolas was watching her. Which was probably worse. The last thing I needed was another attack.

The map had listed the next item as being behind the manor. It had the spot marked next to the old oak tree. As I headed out the back door, I was stopped by a grip on my arm. I spun around with my fist in the air, ready to clobber whoever was attacking me.

CHAPTER TWENTY-EIGHT

Nicolas stood behind me. "Please, let me help you."

I studied his face as he stared. There was a restless energy about his movements. Did it have something to do with the vampire thing? A lock of hair fell forward on his head and I resisted pushing it back. He ran his tongue across his lips as he watched me. The urge to protect my neck came over me. A hunger flashed in his blue eyes.

"I suppose that would be okay," I said reluctantly.

It didn't appear as if I had a choice.

"Where's the book?" he asked.

"The spell book that will make me look like me again?" I asked.

He nodded. "Yeah, that's the one."

"Well, I found this map. It led me to the book that explains what is expected of a leader of the Underworld." The thought of me being the leader caused disbelief to come through in my tone. "The other mark was for outside. I'm praying that it's the book that will fix this. If not, I'll have a whole lot of explaining to do to the Coven."

"I can see where they'd want to know what is going on, yes." The sides of his mouth curved slightly into a grin.

"I supposed if I'm the leader of the Underworld I could just tell them to mind their own business." The thought brought a smile to my face.

Nicolas didn't comment on my snub of the Coven as he walked beside me. We headed toward the tree.

"Who hid these items all over the place?" he asked.

I cast a sideways glance at him. "I don't know what's going on, so I couldn't say for sure. My guess is my great-aunt did it, but why, I don't know. Why don't you tell me? Who was the leader before? It surely wasn't my great-aunt, right?" I asked. She did have all those postcards from people around the world.

"The leader was a powerful witch named Gina Rochester." His voice cracked at the mention of her name.

"Shouldn't she have been in possession of the books?" I asked with curiosity.

Nicolas nodded. "Yes, she should have been. Apparently, somehow your aunt got them. The Underworld has been looking for the books for a long time."

As we neared the tree, I said, "Because it needs a leader?" I asked as we neared the tree.

"Yes," Nicolas said softly.

And that lucky person was me? The Underworld surely wouldn't want me. Nicolas' voice seemed different, more distant, as if his thoughts were a million miles away.

"So where are we looking?" Nicolas asked.

"The map pointed out the spot right here between these two roots. I guess it's buried under there. At least I pray it is."

"Me too, because we have to get your appearance back to normal. Talking to myself is freaking me out."

I nodded. "That's understandable. We need to dig it up? I think there's a shovel in that shed." I pointed across the yard.

"Wait here. I'll be right back," Nicholas said as he turned and walked away.

I leaned against the tree and watched his muscular body as he walked away. It certainly was a nice view. As I waited for Nicolas to find the shovel, I scanned the area. I felt eyes on me and I knew the ghosts were watching. Luckily, if they saw me, they'd think I was Nicolas. They wouldn't confront him. At least I didn't think they would.

It only took a couple of seconds until I spotted the ghosts down by the river, unsuccessfully hiding behind a tree. The three of them stood together, staring at me. I pretended not to notice them. After all, a normal person might not see them, right? They obviously fell for it because they didn't offer to come toward me. They were busy talking to each other, probably plotting on how to get me to change them back to the living.

When I glanced back toward the shed, Nicolas had the shovel clasped in his hand. He didn't appear to notice the ghosts watching him as he walked across the back yard. Would the ghosts think it was strange to see two of Nicolas? Maybe they'd think he was a twin. What must Nicolas think of me? Who was this crazy witch who had changed her appearance to look like him? Wait until Annabelle found out what I'd done.

"Found it," Nicolas said as he approached. "Where should I start?"

"I think right there would be a good spot." I pointed.

I prayed that the map had been correct. I was preparing myself mentally if it hadn't been.

Once back at the tree, Nicolas stabbed the earth with the shovel and dumped the fresh dirt in a pile nearby. The smell of musty earth tickled my nostrils. After several shovelfuls, another box came into view.

"Right there," I said as I pointed at the ground.

Nicolas stood up and plunged the shovel into the ground. He knelt down and dug the rest of the dirt out with his hands. Nicolas reached down and pulled the box from the ground.

"That's it. It looks just like the other one I found," I said breathlessly.

"It's locked," he said.

"The key I found is upstairs in my bedroom. I hid it," I added bashfully. It seemed kind of ridiculous to hide it now that I said it out loud. But I couldn't be too cautious.

"You're something else." He chuckled. "How about I put the shovel away while you get the key?"

I wanted to tell him that I could handle it from here. Having him hang around while I tried a spell from the book would make me nervous. That was if there really was a book in the box. I surely didn't want him around if it didn't contain a book.

"That sounds good," I said finally.

CHAPTER TWENTY-NINE

After grabbing the key, I slowly lifted the lid of the box. A pent-up breath escaped my lips when I saw the book nestled between the velvet lining. It looked exactly like the others. To my relief the table of contents listed more spells. I scanned the list until I spotted the spell that I'd been looking for. Finally, I could be myself again. I clutched the book in my arms and carried it back to the kitchen. At least I didn't have to worry about walking like Nicolas anymore. That had been hard work.

Nicolas was standing in the kitchen when I entered. He was looking through Aunt Maddy's herbs. When he turned around, he smiled. His expression quickly turned into a grimace when he saw his own reflection again.

"I found the book," I said, holding the book up.

"That's a relief," he said. "I can help you with the spell."

"If it's all the same, I'd rather do this myself, if you don't mind." I didn't want to hurt his feelings.

He stared for a beat, then nodded. "Okay, yeah. Let me know if you need anything."

When Nicolas had disappeared out of sight, I flipped through the pages until I had the correct spell. If this didn't work I would be completely screwed. What would the Coven say about this mistake? They'd have to revise the 'what not to do' pamphlet.

I pulled all the ingredients together, dumped them in the cauldron and recited the words faster than ever. This had to be some kind of record for fastest-performed spells. After I was finished and nothing had happened, panic set in.

The click-clack of my shoes rang in my head as I ran to the bathroom down the hall. My stomach was twisted into a knot. I eased the door open and shut my eyes. Slowly, I opened them and said, "Oh, thank you. Thank you."

My own reflection stared back at me. Thank goodness that nightmare was over. One thing I'd noticed though: other witches weren't calling to complain that I'd messed up their spells while performing mine. That was definitely not a coincidence.

***

I woke the next morning to my phone ringing. Without opening my eyes, I fumbled for the phone on the nightstand.

"Halloween, we have a serious problem." My mother had never sounded so freaked out, even when I'd eliminated her eyebrows.

I opened my eyes and sat up. "What's wrong?"

"The Coven wants to speak with you." She rushed her words.

Uh-oh. "What do they want?" I asked innocently.

"I don't know, why don't you tell me?" she asked with resolve.

"I have no idea." I tried to keep my voice casual.

"Halloween, your lying has never worked on me. Why don't you tell me what's been going on." She had that tone I'd heard so many times when I was young. Why was I still hearing that tone as an adult?

I wasn't ready to have this conversation right now. This was something I needed to tell her in person. I threw my legs over the side of the bed and slid my feet into my slippers. Had the Coven told her the truth? Did the Coven know that I'd improved my magic by leaps and bounds?

"I guess I've been messing up my spells more than usual," I said.

"Oh, Halloween. What are we going to do? They may make you stop the magic this time." Disappointment sounded in my mother's voice.

I highly doubted that. I knew what they wanted to discuss, but how did they know that my magic had improved?

"Don't be surprised if you get a visit from the Coven," my mother said.

"What? You mean they're coming here?" I sat up in bed.

What would I tell them when they saw Isabeau? I knew they'd see her because she couldn't mind her own business.

"Do you need me to come over and talk with them when they arrive?" she asked.

I threw the covers off and jumped up. "No, no. I'll come by the store later, okay?"

I didn't want my mother to see Isabeau again either. The more she saw her, the more Isabeau would open her big mouth. For heaven's sakes, this got crazier by the minute.

"Listen, I have to make breakfast for my guests. I'll call you soon," I said while pulling clothing from my closet.

"Please be careful, Halloween," she said around a sigh.

What was that supposed to mean?

"I will," I said and hurried off the phone.

I'd just gotten dressed and locked my bedroom when the doorbell rang. Yeah, I still didn't trust my guests not to take the book. My heart told me that I was supposed to trust Nicolas, but my mind said no. I wouldn't let my guard down.

The doorbell rang loudly through the house. Swallowing the lump in my throat, I made my way down the stairs. I never thought I'd say this, but I was hoping it was the ghosts at the door again and not a Coven member.

When I peeked out the hole in the door, I knew I hadn't gotten that lucky. It wasn't a ghost and I recognized the woman on the other side of the door right away. Misty Middleton and I had gone to high school together and now she was queen supreme in the Coven. I had no choice but to answer the door. I knew she wouldn't go away.

The massive door squeaked as I opened it just a little. "Hi, Misty."

"I guess you know why I'm here."

"Would you like to come in?" I asked.

I spotted the ghosts over her shoulder and wanted to get her inside before they approached.

"Your spells have been going awfully smoothly lately." She regarded me with a strange curiosity.

I shrugged, pretending that it was no big deal. "I guess a little."

Misty had long, straight brown hair that was shiny like she'd finished it off with a clear coat. She wore a black skirt, a black blouse and black heels which made her tower over me. She was tall without them, but now she was the Empire State Building and I was a one-story cottage.

"Please come into the parlor." I gestured.

"Thank you," she said as she scoped out the foyer.

What was she looking for? Misty followed me into the living room. Her heels clicked against the hardwood floor.

"Can I get you something to drink?" I asked.

I had to be a good hostess. I might be nervous, but that was no reason to be impolite.

"No, I'm good. Thank you. This is such a beautiful home," she said with a tight-lipped smile.

I knew by her tone that she wished the small talk was over.

"Thank you," I said, wishing she'd get to the point of her visit.

"It must get lonely staying here all alone?"

I picked at the edge of the wingback chair. "Well, it's okay. I don't mind much."

Footsteps echoed from upstairs. I stopped and met her gaze. I could tell her about my bed-and-breakfast guests, but I really hoped Isabeau stayed upstairs. She was trouble and I didn't trust her not to run her mouth about what had happened.

Misty glanced up toward the ceiling, then looked at me for an answer.

"I guess you're aware that I'm running the place as a bed-and-breakfast?" I asked pushing the conversation along.

"You have guests already?" she asked with shock.

I'd let that comment slip. "Yes, as a matter of fact I do. I was just getting ready to make breakfast. You are out awfully early this morning."

She settled onto the deep red cushions of the chair and crossed her legs. "I do apologize for my timing, but I felt this was urgent."

She couldn't wait to let me know she was on to me. I needed her to get to the point and then leave.

"So what is so urgent that you needed to speak with me?" I wanted her to just cut to the chase.

Her mouth curved into a smile. Whether it was a friendly or pitying gesture I wasn't sure. "What are you doing differently?"

"What do you mean?"

"Your spells don't suck now," she said frankly.

Well, I had wanted her to get to the point.

I shrugged, trying to act innocent. "I guess I've just been practicing and it's finally paying off."

She studied my face for a few seconds. "That's it?"

"You know what they say, practice makes perfect." I plastered the best fake smile on my face that I could muster. "Is that all that you wanted?"

She walked around the room, taking in every detail. Misty ran her finger along the edge of books on the shelves, but remained quiet.

Sweat beaded on my forehead and it wasn't even hot in the room. Did she know about the spell books? She had to, right? That was something the Coven should definitely know about. But if she knew, then why didn't she just come out and say so?

"Well, whatever you're doing you should keep it up. Your magic before was absolutely horrendous."

I stared at her. "Yes, I'm aware."

She folded her hands together and placed them her on her lap. "Halloween, I'm going to stop the charade right now. We know about the book."

CHAPTER THIRTY

I froze. Should I continue to act as if I didn't know what she meant, or should I come clean about what I knew?

I tilted my eyebrow up in mock surprise. "What are you talking about?" I asked innocently.

The beginning of a smile tilted the corners of her mouth. "The Book of Mystic Magic. We know it's here. We know you have it."

I stared for a moment, but her gaze didn't leave mine. There was no way out of this. I would have to tell the truth.

I waved my hand through the air casually. "I may have found a book or two here. But they are mine and you can't have them."

She held her hands up. "Trust me, I don't want them."

I didn't know how to respond. I thought everyone wanted the powers that came with the book.

"Where did you find them?" she asked.

"They were hidden in various places around the house."

Her face lit up with excitement. For someone who didn't want the books, she sure had a lot of questions.

Her tight skirt confined her movements as she leaned forward in the chair. "Well, this is certainly a turn of events for you. I told everyone right away that you couldn't possibly have performed magic that well without some other type of intervention."

Her words stung. Maybe I should have tried harder to be better at the magic. Then I could have proven everyone wrong.

"Has anything strange happened since you got the new powers?" She looked at me expectantly.

"Strange?" I choked out.

She quirked an eyebrow. "Yes, have any of the spells been odd? Because there is one special skill that comes with the powers."

I thought I knew which special skill she was talking about. And the proof that I had that special skill was walking around in high heels upstairs and stuffing her face with cupcakes. "What type of special skill?" I asked.

I wasn't about to give away any details unless I absolutely had to.

"This is something that only a few witches know about, but your new powers allow you to reanimate the dead. Not to mention the many other powers that you probably only dreamed about having."

Now she was just being snarky. Plus, I had to pretend that I was shocked at the news about the reanimating. I widened my eyes and attempted my best Oscar-worthy performance.

"What do you mean reanimating?" I tried to conceal my nervousness.

"I mean you can make the dead living again. I'm not sure about all of the details. Like I don't know how long they stay reanimated, but it's true." She waved her hands through the air. "The Coven is buzzing about the news."

Wow. I was the talk of the Coven and for once it wasn't because I'd screwed up a spell.

"I know why the book was hidden here." She smiled slyly.

"You do? How do you know?" My eyes widened.

"Your great-aunt was a part of the Coven. We knew she was friends with the last leader and there was a rumor that she'd hidden the books for her."

"But why would she do that?" I ran my hand through my hair.

She shrugged. "That I don't have an answer for."

"Well, obviously she didn't tell me anything because I didn't even know about the book or this Underworld thing," I said.

"Maybe she meant for you to find it. She had to know you would when she left you the house." Her voice turned serious.

Aunt Maddy was eccentric but why would she be involved? She had said I was supposed to take my place in the world. But how would she know I would ever find the book? It was probably just a coincidence.

"My mother didn't mention any of this." I said.

"She doesn't know either. You'll probably want to tell her before she finds out from some of the other members," Misty said.

This news might really send my mother over the edge.

"There's something else too…" She hesitated.

"There's more?" I asked.

Misty looked straight at me and said, "You now possess the power of earth, air, water, and fire. No witch holds all four without the power of the book."

"What is the power of earth, air, fire, and water?" I asked in a shaky voice. For a witch I didn't know much about the rules.

She leaned back in her chair. "The ultimate powers. You control who can perform magic."

This was all too much to take in. And I wasn't sure I believed her. I had noticed that she was looking at me entirely differently now. It was as if I was someone worthy of her friendship now. Like I hadn't been in the past. I didn't need fair-weather friends.

"I'm sure the other Coven members will want to talk with you about all of this."

"I'm sure they will," I said drily.

She fingered more of the books, then finally looked at me. "The Coven is extremely happy with your improved skills."

I hadn't expected that comment.

"We'd love it if you'd host the annual Halloween Ball here at LaVeau Manor. What better location than this gorgeous place?"

My eyes were probably the size of saucers. "You want me to host the party?" I asked.

She nodded with a smile. "Yes, with your newfound skills, I know you'll be a perfect hostess. It was planned for the community center, but let's face it, that place is ugly."

What was the catch? There had to be one. I couldn't deny that I was excited about the prospect though. It had always been a dream of mine. Now I would be hosting the ball that all the witches attended. It was the event they talked about all year. So they finally wanted me to be one of them? Would I no longer be an outcast? But did I really want to be a part of their snobby club? It wasn't like I could say no though. It would break my mother's heart if I turned them down.

She studied my face for a reaction. "What do you say? Won't it be fabulous here? It'll be gorgeous with the dim lighting and lots of candles. Of course the Coven will pay for the catering." Misty pushed to her feet and walked the length of the room, her heels echoing across the floor.

I was still had a loss for words, but I finally managed to say, "Sure, I'd love to host the Halloween Ball."

She smiled. "Fantastic. I'll let everyone know. Well, I'd better let you get to work. The ball is in two days." She strolled across the room. "I'll be in touch soon."

Two days? That was a lot of work to get done in such a short time, even for witches.

CHAPTER THIRTY-ONE

When we reached the foyer, I wanted to shove her back into the living room. Isabeau had just stepped off the bottom step and was staring right at Misty. I continued on toward the front door. Maybe if I ignored her she wouldn't speak to Misty.

"Oh hello, I'm Isabeau," she said with her sweet southern voice flowing like honey from her lips.

When I turned around, Isabeau was sticking her hand out toward Misty. So much for ignoring her.

"It's nice to meet you, Isabeau. What a beautiful name." Misty took in Isabeau's full appearance.

Isabeau beamed and looked at me, then back to Misty. "Thank you. It's been in my family for years."

"You must be a guest here?" Misty asked.

Isabeau looked at me, then back at Misty again. "You could say that. Halloween and I are old friends." She plastered a fake smile on her face. "Aren't we, Halloween?"

"Oh really? Are you from around here?" Misty frowned. "You look so familiar."

Isabeau waved off the question with a flick of her wrist. "Oh, I lived here a long time ago, but not recently."

She quirked an eyebrow questioningly. "Did you go to Enchantment Pointe High?"

"No, as a matter of fact I didn't. I was a child when I lived here." Isabeau was growing impatient with Misty's questions.

Misty was so snoopy. Why didn't she just drop the topic? And Isabeau wasn't helping matters either.

"My Great-Aunt Maddy and Isabeau's mother knew each other. Isabeau hasn't lived in Enchantment Pointe since she was a child. Isn't that right, Isabeau?" I glared at Isabeau.

If she didn't go along with my story I would for sure kick her out on her butt.

"Yes, that's right," she said with a fake smile. "Hallie and I know each other from her aunt and mother."

I smiled. Isabeau had just saved her butt.

"Oh, is that right?" Misty said, looking a bit confused. "Well, it was nice meeting you." She waved her hand. "Where are my manners? My name is Misty Middleton."

"I know," Isabeau said.

I shot daggers at Isabeau with my eyes.

"What?" Misty frowned.

"You told me before." Isabeau batted her eyelashes.

Now Isabeau was just messing with Misty. She knew she hadn't introduced herself.

"I did?" Misty asked with a confused look.

"Well, it was nice of you to stop by, Misty. Let me know when you have more details." I ushered her toward the front door.

She kept glancing over her shoulder at Isabeau. "Yeah, I'll let you know," she said, distracted.

"Nice to meet you," Isabeau said in a sweet voice.

When I'd practically pushed Misty out the door, I turned around and glared at Isabeau.

"What's for breakfast? I'm starving." Isabeau flashed a wide grin.

"After what you just did I shouldn't make anything for you," I warned with a wave of my finger.

She stuck out her bottom lip. "What? I was only being polite."

Yeah, like she was only being polite to Nicolas and Liam too. She couldn't keep her hands off them.

"Just don't let it happen again," I warned.

She glared at me with one of the evilest looks that I'd ever seen before. It sent a chill down my spine but I wouldn't let her think that she was intimidating me. I stomped off toward the kitchen, hoping that she wouldn't follow. But she walked along behind me, her presence a constant by my side. Having a sit-down breakfast with Isabeau, Liam, and Nicolas should be interesting.

I still couldn't believe what had just happened. Even the Coven had now taken an interest in my new badass witchcraft skills. What a crazy turn of events.

CHAPTER THIRTY-TWO

Isabeau ate Liam and Nicolas' breakfast. Apparently they had business and skipped breakfast. They did that often. Should I take that as a hint of my cooking ability? Maybe I should try the magic more in the kitchen. But at the rate Isabeau was stuffing pancakes into her mouth, I wasn't sure I really needed it.

When Isabeau wasn't looking, I slipped out of the house. I hurried behind the wheel and cranked the engine. If she found out that I'd left without her, she'd be furious.

As I drove down the driveway, the ghosts followed behind the car. They stared and scowled. I was pretty sure they were plotting against me. I punched the gas and pulled out onto the road before they had a chance to catch me.

On my drive to the store, I called Annabelle and asked her to meet me there. Annabelle pulled up behind me just as I'd shoved the car into park. I was happy to have her with me when I broke the news to my mother. She might faint and I'd need help lifting my mother off the floor. Annabelle looked bright and cheerful in her red sweater and jeans.

"You got away from your unwanted guest?" she asked as she approached my car.

"It wasn't easy. I made a batch of cupcakes and left them out where she could see them."

Annabelle laughed. "By the way, I did more research this morning."

"What did you find out?" I asked.

"Nothing," she replied.

My stomach sank. "Nothing?"

"Nothing. There was no death certificate for anyone by that name. Not that I could find anyway." She sighed.

I didn't want to question her research abilities. After all, she had done this for me out of the kindness of her heart.

"I even searched the birth certificates too. Of course it could be so old that it's hard to find or doesn't even exist. It may be hard to find out anything without more information."

I sighed. "Yeah, and I doubt she'll be willing to give me any more info."

Annabelle huffed. "You should tell her to tell you more details about her life or to get out."

It wasn't quite that simple, but Annabelle was right. I needed to demand more information.

"I'll have to do more research on the house too. Maybe I can find out if there's any connection."

"It's worth a shot," Annabelle said.

Why would she be haunting LaVeau Manor? She didn't just pick it at random.

"Come on. Let's go inside," I said.

"So what's going on? Why did you need me to be here?"

"I want to tell both of you something. I figured it was better to do it at once. You two can support one another." I offered a big smile.

"You're scaring me," Annabelle said as I held the door to Bewitching Bath and Beauty open for her.

"Don't panic. It's just something I need to share with the two most important people in my life."

I tried to soothe her fears with a smile. She gave a weak smile in return.

My mother rushed toward us when we walked through the door. "Well, what happened?" she asked impatiently. "Did they come to see you? I heard Misty Middleton was there?"

I tried to read my mother's expression. Apparently, they were keeping her in the dark about what was truly happening. Didn't she know about the book that Aunt Maddy had hidden?

"What's going on?" Annabelle asked as she sniffed an aromatherapy candle.

"Why don't you both have a seat?" I pointed at the stools.

Annabelle looked at my mother. They both walked over and sat on the stools behind the counter. I stood in front of them, searching for the right words. My mother waved her hands, telling me to get on with it.

I shrugged then said offhandedly, "The Coven just had some questions about my new magic skills."

My mother's face was all smiles.

I stared at her. "Do you know about the books?"

She smiled wider and nodded. "I just found out. I am so proud of you."

I frowned. "For what? I didn't do anything? It's not like I made the books or something."

"What's going on? What books?" Annabelle's brow creased with worry.

I didn't answer and my mother continued.

"Don't you see, Halloween? You were chosen for this. That's why your magic was bad for so many years." She pasted on smile of nonchalance.

I shook my head. "I don't believe that."

My mother shrugged. "Well, believe it or not, it's the truth."

"Will someone please tell me what's going on?" Annabelle frowned.

"There's an Underworld. As far as I can tell it's not really underground," I said, trying to sound casual.

My mother shook her head.

"Anyway, it's like the overseers of the paranormal world. And yours truly is now the leader of it."

Annabelle started choking. My mother handed her a bottle of water and I patted her on the back.

"Are you okay?" I asked.

When she finally caught her breath, she said, "Are you kidding me? Is this a joke?"

I shook my head. "Unfortunately, I am not joking. I don't even want this."

"But you can't turn it down now," my mother said in a panic.

"What if I gave someone else the book and let them be the leader? I just want a normal life."

My mother gasped. "You can't do that. No, no, no."

"You're not the one thrown into this crazy world," I said.

"I realize that, but if you're meant to do this, then you need to give it your best shot. Now I know I didn't raise a quitter."

She always threw that line at me.

"So what does this leader of the Underworld do?" Annabelle asked.

I shrugged. "How am I supposed to know? I didn't get an orientation packet. I have a couple of strange men running around, one telling me not to accept it, and the other one saying the same thing but he wants the book for some reason. He claims he'll destroy it."

My mother shook her head. "No way, don't let him have that book. I wouldn't trust him."

I let out a deep breath. "Don't worry. I didn't give it to him and I don't plan on it either." I looked at Annabelle, then to my mother. "Part of the special skills is that I can reanimate the dead."

"That's the part I don't like," my mother said. "You should stay away from that."

"I'm trying to stay away from all of it. But I accidentally turned the ghost that was living in the manor back into a living, breathing annoying snot of a person. It's like the freakin' pet cemetery at my house," I said.

"What? There's a ghost in the manor with you?" My mother swayed a little then sat back down on the stool.

I rushed over and steadied her.

"Well, she's not a ghost any more. It was the woman I brought by here. Her name is Isabeau and she is a pain in the butt."

"Can't you get rid of her?" Annabelle asked.

"Well, I haven't found the counter spell. Besides, I don't think the spell lasts forever. Soon enough she'll be gone."

My mother shook her head. "No, you need to get rid of her. I'll come over today and help you find the spell that gets rid of her."

I picked up the sampler for the new lip gloss that my mother had made. I smeared it across my lips then puckered in disgust. "This stuff is terrible."

She snatched it from my hands. "Well, it's not finished yet," she said defensively.

I didn't even try to argue with my mother about finding the counter spell for Isabeau. When she set her mind to something there was no stopping her. Must be where I got my stubbornness from.

"There's something else I want to tell you," I said looking at my mother.

"I don't know if I can handle much more, Halloween." She clutched at her chest.

"I think you'll enjoy this news."

Her eyes brightened and she sat a little straighter. "I'm listening."

"The Coven has asked me to host the annual Halloween Ball," I announced.

My mother gasped and clasped her hands together. "I can't believe it. My one and only daughter is finally being welcomed by the Coven." She waved her hands in front of her face to fend off the tears.

This was what made her proud? What about that I'd started a small business? I didn't need the approval of some club. Or did I? Why was I so excited about hosting the Halloween Ball?

Annabelle sat up straighter. "I don't know, Halloween. I don't think you should give them the time of day."

I cast a glance at my mother. She would not be happy with Annabelle for that statement. I gave a warning glare to Annabelle, but she didn't take the hint.

Annabelle scoffed. "They didn't want you before, so why should you allow them into your life now?"

There was no way I could let my mother down now. The look of happiness on her face was priceless. As much as I'd disappointed her with my magic in the past, I owed her this one. Besides, I couldn't deny that I liked being wanted for a change. I was popular and it felt good.

"I see your point, Annabelle, but this way I can show them I am in charge. I can finally prove myself."

My mother beamed. Annabelle shrugged. She'd come around to my way of thinking soon enough. I gestured with a tilt of my head for Annabelle to look at my mother.

When she noticed my mother's smile, she nodded in understanding. "Well, I guess now that you've explained it, the party at the manor does sound like a good idea."

CHAPTER THIRTY-THREE

When I returned to the manor that evening for my date
with Liam, Isabeau had Nicolas cornered in the library.
She was running her hands through his hair. Why didn't
Nicolas just tell her to get lost? I was all for manners and
Southern hospitality, but I had to draw the line
somewhere. Isabeau had to go. My movement must have
caught Isabeau's attention because she turned around and
glared at me. Nicolas' fangs reached over the bottom of his
mouth and his eyes had a glazed-over look. I wouldn't
even bother to ask what was going on.

Isabeau smirked and laughed. "Good evening,
Halloween." She said my name with disgust. "Are you all
ready for your evening with Liam?"

She touched Nicolas' face as he stared at me. I couldn't
read his expression, but it looked like there was hurt in his
eyes. I hadn't told him of my plans with Liam. I hadn't
planned on it either. There was nothing to my date with
Liam, right? I'd wanted to get more information from him.
That was all. He seemed more forthcoming about the
whole situation with me anyway.

Nicolas shouldn't be jealous when he was flirting with
Isabeau. I didn't hang around and give Isabeau another

chance to mock me. There was no telling what she had said to Nicolas. I had to get rid of her right away. No more feeling sorry for her and no more Ms. Nice Girl.

I turned around and ran out the front door. Now more than ever I needed fresh air and to get away from everyone. All I wanted was to be alone with my thoughts.

Nicolas called out to me, "Halloween, please, I want to talk with you."

I glanced over my shoulder as I ran. Nicolas moved with lightning speed after me. I knew I wouldn't be able to outrun him. What did he want? There was nothing to talk about. Up ahead, the ghosts waited for me. They didn't even try to hide this time. They were becoming bolder and obviously losing their patience waiting for me to perform magic. If they were anything like Isabeau there was no way I would ever turn them.

My side hurt and my legs couldn't move any faster. My speed was slowing. When I reached the line of trees, Nicolas grabbed my arm from behind. He spun me around and pulled me toward his chest. His eyes were clear and focused on my face. His gaze slid down to my lips and he pressed his mouth against mine. I sucked in a sharp breath. My heart raced as his tongue met with mine. I couldn't stop myself. His lips were warm and delicious and I relished every moment of it. His tongue traced a sensuous path down my neck and I sucked in a sharp breath. The tips of his fangs eased against my warm flesh.

Finally, I let my mind break free from this moment. I pulled away and stared at him.

"Halloween, don't go out with Liam tonight," he said.

"Is that what all of this is about? You just don't want me to go out with him?"

"No, that's not what all of this is about." He stepped closer to me and I moved back a few steps.

I stared at his fangs and then back at him. "This is just all some weird macho game you all have going on, isn't it? You don't care about me at all."

200

"That's where you're wrong. I do care about you." His gaze fell to my neck..

"Then why shouldn't I go out with him tonight?" I stared at him waiting for an answer.

"Because I want you to go out with me. I want to be with you."

The ghosts had found us. I looked around and they had me surrounded. It was like they were planning their attack. Nicolas didn't seem to notice or, if he did, he didn't care.

"What is going on with Isabeau? You looked awfully cozy together." I tried not to sound accusing.

He shook his head. "There is something going on with her and I'm not sure what."

I looked around at the ghosts and they stepped closer. I would have to get out of there soon or I wasn't sure what they would do next.

"What do you mean?" I asked, glancing over my shoulder again.

"There is a bad vibe about her," Nicolas said.

"You can say that again."

"Where did she come from?" he asked.

"I don't know. She was here when I got the house. I don't know how long she's been here or what she wants. I don't know why she is here."

"Have you asked her to leave?" He looked at me intently.

I glanced over my shoulder again. "Not exactly. It isn't that easy. She has nowhere to go. I didn't want to kick her out with nothing. I have tried to find out about her. I looked for a death certificate, but I can't find anything. She says she was from Enchantment Pointe, but I can't find any proof of that."

Nicolas reached for my hand again. Maybe it was my imagination, but I thought he was staring at my neck with a hunger in his eyes. Did he want my blood? It would make sense that he did. After all, he was a vampire.

I peeked over my shoulder again. The ghosts had moved closer. There was no more time left. I had to get out of there.

I pulled away from Nicolas. "I have to go."

He touched my arm. "Halloween, don't go. It's not safe."

Yeah, he was telling me. It wasn't safe anywhere I went. My life wasn't safe anymore. I felt like the walls were closing in on me and I was running out of places to go.

I ran toward the house and didn't look back. If Nicolas followed me, I didn't know. It didn't matter. I burst through the door and toward the stairs.

Isabeau was standing in the foyer. "You look like hell."

I didn't hurl the insult at her that I wanted to. I bit my tongue and continued upstairs. Maybe I was just jealous of Isabeau's flirting with Nicolas, but it was my home and I could toss anyone I wanted out on their butt.

I'd take a shower and get ready for my evening with Liam. Maybe he could help me figure out what was going on. I could trust him, right? After all, he was a witch like me. Witches had to stick together. He wouldn't lie to another witch. He'd done nothing but offer to help me since he arrived at the manor.

I slipped under the water and tried to erase the crazy thoughts from my mind. It was no use though. I was more confused than ever. My thoughts were consumed with Nicolas' lips pressed against mine—the heat from his body and the tips of his fangs touching my mouth.

I climbed out of the shower and into a blue dress and heels. I wasn't sure where Liam was taking me, but I hoped it was away from this place for the evening. If I had some distance, maybe I could stop thinking about it for a while.

But the reason for my date was to find out more about what was going on and nothing more. I'd push romance away. Discovering Nicolas and Liam's true agenda was my main concern.

When I stepped out of the door, I heard movement coming from Isabeau's room. I walked over and pressed my ear against the door again. She was reciting another spell. What was she up to? I needed to ask the Coven about her. Surely someone knew of a witch who had died and was possibly haunting the manor. Perhaps if I tried to find out more history about the manor it would give me clues about Isabeau. There had to be more information about the manor other than the rumors I'd heard over the years.

CHAPTER THIRTY-FOUR

Liam was supposed to meet me in the parlor. When I reached the entrance to the room, he was already there, looking out the window. He seemed deep in thought.

"What are you looking at?" I asked.

He turned around and drank in my appearance. "You look beautiful."

I smiled. That was a good way to start the evening. Had he been looking at the ghosts? I hoped they weren't waiting for me when we went outside. I was glad that Nicolas hadn't been downstairs when Liam and I left for our date. It would have been awkward to see him.

"Where are you taking me?" I asked as we stepped out onto the veranda.

"I thought we'd eat at a great little place in town." He held the car door open for me.

"That sounds lovely."

We slipped into Liam's sleek black car and eased down the driveway. When I glanced in the side mirror, I saw Nicolas looking out the library window at us. My heart sank. What had he tried to warn me about? Why was I in danger?

A strange vibe buzzed around us, but I wasn't sure what feeling was or where it came from. It was a different sensation from what I felt from the books. I glanced over at Liam and he smiled. Could he be what Nicolas was warning me about? No, he just didn't want me to go out with him. Nothing more.

"Have you always been great with your witchcraft powers?" I asked.

Liam glanced over at me as he steered around the corner. "Um, I suppose so. Like with everything I improve with practice. Why do you ask?"

"I don't think it's any secret that my magic wasn't the best before I got the spell book."

He stared at the road. "No, it wasn't a secret. But that's the past now. I wouldn't worry about that."

I studied his handsome profile. "Speaking of past, you and Nicolas are still enigmatic about your past. Why don't you tell me more about yourself? After all, people having dinner together usually talk about themselves and share details."

He glanced over again. "There's not much to say. I'm just a boring guy. After college I began working for the Underworld. I've been there for ten years now."

"Do you have a ton of cases?"

"I keep busy, yes. You're the most interesting so far though." A smile played at the corners of his mouth.

I would have said that he and Nicolas were the most interesting guests I'd had so far, but they were the only guests. If any future guests were more interesting I would definitely reconsider the bed-and-breakfast business.

We made it into town and parked along the curb in front of the little restaurant. Liam opened the car door for me and I slipped out. With his hand on the small of my back, he guided me toward the restaurant's entrance. Stars sparkled in the black ceiling of sky.

"I'm glad you agreed to go out with me." Liam's presence was resilient as he walked along beside me.

I glanced over at him as we walked into the restaurant.

"I wasn't sure if you just wanted to go out because of your weird competition with Nicolas."

"There is no competition," he said with a smile.

Checkered tablecloths covered the tables dotting the room. Candles were placed in empty wine glasses with wax dripping down the sides in the middle of the tables. Luckily, Liam had made reservations or we probably would have been waiting for a long time. We weaved around tables full of people and were seated at the back of the restaurant. We ordered pasta and wine from the menu.

Taking a sip of my wine, I studied Liam's handsome face. "Why did you come to LaVeau Manor?"

I didn't want to beat round the bush any longer. I'd just come out with it.

He sipped his wine then offered an easy smile. "You don't waste any time."

"I feel like I've waited long enough to ask. I trust you'll give me honest answers." I folded my hands in front of me on the table and waited for a response.

He set his glass down. "The law in the Underworld doesn't want a witch to rule who shouldn't be in that position. They sent me to make sure the book didn't get in the wrong hands."

"Then why do you want to destroy it? Wouldn't that end law and order?"

He shrugged. "Maybe it's time for a change in the Underworld."

"A change for the worse? How long have things been tumultuous?" I asked.

"Not long," he offered. "It didn't take long for things to get out of control."

"So why change now?"

He shrugged. "Things change. Why not make it now?"

"I haven't seen anyone show up other than you and Nicolas who want the book. So why should I take your word for it?" Maybe there was too much distrust in my voice, but I felt it was justified.

Well, no one other than the men and Isabeau had shown up. But I didn't think she had any interest in the book other than wanting to make sure she wasn't turned back into a ghost, although I didn't know that for sure. She had been performing a lot of spells.

"Mara hasn't tracked you down yet, but she will." His tone was apologetic.

"How were you able to find me before she was?"

"That's my job. That's why I was hired as a detective for the Underworld and she wasn't."

I guessed he did have a point.

"Who is this Mara?" I asked as our food was placed down in front of us.

I didn't waste any time sinking my fork into the food. Planning the Halloween Ball, running from ghosts and vampires, and having dinner with mysterious gorgeous men was hard work. It made me hungry.

"She's the estranged sister of the last leader. Mara feels she should be the one in charge, that her sister's death somehow made her in line to get the book. She'll eventually be able to track down where the book is," he said.

"Why wouldn't she be the new leader then? How is this decided?"

"It's usually decided by the current leader and a team. That's if the leader retired, but if something happens to the last leader, then it's a completely different scenario. Apparently the last leader felt that her sister would get the book—that was why she had your aunt hide the book."

"What happened to the last leader?" I asked, almost afraid to find out the answer.

"She was murdered," he replied softly.

207

CHAPTER THIRTY-FIVE

I choked on my wine.

"Who murdered her?" I asked when I'd recovered.

He stared at me. "We don't know. It was rumored that her sister killed her."

I swallowed hard, then asked, "For the book?"

He nodded. "Yes, for the book."

And now she was coming for me? This couldn't end well. And I thought I had problems before. If what he said was true, I had a lot more to worry about than a few botched spells.

"Have you always lived in New Orleans?" I'd play the same question game with Liam as I had with Nicolas.

"No, I lived in Bayou L'Ourse," he offered casually.

My eyes narrowed. "So you are both from the same town? You know each other well, don't you?"

"No." He didn't meet my stare.

"You are both from the same town, currently live in New Orleans and show up on my doorstep within hours of each other, but you don't know each other?"

"I didn't say we don't know each other," he said.

"Yes, you did. When I first met you all." I pointed my fork at him.

"I may have crossed paths with Nicolas at the coven meetings."

My heart rate increased. "Wait. Why would a vampire be at the coven meetings?"

"Didn't he tell you? He's a witch too," Liam replied as if this was common knowledge.

"He didn't tell me," I said softly.

Why had Nicolas left out that detail about his life?

"So if you didn't ask me out just because of Nicolas, then why did you ask me out?" I cast a glance his way.

He smiled. "I asked you out because I think you're a fascinating person. With a name like Halloween how could you not be?"

I tried to hide my smile. "Having a name like Halloween isn't easy."

"You certainly make it seem easy." He grinned then took another drink from his glass.

"Why does Nicolas tell me that you're dangerous, then you warn me that Nicolas is dangerous?"

"I can assure you I am not dangerous." He placed his hand on mine. "I'm a sucker for a pretty face though."

"Flattery will get you nowhere, Mr. Rankin." I pointed with my fork.

"It's not flattery, Hallie. It's a fact." He took a drink of wine.

"That doesn't really answer my question though. Why should I be afraid of Nicolas?" I wouldn't take my eyes off him until he answered.

He leaned forward, placing his elbows on the table. "I'm just not sure he has your best interest at heart."

"But you do?" I asked with a raised brow.

"Absolutely." He took another bite from his plate.

I'd taken the last bite of my tiramisu when I felt eyes on me. The ghosts had entered the restaurant. This was not good. How had they gotten in? If they could come in here, then I would probably no longer be able to keep them out of the manor. I had to find a way to protect myself from them. With scowls on their faces, they looked like they were completely pissed off. This was no longer about being reanimated. This was now more about revenge against me.

"Do you see them?" I asked with a tilt of my head.

Liam looked toward the restaurant's entrance. "You mean the gang of ghosts over there?"

"Yeah. They want me to reanimate them." I blew the hair out of my eyes.

He shrugged. "So do it."

"What? Are you crazy? I don't want the one I've got. Why would I want to add more to my list?" I loudly whispered.

He finished his last bite. "Did you tell them to go away?"

"Of course I did," I said.

"I'm not sure there's anything else you can do then," he said.

"Can you please get me out of here? And without the ghosts seeing us?"

"Come on." He grabbed my hand and I couldn't deny that this touch felt fantastic. "We'll go out the back door."

"I don't think we're supposed to do that," I warned, glancing over my shoulder.

"We aren't supposed to do a lot of things, but sometimes it's necessary." He pulled on my hand.

I hid my smile. Liam was definitely the bad boy type. And that was a bad thing for me. With some dirty looks from the chef, we slipped through the kitchen and out the back door into the alleyway. We made it around the side of the building and Liam peeked around the corner.

"Are they there?" I whispered.

"No." He shook his head. "The coast is clear."

Running from ghosts was getting the better of me. Something had to be done.

"I'm so sorry, but I think I need to get home so I can find a spell that will protect me from the ghosts."

"If you say so," he said. "I still think it wouldn't do any harm to help them."

"I'll make my own decisions, thank you very much."

Before I had a chance to step forward, he grabbed my hand again and swung me into the circle of his chest. His arms held me in a tight embrace. Then he pressed his lips against mine. My heart raced. This was crazy... kisses from both men. Liam's lips moved across mine with a sense of urgency. I reluctantly pushed at his hard chest and backed away him away.

"We need to go," I said softly.

The warmth of his lips lingered on my mouth. Liam nodded and helped me into the car.

During the ride home Liam tried to keep the conversation light. I knew he sensed my tension. He asked about the process of running a bed-and-breakfast and about my mother's business. I was thankful for the easygoing chat.

Nicolas' car wasn't there when we'd returned to the manor. My heart sank a little. I was so torn as to what to do.

Liam held the door open for me. "Do you want me to help you with the spell?"

I shook my head. "I think I have to do this on my own."

He brushed my cheek with his hand. "Let me know if you need help."

I nodded. Liam walked up the stairs. When he turned the corner, I slipped into the kitchen. I'd been through the spell books and hadn't seen anything to keep the ghosts away. I was sure Aunt Maddy had a protection spell though. It would have to do.

I pulled the book from the shelf, then collected the ingredients that I needed.

After performing the spell, I headed upstairs. It had been a long day. Tomorrow I had to begin preparing for the Halloween Ball. There was only a day until the party. I should have told them that there wasn't enough time, but I had been so thrilled that they'd asked that I couldn't possibly have said no. How pathetic was I? I'd show them how to really throw a party though. It would be the party of the century.

CHAPTER THIRTY-SIX

I woke in the middle of the night with a strange pull willing me out of the bed. The overwhelming desire to go outside compelled me from bed, down the stairs and out the front door. The wind was cold against my exposed skin. I had no idea what was bringing me out here.

I stopped in the middle of the front driveway. I looked up at the rolling clouds. They zoomed past at a million miles a minute. Was I dreaming? No, this seemed all too real. A tingling sensation started at my feet and moved slowly up my body, flowing up my legs, through my torso, over to my arms and up to my head.

I collapsed to my knees. My body was drained and my limbs were lifeless. I fell forward onto the ground and couldn't move. The smell of grass and dirt assaulted my senses. It felt as if something was draining all the energy from my body. The clouds zoomed past above me. The wind whipped around my body, yet I still couldn't move. I willed my body to move, but nothing happened.

My thoughts became foggy and I only remembered bits and pieces. Someone swooped me up and into his strong arms. I couldn't open my eyes to see who it was. I smelled the familiar spicy scent. It was definitely a male. He carried me across the yard.

We moved up the stairs of the manor and through the front door. He carried me up the stairs and into my bedroom, laying me gently on my bed. He pulled the cover up over me and tucked it tight against my body. I was warm again and drifted off to sleep easily.

When I woke in the morning, I wasn't sure if it had all been a dream. I opened my eyes and looked around. Nothing was out of place. When I pulled the covers back though, I realized it hadn't been a dream. My gown was stained with dirt and grass. Who had carried me inside? And what had happened?

Throwing back the covers, I jumped out of bed and threw on a white long-sleeved shirt and jeans. When I stepped into the hallway, everything was quiet. No noise came from Isabeau. Today was the day when I would talk with her. She had to be out of the house by the Halloween Ball. I didn't want her to ruin it for me.

In my bare feet, I eased down the stairs, careful not to make a noise. When I stepped into the parlor, I was startled to see Liam and Nicolas talking to each other. Were they challenging each other to a duel? They didn't notice me at first and I thought about sneaking back out and listening to the conversation from the hallway. Unfortunately, they were talking so quietly I couldn't make out what was being said.

My contemplation was over though because both men turned to look at me at the same time. The solemn looks on their faces had me nervous.

"What's going on?" I asked.

I wanted to ask which one had brought me inside, but it would have to wait.

They exchanged a glance, then glanced around.

"What are you all looking for?" I asked.

"Where is Isabeau?" Nicolas asked.

"I have no idea. Why? I guess she's in her room." I frowned.

"She must leave right away. Your life depends on it." Liam didn't take his eyes off me.

I felt my chest tighten. "What? What are you talking about?"

"We've discovered information about her." Nicolas' face darkened.

"Such as?" I asked, motioning for them to spill it.

"Isabeau isn't just a witch, she is a demon... and demons use their powers to drain energy away from witches," Nicolas explained.

"Wait." I massaged my temples. "Just let me wrap my mind around this. What you're saying is she is here to hurt me?"

They both nodded.

"Why me though?" I asked.

"Isabeau was sent by Mara to take your power," Nicolas said.

I glanced over my shoulder, looking for Isabeau. Was this true? The thought sent a chill down my spine. And to think I'd made her cupcakes. I was furious. But a demon? How did I begin to get rid of a demon?

"Was that what happened last night?" I looked from Nicolas to Liam. "I was outside. Something pulled me out there. I couldn't stop it. It felt like all the energy was being drained from my body."

Liam nodded. "She is using magic against you. She'll take all your power. That opens you up to allow Mara to get the book."

"So Mara knows where I am? I thought she hadn't found me yet? I thought you were such a great detective that you found me first." Panic rose in my voice.

Liam stared at me. "Well, did I not arrive before Isabeau?" he asked.

I paused, then finally had to say, "Yes, I guess you did."

"She figured with me here that she'd have to find another way to get the book. With the magic Isabeau is doing, they hoped you'd be so weak that you'd just give them the book."

"Fat chance of that." I scoffed.

"They counted on you getting rid of us before now too," Nicolas said.

"What do I do now?" I asked.

"You have to use your powers to banish her from the house. It won't be easy," Liam said.

"I'm here to help you," Nicolas said.

Liam glowered at Nicolas. "I am here for you, Hallie."

Nicolas glared back at Liam. Nicolas stepped closer to Liam and he puffed out his chest. I held my breath waiting for the first punch to be thrown.

I threw my hands in the air. "Enough! You all need to stop. I have enough to worry about right now without you two fighting."

They backed off, but didn't apologize. Tension still hung in the air.

"Is there a spell in the book for this?" I asked.

"Yes, there should be something for banishing the demons. But I'll warn you now. It's not an easy one. It'll take all the energy you can get. You're already depleted from last night." Liam rubbed the back of his neck and let out a deep breath.

"This is your fault, Liam." Nicolas clenched his jaw.

I walked out of the room, leaving the men arguing. They could waste time if they wanted, but I had problems to solve.

I needed to do this right away before she came down in search of doughnuts. I hadn't known a demon would eat so much. I hurried upstairs and didn't wait for Liam or Nicolas. They could argue over what I needed to do next if they wanted, but I had to get rid of Isabeau.

I'd have to use the darkest spell I could find to force Isabeau off the manor grounds. Isabeau had vowed to return. I knew she'd keep that promise.

I'd had a confrontation with Isabeau—and I hadn't even known it. I'd learned the hard way that bad spirits can steal power from witches.

CHAPTER THIRTY-SEVEN

After retrieving the spell books from the hiding place in my room, I scanned the contents until I found the section on demons. This wasn't a sweet little spell to make cupcakes. This would require a lot of my energy and top-notch powers. I wasn't sure if I had what it took, but I had to give it a shot. There were no other options. I had to rid my home of this demon witch. And to think I'd been feeding cupcakes to a demon. How bizarre was that?

When I reached the library again, Liam and Nicolas were pacing on opposite sides of the room. I ignored their stares and headed straight to the kitchen to gather the items I needed. I grabbed the spices and herbs and moved through the library again. The men still paced back and forth. Heck, they didn't even seem to notice what I was doing this time.

The spell required that I perform it outside. If it worked like it was supposed to, then it would lure the nasty demon outside. Isabeau wouldn't be able to set foot on the manor's grounds when I was done.

After setting up my items in the middle of the front lawn, I looked up at the manor and as if on cue, Isabeau glared down at me from her bedroom window. She knew what I was about to try. Somehow she knew. For a moment, her face skewed into that of a dark monster, twisted and gnarled. In the blink of an eye, she morphed back to the beautiful Isabeau, offering me a sweet smile. I wasn't falling for that act any longer though. She could run back to Mara and tell her that this witch wasn't playing their games any longer.

Energy and current flowed through my body like a live wire. Pulling every bit of power from within, I recited the spell over the ingredients that I'd mixed together.

The wind whipped and whirled and the clouds zoomed past as if I'd pressed the fast-forward button. Rain fell from the heavens in a light mist against my face. Gathering the mixture into my hands, I walked the perimeter of the grounds. I'd call the elemental four corners. After all, Misty said I possessed that power now. What better time than now to see if she was correct?

Looking down, I was careful of each step. As I walked, I sprinkled the mixture onto the ground and chanted. Facing north, I began to recite the words: "Element of Earth, I call to you. Empower me with your energy to banish the wicked." As I turned the corner, facing west, I recited the words: "Element of Air, I call to you to push the unnatural force from this place." Walking more, I turned to the south and recited the words: "Element of Fire, I call to you for warmth and protection. Help me have the knowledge." To complete the spell, I turned one last time to the east and recited the words: "Element of Water, I call to you for force and tranquility. Give me the force to change the power and banish the evil."

Each time the mixture of herbs and spices hit the earth, tiny flames flicked and quickly burnt out. I glanced back at the window where Isabeau stood. She looked down at me with venom in her eyes. No matter her look of hate, I wouldn't let her get through to me. I concentrated harder and continued my walk around the grounds.

When I'd completed the full circle, I returned to the front of the yard, praying that what I'd done had been correct. I looked up at Isabeau. Her smile was gone and she hissed at me through the glass. I pushed the wet hair out of my eyes and continued. I repeated the words over and over.

The front door of the manor swung open with a fury and Isabeau marched toward me. Nicolas and Liam gazed on in shock from the library windows. There was nothing they could do to help me. I had to do this on my own. I sucked in a deep breath as Isabeau continued her advance toward me. If the spell wasn't working, then I might have a fight on my hands. I'd really pissed Isabeau off this time. No amount of cupcakes would make her happy with me again.

As she continued walking toward me, I steadied myself for a fight. I repeated the words, not allowing her nasty glare to stop me. She hissed and snarled, twisting her lips into a contorted expression that only a demon could make. Her eyes glowed a deep red as she approached. I'd be lying if I said I wasn't terrified. What if she ripped me limb from limb? How would I fight a demon? I was sure she was stronger than me.

As Isabeau neared me, she stretched her arms out toward me, but just as she grew close enough to wrap her hands around my neck, she kept walking. I whipped around to watch her. She twisted and jerked, but it was as if she couldn't control her movement forward. The spell was working.

Adrenaline rushed through my body and my heart pounded. The spell was actually working. Isabeau walked across the drive and out the gate onto the road. Once outside the manor's gate, she stopped abruptly and glared again. The red glow in her eyes diminished. She moved forward, attempting to come through the gate again. But she was zapped back and landed on her butt.

She pointed at me, then yelled, "This isn't over. I'll be back. You can't banish me."

"I just did," I yelled back.

I'd gotten a little cocky after that spell had worked. I guess I'd shown her. Don't mess with Halloween LaVeau! I came back down to reality though when I remembered Mara. She wouldn't be happy when she found out what I'd done. She'd be here for me soon. How many demons would she bring with her? I was able to banish one Isabeau, but how would I handle multiple ones?

I gathered up my things and headed back to the house. When I reached the door, I turned around. Isabeau had disappeared. I looked around in a panic thinking that the spell had faded, but she was nowhere in sight. The ghosts weren't around either. Were they demons too? I released a deep breath, then headed inside.

Liam and Nicolas were waiting for me in the parlor.

"That was impressive," Liam said.

I stood a little straighter. "Thank you."

Nicolas smiled. "You were amazing."

"If you'll excuse me, I need to go collapse now." I pointed toward the stairs and didn't turn around as I made my way to my bedroom.

Now that was one heck of a magic spell.

CHAPTER THIRTY-EIGHT

Now that Isabeau had left the manor, Annabelle agreed to come back. The next morning, I insisted that Liam and Nicolas come down to breakfast. Annabelle was coming over and I thought it would be great to sit down to a lovely breakfast that I whipped up with my new magic skills. Yeah, I just wanted to show off a little. Having Nicolas and Liam at the table to look at wasn't so bad either. Sure, the tension was high, but they were nice to look at nonetheless.

I intended on whipping up the magical breakfast and having it all set up on the dining table before my first guest could say 'pass the maple syrup.' The house felt different as I made my way downstairs. I suspected it had something to do with the fact that Isabeau was gone. Certainly a weight had been lifted from my shoulders.

I knew the relief would be short-lived though. I was waiting for the moment when Mara would show up. But maybe Liam and Nicolas were wrong. Maybe she would never come to the manor. Yeah, that was probably wishful thinking.

Cooking without the mess and not burning the food would be something that I'd have to get used to. I smiled as I stepped into the kitchen and pulled the items for my breakfast feast out from the refrigerator and cabinets.

Gathering the recipe spell book and setting it on the counter in front of me, I recited the words for the spell. The wind whipped and whirled as the ingredients performed their magic. But soon, the wind diminished to nothing more than a whisper. The food hadn't finished its preparations.

What was wrong? Why was this happening? My heart rate increased and I began to panic. What would I do now? Had I done something wrong? Sure, that had to be it. I was just tired from the day before. I'd try the spell again and everything would be fine. I recited the words again and everything exploded. Food was everywhere in the kitchen. This was worse than ever. My heart thumped wildly and sweat broke out on my forehead. *Don't panic.*

What had happened to my fantastic new powers? I should have known this was too good to be true. What would I do now? Isabeau would probably return and pulverize me for banishing her. Mara would show up and take the books. She'd be the new leader and it would all be my fault. Footsteps sounded from behind me and I whirled around.

"Oh, dear, what happened in here?" Annabelle asked with wide eyes.

I fought back the tears as I said, "My magic is gone. The mojo left."

"Oh, honey. I'm so sorry. Let me help you clean it up." Annabelle rushed to my side.

What would I do without her?

"What do you think happened?" Annabelle asked as she wiped pancake batter from the wall.

I shook my head as I mopped fruit compôte from the floor. "I have no idea."

Annabelle helped clean up the rest of the mess and then we hurried together what resembled a breakfast. I'd just set it out on the dining table when Nicolas entered the room. Annabelle was in the kitchen, so it was just the two of us. This was the first time I'd been alone with Nicolas since we'd shared the kiss. His eyes held a dark hunger as he stared at me.

Nicolas didn't say a word as he closed the distance between us. Once in front of me, he looked down at my face. The butterflies danced in my stomach. My gaze was fixed on his lips as he placed his lips against mine. His kisses felt so right and so wrong at the same time. I didn't know enough about him. How could I have these feelings for someone I didn't completely trust? I was lost in Nicolas' kiss when someone cleared their throat, forcing us out of our own little world.

Liam glared at us from the other side of the room. My heart sank a little. Why did I have such conflicting emotions?

"I'm sorry if I've disturbed you, but there's something I need to discuss with Ms. LaVeau." His tone was very businesslike. "It's very important," he added.

"Can't it wait?" Nicolas glared at Liam.

I stepped away from Nicolas. "Is something wrong?" I managed to ask softly.

"Have you noticed anything different this morning?" he asked.

I exchanged glances with Liam to Nicolas. It was hard to wrap my mind around the fact that as soon as Isabeau had left my powers had dissipated, but it wasn't a coincidence, right? Did Isabeau's leaving have anything to do with it? How had he known my magic sucked now? I had hoped it was just a fluke, but this was serious; I knew by his expression. He was upset about the kiss, but there was more to his demeanor than that.

"I think I lost my special powers," I said quietly with my head lowered.

Liam nodded. "Just as I suspected. I did some research—"

Nicolas cut off Liam's words. "Don't put ideas into her head."

I glared at Nicolas.

Liam cleared his throat and said, "I discovered that there was more to Isabeau's visit than we suspected. Isabeau had been slowly drawing out your powers while she stayed here in the manor and now she's taken them with her. Once the powers are drained, it takes a special spell to get them back."

"Wait. So there's no way to get them back?" I asked.

"There is a way but we just have to find the spell." He crossed his arms in front of his chest.

"Is it in the book?" I asked as I exchanged a look with both men.

"Only you can tell me that. I don't have the book, remember?" He gave a forced smile.

"Yeah, well, you wanted to destroy the book, remember?" I asked.

"I've changed my mind," he said firmly.

I stared at him. "Why would you do that?"

"I have my reasons. Please let me know if you need any help with the spell." He turned around to leave.

"Liam, wait." I ran after him, but he didn't stop.

Nicolas had followed after me across the room. He grabbed my arm. "Hallie, please. Why don't you give me the book?" His voice was barely above a whisper. "I don't want you involved in this anymore."

My head was spinning. "Why do you both insist on playing these games with me? First you didn't want to destroy the book and Liam did. Now you want to destroy it and he doesn't. I don't understand."

"Sometimes things change, Hallie." There was an underlying sensitivity in his voice.

I stared at him. "Sometimes they shouldn't change, Nicolas. I need to check the book for whatever spell this is that Liam is talking about."

Annabelle entered the room and eased the plates of food onto the table. She shrugged and mouthed, "What's going on?"

"I don't think anyone will be eating breakfast this morning." I grabbed Annabelle's hand. "Come on, Annabelle. Why don't you help me look for something?"

"Does it require going upstairs? Because I still can't do that." She waved her hand.

Oh yeah. I'd forgotten about her fear.

"Halloween, please." Nicolas pleaded with his eyes.

"Why don't you two sit down and eat. Hallie, surely whatever you have to do can wait, right?" Annabelle pulled a chair out and pointed for me to sit.

I hesitated. "I guess it can wait a few more minutes."

I'd already wasted the morning. What was a few more minutes?

"I'd love to stay," Nicolas said. "But I really need to check on something."

Was he being honest? Or was he just upset because I wouldn't allow him to have the book to destroy it? Nicolas paused at the door. He stared at me for a second, then walked out of the room.

"What was that all about?" Annabelle asked.

I shook my head. "I'm so confused. Apparently, I've lost the improved magic because of something Isabeau did."

"Well, that's not so surprising because she was bad."

"I need to check the spell book to find the spell to stop her. Now Nicolas has flopped and wants to get rid of the book and Liam doesn't care either way, I guess."

"Why do you say that?"

"He caught me kissing Nicolas."

She sat up straighter. "Oh, is he a good kisser?"

I nibbled on a piece of toast. "The best." I stood. "I really need to check that book. If there's a spell, then I need to do it right away."

Annabelle stared at me. "And if there's not a spell?"

"I don't even want to think about that. I'll be back in a few."

"I hate being down here alone." She shivered.

"You're fine now. The ghost is gone now, remember?"

She nodded. "I guess. I'll just take these dishes into the kitchen."

"Thank you, Annabelle. You're the best," I said.

She smiled. "Now go find that spell." She shooed me away.

CHAPTER THIRTY-NINE

My thoughts ran wildly as I hurried up the stairs. I wished I could talk with Liam and Nicolas and get everything sorted out. But that was hopeless. I didn't even know what my feelings were, so how could I possibly get the men sorted out?

I closed my bedroom door and pulled the books from their hiding spot. I carried them over to my bed and went through the table of contents. There was nothing that dealt with losing the power. How could it not be there? This was something that had to have come up in the past. What would I do now? I had to show the books to Liam. I hoped that I could trust him not to destroy them now. He'd be able to tell me if the spell I needed was really there. Maybe I'd just overlooked it.

I grabbed the books and headed up the next flight of stairs. A male voice floated down the hallway. I recognized Nicolas' voice right away. Who was he talking to? I stepped over to his shut door, and pressed my ear against the wood. I couldn't make out much, but I heard enough. He was talking about me, telling someone that I wouldn't give up the book. Who was he talking to? Since I didn't

228

hear another voice, I knew he was speaking with the phone.

When his voice stopped, I hurried away. I knocked on Liam's door and he answered right away.

"You said if I needed help to ask you." I half-heartedly grinned.

He looked down at the book. His eyes widened and he looked back up at me. I guess he was surprised that I'd brought the books.

"I can't find any mention of a spell to bring back the power." I gestured toward the books in my arms.

His expression darkened—not what I'd wanted to see. This couldn't be good news.

"I hope that I've just overlooked it," I said.

"Would you like to come in?" he asked with a tilt of his head.

I glanced over toward Nicolas' door. No noise came from the hallway, so I stepped into Liam's room. I stepped into his room and looked around. Everything was neat and his suitcases were by the door. The bed had been made.

"Are you checking out?" I asked.

"Now that Isabeau is gone…" His words trailed off.

"I can't believe you. You claim that my powers are gone, Mara still wants my head on a stick and you're going to bail on me? Why did you even offer to help me?" I poked him in the chest. It was way harder than I'd expected.

He grabbed my arms. "Calm down. I'm not going anywhere. Yes, for a moment I thought about leaving, but I realize that would be a mistake. I had a job to do and I need to see it through."

"You're darn right you need to see it through." I poked him in the chest again. It was like touching a rock, by the way.

He stared as if he had something else to say, but didn't.

Finally, he said. "So the books don't have the spell you need?"

I nodded. "Not that I can find."

"You're going to trust me with the books?" His left eyebrow rose a fraction.

I watched for a few seconds, then said, "Yes, I suppose I am."

The edges of his mouth barely turned upward. But it was a start. I handed him the books. I wouldn't lie and say that I didn't have a moment of hesitation, but it needed to be done. I was out of options. Liam sat on the edge of the bed and I stood by the door.

He looked at me. "I won't bite." He smiled.

This was heading into dangerous territory. I stepped toward the bed. I wasn't sure why I glanced over at the door on my way there. Wait. I knew why. Nicolas was the reason. Why did I care if he saw me in the room? He was acting strange anyway.

I eased down onto the bed next to Liam. My heart rate increased. I shouldn't have been that close to him. I needed to distance myself from both men. Liam handed me one book while he opened the other. I opened my book and began flipping through the pages.

After a few minutes of silence, Liam looked at me. "May I?" he asked while holding out his hand for the other book.

I handed it to him and he handed me the other one. More silence surrounded us. Finally he closed the cover and looked at me. The expression on his face said it all.

"You may need to get some outside help on this one. Maybe there is a spell another witch knows of that we can modify." He ran his hand through his hair.

I nodded. It wasn't the news I wanted to hear, but it was the news I had to deal with.

"I'll see what I can do," he said, "but maybe you can ask around too."

I nodded. "I will. I'll contact the Coven."

Liam stared at me, then reached up and brushed my cheek with the back of his hand. "I'm sorry if I was upset earlier. It's your business who you kiss."

I nodded, but I didn't know what to say. He was right, it was my business. He leaned forward and kissed me gently on the lips. I closed my eyes, but he didn't kiss me more. He stopped with the soft gentle kiss. I had been expecting more, or maybe wanting more. When I opened my eyes, he touched my lips with his finger.

Then Liam stood. "I'd better see what I can find." He handed me the books.

"Thank you," I said.

I stood and made my way to the door.

"I'll call you when I know something." His dark hair gleamed in the light.

I nodded and walked out of the room without looking back. I didn't want to see his handsome face.

231

CHAPTER FORTY

After hiding the books yet again, I headed back to the kitchen.

"What did you find?" Annabelle asked when I stepped back into the room. She closed the magazine she'd been looking at and waited for me to answer.

I shrugged off her concerned look. "Nothing. I think I'm in serious trouble. But I won't worry you with that now. You didn't come over here to hear me complain about magic."

She waved her hand to get my attention. "Hello. I'm your friend. That's what friends do."

I tried to smile, but came up short. "Liam is trying to help me figure out the spell, but right now it doesn't look good."

She sighed. "How about we take your mind off it for a few minutes? We can plan the party."

I nodded. "Okay, yeah, maybe that is for the best."

It should have been a wonderful breakfast, but it had turned into little more than another bizarre game of tug-of-war between two men. Annabelle and I sat down to plan the Halloween Ball. There was a lot to be done before the party tomorrow. Too bad I couldn't use any of my fantastic magic to help me with the planning. I'd have to do it all without the magic. What if the Coven found out that I no longer possessed special skills? They'd cancel the party and my mother would be heartbroken.

"Are you okay?" Annabelle asked.

I shook my head. "Yeah. I guess I'll figure this out."

"It's not so bad," she said. "I mean, you were doing fine before your magic changed and you'll do fine without it. You were happy without it, right?"

I looked at her. "Yeah, you're right. I was happy without it. I don't need it, right? I was just trying to please everyone else."

"Sometimes you just can't please others though. You need to do things for yourself." Annabelle's cheeks glowed rosy as a smile spread across her face.

"If I'm happy, then I can make others happy too, right?" I leaned back in the chair.

"Yes, that's the way to think of it."

I smiled. "Thanks, Annabelle. I appreciate that you always stand by me."

"That's what friends are for. Now, what type of theme did you have in mind for the party?" she asked, pointing at the blank pad of paper in front of me.

"I want a traditional costume party with lots of candles and gauzy material hanging around… all done in black and white." Visions of the grand ball flashed in my mind. Of course, in my mind the night turned out fantastically. Unfortunately things didn't always turn out as I planned.

"Oh, that sounds beautiful," Annabelle said.

I waved my hands through the air. "I want lots of pumpkins too. Spooky meets elegant is the theme. The men can wear tuxedos and the women can wear elegant ball gowns with elaborate feathered masks."

"It sounds beautifully haunting," Annabelle said wistfully.

"The good thing about the manor is it doesn't take much to dress it up for the party." I pinched off a piece of the now stale toast and popped into my mouth.

"That's true." Annabelle tapped the pen against her lip. "What about invitations? I guess everyone knows where the party is being held."

I nodded. "Yes, but they still need official invitations. Considering they need to deliver them in the morning, I know there is magic involved. But I just have to design them. They'll be hand-delivered."

Annabelle reached for my pad of paper and began writing. "How about if they say something like this?" She handed the paper back to me.

In her pretty handwriting she'd written,

You're invited to a party under the moon and stars for an evening of enchantment and celebration. Your face should not be seen on this Halloween. Your presence is requested at LaVeau Manor for Enchantment Pointe Coven's annual Halloween Masquerade Ball.

"That is perfect," I said. Annabelle had always had a way with words.

"How many people will be here?" she asked.

"Over a hundred, I think." I shrugged.

"Wow, that's a lot. What do you do for food?" Annabelle asked.

"The Coven has hired caterers. They'll be here the day of the party to set up." I scribbled more notes on the pad.

"Thank goodness," Annabelle said, then immediately covered her mouth with her hand. "Oops."

I quirked my eyebrow.

She held her hands up in surrender. "I wasn't saying that you would be bad at preparing the food."

I glared, then laughed. "You don't have to say it. We all know it."

She shook her head. "Well, yeah. I guess we do."

After another hour, I walked Annabelle to her car. "Are you sure you'll be okay?" she asked.

I nodded. "Yeah. I'm okay."

"Call me if you need anything," she said as she climbed into her car.

"I promise I will." I watched as she pulled out of the drive and onto the road. Nicolas' car was still parked in the drive. It would be just the two of us in the house. The thought made my stomach flip. I wanted to see him, but there was the little matter of finding a spell that was weighing on my mind.

I had to find the spell before it was too late—a spell that none of the witches at Enchantment Pointe knew how to perform. The fact that I'd lost the powers was devastating. Not because I'd lost the magic, but because the Coven would once again think I was a failure. My mother would be so disappointed.

When I turned around to go back inside, Nicolas was standing at the front door. Why did I feel the need to run into his arms? I wanted to find comfort in Nicolas' embrace. Was what Liam and Nicolas said true? That Mara would use my power to take over the Underworld? I should trust Nicolas, so why did I doubt him? All Mara needed was to get the book and get rid of me. Given what they'd said about her apparent determination, I figured she could easily achieve this.

Nicolas wanted me to give him the book to destroy, but I wanted more answers. There had to be another way. How did he know all of this anyway? Why was he getting involved in the first place? Why was he being so secretive? I still couldn't trust him completely, no matter how much I wanted to.

CHAPTER FORTY-ONE

I forced my legs to move slowly, but it was impossible not to walk straight toward Nicolas. My gaze was locked with his and my heart pounded. I wanted to feel his lips pressed against mine; I couldn't stop the feeling.

When I reached the door, he pulled me into him and wrapped his arms around me. He kissed me passionately, urgently, his lips moving over mine with swiftness.

When he lifted his lips from mine, he looked me in the eyes and said, "I just want to help you, Halloween. I don't know what the right answer is for this problem, but I want to try what I think is best for you."

"I don't know…" I whispered.

"What Liam says is true. Isabeau intends to give your power to Mara. It'll complete her plan to take over the Underworld. Her only goal is to be the leader."

"She sounds like a lovely person," I said drily.

"She'll stop at nothing to get what she wants. I've seen it before," he said.

"There is something that you haven't answered for me." I whirled the words in my head, trying to think of just the right way to ask.

He looked at me. "What is it?"

"I know why Liam is here. He said he's a detective sent to find the book before Mara gets it. But why are you here? Are you a detective too?" I pushed.

He paused, then shook his head. "No, I am not a detective."

"Then why are you here?" I asked.

"I'm here for the same reason as Liam." He gestured with a tilt of his head toward the staircase.

"That's not what I want to hear. I need answers from you. Before I can go any further with whatever this is we have"—I motioned between us—"I have to have answers from you. I want honest answers, not vague hints."

"I don't know what else you want me to tell you," he said.

"The truth," I said.

"Hallie, I haven't lied to you about anything." He ran his hand through his dark hair.

Well, he had me there. As far as I knew he hadn't lied about anything. The door remained open and I thought back to the fateful night when Nicolas had appeared at my front door. What would have happened if I hadn't answered the door?

"But you aren't telling me what you're doing here. How did you just happen to show up one night? It wasn't a coincidence, we both know that."

He hesitated, then said, "I came for the book."

I threw my hands up. "This is hopeless."

He was just talking in circles and it was doing nothing but making me angry and sad at the same time.

"I think you need to give me the book so that I can get rid of it." The sentence slipped from his tongue as casually as if he'd asked about the weather.

I glared at him. "So that's what this is all about? You wanted to fool me into thinking you're here to help me, but really all you want is to get rid of the book," I said.

He looked down, then back up at me with a hurt look in his eyes. I no longer knew what was real or fake. My life had been turned upside down and I didn't know who to trust.

Movement caught my attention and I looked over my shoulder. The ghosts had returned and paced back and forth. They were on the edge of the property, just waiting for their chance to come closer. Didn't they know that I could no longer bring them back to the living? Did they fail to get the memo in the afterlife? They made me nervous.

"What could you getting rid of the book do?" I asked.

"If the book is gone then you are no longer obligated to be the leader of the Underworld. I don't know if you know what you're taking on by agreeing to take that position." Something dark and unfathomable flashed in his eyes.

I waved my hands. "Whoa. I never agreed to take it on yet. No one has even asked me to do that. All I have is Liam and you telling me what will happen and my Coven being excited that I have the book. I've not heard of this so-called law that you all talk about. And I've been a witch for years—why have I not heard of this until now?"

He shrugged. "I guess there was no reason for you to know."

"Meaning that my witchcraft sucked so I didn't need to be included in something like that." I glanced over my shoulder again.

The ghosts had moved to the other side. Hostility encircled them and snaked its way to where I stood.

"That's not it at all. The more I thought about it the more I realized that I don't want you to have to deal with all that. You're so happy here at the manor. It would be adding too much chaos to your life." Nicolas stood in front of me and I became acutely aware of his tall, athletic physique.

"I guess I should be the judge of that, right?" I said, placing my hands on my hips.

"Yes, I suppose that is your decision." He looked up at the sky. "Mara will be here soon."

"What? Does she fly on a broom?" I snickered.

He shook his head with a slight smile. "No, I can sense it. She's on her way."

My heart rate increased. "Well, I'm ready for her. Whatever happens, happens."

I started to walk past him. I wanted inside before the ghosts caught up to me. They would be angry if I had to tell them I couldn't do the magic anymore. There was no telling what they would do. Drag me away to the afterlife maybe.

Nicolas grabbed my arm. "Hallie, I will help you any way I can."

My knees went weak every time he touched me. Why did he have that effect on me?

"I appreciate that, Nicolas. Thank you for trying, but I won't get rid of the book." I pulled away from him.

He shook his head. "I know you think that is the wrong decision and I'm sorry."

Even though I wanted to stay with him, I pulled my arm away. Without looking back, I rushed upstairs and slammed my bedroom door. The sound of footsteps moving downstairs let me know that Nicolas was pacing. No matter, I couldn't talk to him about this anymore. My room was the only safe place I had. I collapsed onto the bed and before I knew it, I'd drifted off to sleep.

When I woke three hours later, my cell phone was ringing loudly in my ear. Confusion filled my thoughts. What day was this? What time was it? Soon enough the memories came flooding back. The conversation that I'd just had with Nicolas popped back into my mind. Where was he now? I couldn't believe I'd fallen asleep. I fumbled for the phone and answered in a groggy voice.

"Where have you been?" my mother asked with a panicked voice.

"I fell asleep," I said.

"I've been trying to call you for the past two hours," she screeched.

I felt as if I'd been drugged. "I never heard the phone," I said. "What's wrong?"

"I need you to come to the shop right away." Her words were a command and not a request.

"You're scaring me. What happened?" My voice shook.

"I have something to show you. Just get here as soon as you can. And be careful," she added.

I didn't know what all of this was about, but obviously she wasn't going to tell me over the phone. I hoped she didn't want me to use my new magic skills. Knowing her, she just wanted to talk about preparations for the party and thought that decoration selection was urgent.

When I went downstairs, the house was empty. That hadn't happened since that night when Nicolas first showed up. Just thinking about his gorgeous face at my front door in the rain made my stomach twist. Why did it have to be this way? Why couldn't I find a normal man to date?

Nicolas' car wasn't there. But the ghosts still stared at me from just behind the trees. Ignoring the ghosts, I hopped into my car and hurried out of there. Had what Nicolas said about Mara been true? Would she be here soon? And if so, what would I do? What would I say to her? I could tell her one thing, there was no way in hell she was getting the books.

I tried Annabelle's number on my way, but she didn't answer. I really needed to talk with her about Nicolas and Liam. Maybe she could help me figure out who was being truthful. Okay, I wasn't sure how she would do that, but it would help to get everything off my chest.

I pulled up to the shop and hopped out. The wind had picked up and the dark clouds rolled in from the west. A storm would be beating down on us soon. I wasn't sure what my mother wanted, but I knew it was time I confided in her. I had to have help with this, and even though she'd pushed me to improve my magic, I knew she only wanted the best for me.

When I walked through the door, I was surprised to see Annabelle was there. My mother stood beside her. Was this a magical intervention?

My mother threw her hands up and said, "Oh, thank goodness you are finally here."

"What are you doing here?" I asked Annabelle.

She looked at me sheepishly.

My mother placed her hands on her hips. "Now don't get mad at her. She's only trying to help and she was worried about you."

I frowned as I looked between Annabelle and my mother.

"What have you done?" I asked.

"I'm sorry, Hallie. I just didn't know what else to do. I felt like my hands were tied." She exchanged a glance with my mother.

I motioned for her to get on with it. "And? What did you do?"

"Well…" She looked down at her shoes. "I told your mother about everything. How you lost the powers and how the guys are being weird and you can't find a spell to get rid of Isabeau and Mara."

I looked at my mother.

"I wish you'd told me this right away," my mother said.

I let out a sigh. "I didn't want to worry you. There was nothing you could do."

She pointed her finger. "That's where you are wrong."

"What do you mean?" I stood next to the counter.

My mother pulled a book from under the counter. It was a large brown leather book with gold-embossed letters and details. It took both arms for her to hoist it onto the counter.

CHAPTER FORTY-TWO

"What's that?" I asked.

"This book…" She tapped it with her brightly polished fingernail. "This book has the spell that you need to fight off this Isabeau demon and that bitch of a witch, Mara."

My eyes widened. "Are you serious? How did you find it?"

She wiggled her eyebrows. "I'm good. Never underestimate your mother."

"Well, let me see it," I said, spinning the book around and flipping the cover open.

At least this one was in English.

"I wish there was something more I could do." Annabelle said. "I feel like a bum since I can't do any magic to help you."

I patted her hand. "You did enough by telling my mother."

"You're not mad at me?" she asked.

I frowned for a second, then released a smile. "Well, normally I would be furious, but since it all worked out, I'm not mad."

She shook her head. "Whatever. That works for me."

A ton of spells stared back at me from the pages—everything from love, gardening and cooking to getting rid of demons.

"Where in the heck did you find this book?" I asked my mother.

She offered a sly smile. "I have my ways, but I can't divulge my secrets."

I shook my head. "Okay, whatever you say."

I'd eventually get the info from her.

My mother grabbed the book and turned it around. "Here's the spell you need." She tapped the page.

I looked at it and flipped to the page. "Where is the other page?"

My mother's eyes widened. "What do you mean?"

"The page that has the rest of the spell is missing." I tapped my finger against the book.

My heart sank. What would I do now? I had had so much hope and now it was burst.

"I have no idea," my mother said.

Annabelle sank back onto her stool. "I'm sorry, Hallie."

"I guess I got so excited that I didn't pay attention to that detail." My mother blushed.

"So where is it?" I asked.

"I don't know. The book has been on the shelf at my home since your Aunt Maddy gave it to me."

Why was I not surprised that it had come from Aunt Maddy? I wished I'd never gotten LaVeau Manor now. It had caused nothing but problems with my life. And I included Nicolas and Liam as part of those problems.

My mother grabbed the book again. "Well, maybe I can figure out what the rest of the spell is."

She flipped through the pages, studying each one intensely. This was not going to end well, I just felt it. Annabelle and I stared at her.

After several minutes of her flipping the pages, she closed the cover. "Well, I just need a little more time to find something. I'll figure it out though." She didn't sound confident.

"You know I appreciate your help," I said.

My mother patted my hand. "I know, dear. Now in the meantime, maybe you need to try a few spells to warm up before you try this big one."

My mother knew I was going to screw this up. But what could she do? I had to be the one to do it. She couldn't do it for me. Believe me, if she could, she would have. She'd bypass me altogether.

"What kind of spells?" I asked.

"Oh, I don't know, something simple." My mother waved her bangle-covered arm through the air.

I stared at her.

"Oh, well, okay, I know the spells aren't simple, per se."

What she meant to say was that no spell was simple for me. She was just feeling sorry for me and protecting my hurt feelings. The truth hurt sometimes, but sometimes it was necessary to go through that pain.

"How about you just do a spell to make these flowers fresh again?" She pointed at the vase of roses she had on the counter. She opened the book and pointed at the page. "I even have a super-easy spell here that you can use."

It was like she was teaching magic to a five-year-old witch trying a spell for the first time. I pulled the book closer and looked at the page. "Yeah, I guess I can use this spell."

I knew she wouldn't stop asking until I tried the spell. I lifted the vase and set it in front of me. With a wave of my hand, I said, "Life is new and fresh, make no distress. Bring the flowers back many hours. So mote it be." The flowers drooped even further. They almost touched the counter they'd fallen over so far.

"Oh dear," my mother said as she held her chest.

She could be overly dramatic sometimes.

"Okay, that didn't work so well." I released a heavy sigh.

Annabelle gave me a pitying look.

"Maybe you should try something else," my mother said. "Those flowers were almost dead anyway."

How many attempts would my mother insist I make before she accepted the fact that my magic wasn't going to work? I wasn't meant to be a witch and I certainly wasn't meant to be the leader of the Underworld. The sooner she accepted that the better off we'd be.

"What do you want me to do now?" I asked with deflation in my voice.

We were trying spells that first-graders could do easily.

"Can you turn this pencil into a pen?" she asked.

This was just silly now. I stared at her. "Honestly?" I asked.

She pushed the pencil toward me. "Come on. At least give it a try."

I let out a deep breath and took the pencil from her outstretched hand. After I repeated the words and the pencil was still a pencil, my mother gave up. She looked like she wanted to cry. And she wasn't the only one. I wanted to hide away and cry my eyes out.

So I'd tried multiple spells, but none of them had worked. What else could I do? The magic was gone. The spells had done nothing but fizzle out. I didn't think it was possible, but my powers were even worse than when all of this had started.

"Can you watch the store?" my mother asked, after she'd finally given up on my magic. "There's somewhere I need to go."

"Yeah, sure," I said dejectedly. What else did I have to do?

Rain pounded against the windows and the wind blew with a fury.

"Just be careful out there. The weather is wicked."

"I'll stay with you," Annabelle offered.

The store wasn't busy because of the bad weather, so Annabelle and I spent our time smelling the candles and testing out the sample lotions. That bad vibe still pulsed around me though. I knew it was only a matter of time until I discovered what this strange feeling was all about.

CHAPTER FORTY-THREE

After a couple hours, my mother burst through the door with a look of determination in her eyes.

"Are you okay?" I asked.

"Okay. I couldn't find out what the rest of the spell calls for, but that is no excuse. You should at least give it a try."

I climbed off the stool and stepped out from the counter. "Okay. What do you need me to do?"

There was no point in arguing with her. I might as well do the spell like she wanted and get on with it. It was getting dark and I needed to get home. A strange feeling enveloped me and I couldn't quite put my finger on it. It was different than anything I'd felt before. LaVeau Manor needed my protection... but protection from what? Mara?

My mother pulled the ingredients from the shelves and placed them in a bowl in the middle of the room. She pulled the book over and placed it in the middle of the floor.

Once she'd locked the door and flipped the sign to say *Closed*, she motioned for me to start. "Give it your best shot, dear."

I wanted to laugh, but that would have just been mean. My mother grabbed my hand and motioned for Annabelle to join us.

"We'll make a circle around the bowl in the middle of the room," my mother said.

As I recited the words, the light show began. Blue and red lights swirled up from the floor and began to make a circle around us. But when it was halfway around, it just fizzled out and disappeared. I half-heartedly repeated the words on the pages, but nothing happened. It was no use.

Annabelle stood with us, holding my hand. I knew she had no idea what she was doing, but I gave her credit for trying. That was a lot more than a lot of friends would endure. I owed her for this.

My mother released my hand with a sigh. "At least you gave it a shot. No one can say that you didn't try."

I nodded. "You got that right. I think I should go home now. I think the place is calling to me."

"Are Nicolas and Liam still there?" my mother asked with a wiggle of her eyebrow.

I shrugged. "I don't know. They said they would stay and help me figure this out, but I just don't know what to believe."

"Just go with your heart," my mother said.

"How am I going to get rid of the demon and Mara?" I asked around a sigh.

"I don't know, honey, but we'll think of something." My mother smoothed down my frazzled hair. "Do you want some of my special conditioner?"

Leave to my mother to be worried about my frizzy hair at the moment.

"I'll see you later." I hugged my mother, then waved over my shoulder on the way out the door.

As soon as Annabelle and I jumped into my car, she asked, "What are you going to do now?"

"Well, since the party is in two days, I need to pick up some of the supplies that I ordered. I thought I'd grab dinner and go home after that. Like I said, something is calling me at the manor and I don't know what it is." The idea sent a chill down my spine.

I hoped it wasn't the ghosts. I wanted them to go away just like Isabeau.

"Do you think this Mara person is there?" Apprehension colored Annabelle's voice.

My stomach twisted into a knot at the thought. "I sure hope not. I think Liam or Nicolas would call me if she was. Well, that's if they are still there."

What if they were in on this with Mara? I'd just blindly trusted them. This could all be an act leading up to when she showed up.

"Do you want me to go with you? We could hang out downstairs in the parlor. Maybe watch a movie? We haven't had a girls' night in a long time... but no scary movies," she warned with a wave of her finger.

"I'd really like that," I said with a smile.

It was a big deal for Annabelle to be inside my house at night. She must really feel sorry for me.

After picking up the supplies for the party, we loaded them into the trunk, then decided to pick up a pizza and a bottle of wine.

On the way to the local pizza shop, Annabelle asked, "So what are you going to wear to the party?"

"Hmm. I hadn't even thought about that." I tapped my fingers nervously against the steering wheel.

What would I wear? I didn't have anything formal other than my prom dress from ten years ago and an ugly teal bridesmaid dress from my cousin's wedding last year. There was no way I could wear either one of those.

Annabelle clapped her hands together. "Okay. That does it. Before we pick up the food and go home I know where we have to go. There is the perfect dress for you at that boutique in town. I saw it in the window and thought it would look great on you."

249

I hesitated. The light turned green and the car behind me honked.

"Do you think I should get a dress?" I asked, biting my lower lip.

"You just said you didn't have one to wear." Annabelle pointed at the green light.

The car honked again and I punched the gas.

"What are you going to wear?" I asked as I turned down the street toward the boutique.

"Me? I'm not coming to the party, am I?"

I glanced over at her. "What do you mean? Of course you're coming to the party. Why wouldn't you?"

"I thought it was only for witches... you know, members of the Coven." Annabelle frowned.

"You're my guest. Other witches bring guests who aren't paranormals." I made a right turn.

"I think I would feel out of place." She chewed on her bottom lip.

"Oh, come on. I can't have a big party at my place and not have my best friend there."

She sighed. "Okay. You've convinced me. I have a beautiful green evening gown that I wore to my mother's real estate award banquet last year."

"Oh yeah, I remember that dress. It's beautiful and the color looks great on you. So it's settled. You're coming to the party," I said as I pulled the car into the parking space in front of the boutique.

"I wouldn't miss it for the world. You are going to love this dress," she said as she got out of the car.

Bubble and Bunny Clothing Boutique always had the latest fashion. Most of the time I window-shopped. But as soon as I saw the dress in the window, I knew I had to have it. It practically called to me.

"How did you know I would love this?" I asked as we walked through the door.

"Hey, we've been friends for a long time. I know what you like." Annabelle waved her freshly-manicured finger.

The interior of the store was just as hip as the clothing they sold. A soft lavender color covered the walls and the light hardwood floor shone under the abundance of track lighting. The red dress in the window was satin and fit tight through the bust and hips, then fanned out at the bottom. At the back was a small train.

After rushing into the dressing room, I slipped into the dress and it fit perfectly. I took that as a sign that it was meant to be. I stepped out from the room and spun around.

"It's perfect. Nicolas and Liam will love it," Annabelle said with glee.

"Oh no. I don't want them to love it," I said, avoiding her glare.

"Yeah, you don't want them to love the dress as much as I hate chocolate," she snorted.

After I paid for the dress, the woman wrapped it up in a box, placed it in the gift bag and I was on my way. I had second thoughts about eating that pizza though. I wanted to still be able to fit into my new dress. Annabelle loved chocolate and I knew she was right; I couldn't wait to see Nicolas' reaction when he saw the dress. It was just a coincidence that he said his favorite color was red.

We picked up a large pepperoni pizza and the wine and made our way back to the manor. The golden sunset was waning and the last, faint color of the day faded as we pulled into the driveway. The house was shadowy and inscrutable, appearing especially creepy. Annabelle's apprehension filled the air.

"It won't be nearly as spooky-looking when I turn all the lights on," I said.

I expected her to back out of our plan for movie night at any moment. But so far she was still game. I didn't see the ghosts and for that small favor I was thankful.

"Where do you think the guys are?" Annabelle scanned the surroundings and shivered.

"I don't know," I said as I pulled the dress from the back seat of the car.

Annabelle grabbed the pizza and the wine. I'd get the party supplies later. There was a break in the rain and I wanted to get inside before the downpour started again.

"I was thinking," I said as I unlocked the front door. "Do you think both men could be lying to me? Do you think they are in on this plan with this Mara woman?"

With any luck she'd tell me I was crazy and that I had nothing to worry about.

"What do you think?" Annabelle asked. "Do you feel like they are doing that to you?"

I glanced over at her. "Honestly? No, I don't feel like they would do that."

"Well, then there's your answer," Annabelle said.

Her expression didn't instill much confidence though.

CHAPTER FORTY-FOUR

Annabelle and I had just turned on the movie, poured the wine, and plopped down on the oversized white sofa when a loud crash rang out from the front of the house. We both jumped from the sofa.

"What the hell was that?" Annabelle asked.

"I don't know." I ran toward the front door.

I prayed it wasn't Isabeau or Mara. Heck, it could have been the ghosts too. They seemed to grow angrier by the minute.

Nicolas burst through the front door with a wild look in his eyes. His wet hair and soaked clothing clung to his body. I had to admit it wasn't a bad look on him. His breathing was heavy.

"What the hell is going on?" I asked.

"Hallie, you have to give me the book." He motioned for me to hand it to him.

"I don't have it," I lied.

This was getting way more bizarre than I was comfortable with. And I'd put up with a lot of weird things in my life. This was too much though.

The worried lines on his face deepened. "Where are the books?" he asked with authority.

"I hid them at my mother's shop," I said with satisfaction.

It wasn't the truth, but I couldn't let him think the books were still at the manor.

"We have to go get them now." Nicolas motioned for me to follow him.

I shook my head. "No way. And you're not telling me what to do."

"But it's for your own good," he said in a strained voice.

"Hallie, what's going on?" Annabelle asked in a panicked tone.

"It's okay. Nicolas was just leaving." I studied his face.

I didn't want him to go, but I wanted him to know that I was serious. Why did he seem so frantic?

"You have to let me destroy it," he pleaded.

"This is getting too weird, Hallie," Annabelle said.

She was telling me.

"I told you before that isn't happening, Nicolas. You have to stop asking me. Now I think it's best if you leave." I folded my arms in front of my chest.

He frowned. "You don't want me to leave."

"I don't?" I asked with a frown.

He stared.

"I'll just leave you two alone," Annabelle said. "I need to get home and feed my pets anyway. Are you sure you'll be okay?" Annabelle asked as she looked from me to Nicolas.

I nodded. "Everything will be fine."

Once I hugged her goodbye, I continued my showdown with Nicolas. I wasn't going to give in about the books.

"You tell me why you're here and maybe I'll consider giving you the books."

I knew that would get him to stop asking. For some reason he refused to tell me the true reason he was there. More and more I was beginning to think he was there for nefarious reasons. I wanted to trust him, but he'd left me no choice.

"I was sent here to protect you. If that meant not getting rid of the book, fine. But things changed and now I need to get rid of it," he explained.

As suspicious as I was, he looked like he was telling the truth. Maybe I just wanted to believe that though.

"Please, Hallie." He stepped closer. "If we destroy it, the book will be gone forever. Your problems will stop and Mara will not come here to harm you."

Maybe he really was here to protect me. Why would he be so concerned about stopping Mara if he was working with her?

"How would you get rid of the books forever?" I asked with a shaky voice.

"We would burn them." His voice remained calm.

I guessed that would certainly get rid of them for good. I sighed. "I'll think about it, okay?"

"We don't have much time," he pushed.

I didn't respond to his statement. Instead, I said, "Who sent you here to protect me?"

He paused, then said, "Someone who wants to protect the Underworld."

"But you can't tell me who this person is, right?"

He shook his head. "I'm sorry. It's part of my job."

"Well, I don't think I like your job very much."

Until he could tell me who this person was, I doubted very seriously that I would ever turn the books over for him to destroy. I was just surprised that the books hadn't been destroyed before now. All these years and the first time I got near them everyone wanted to get rid of them. That sounded about right. What would Liam say?

"What is Liam's role in all of this?" I asked. "Who sent him?"

"Liam's job is different from mine and I have nothing to do with that," he said matter-of-factly.

"But is he here to protect me as well?" I pushed.

"He is here to get the book and that is all. He's here to protect his ass and he doesn't care about anyone else. The only reason he is protecting you is to ensure that he keeps his job." Nicolas' whole body tensed.

"But that's not why you're here?" I asked with a raised eyebrow.

He stared at me. "No, it's not. I must admit I didn't know what I was getting into when I first came, but now that I know you, I want what's best for you. The Underworld be damned."

His proclamation made my stomach dance. It was one of the most romantic things anyone had ever said to me.

"Do you still want me to leave?" he asked with puppy-dog eyes.

I shook my head. "No. I don't." After a couple seconds, I asked, "Would you like pizza and wine?"

A smile slipped across his face. "I'd love that. I'll go change and be right down."

When Nicolas came downstairs, he was dressed more casually than usual. And it looked good on him. He wore torn jeans and a tight blue T-shirt. His muscles looked delicious under the fabric. I handed him a wine glass after he sat on the sofa, then I slipped beside him. My heart rate increased. Nicolas grabbed a slice of the now cold pizza.

"Sorry it's cold," I said.

"That's okay," he said, taking the plate.

"Would you like to watch a movie?" I waved the DVD case.

He looked over his shoulder out the window as if he'd heard something. He didn't exactly seem relaxed, but I wasn't surprised.

"I'd like that. What are we watching?"

"*Pride and Prejudice*. Annabelle and I have seen it a million times, but it's fun to re-watch it."

It didn't take long after the movie started until the wine kicked in and I found myself yawning. And I thought Nicolas would be the one falling asleep while watching the movie. My head rested on Nicolas' hard chest and the next thing I knew, I'd fallen asleep on the sofa in Nicolas' arms. It felt so right.

CHAPTER FORTY-FIVE

The next day arrived and it was time for the annual Halloween Ball. Annabelle had helped me set up the candles around the house. We'd draped black gauze around the room and the house positively sparkled. The guests would start arriving soon. The caterers were sitting up the food on tables that had been draped with white cloths.

I slipped off upstairs to get ready. I couldn't wait to wear the red dress. After sliding into the dress, I added the red feathered mask that Annabelle had found. I'd always wanted to attend a masquerade ball.

Footsteps caught my attention. Someone was going down the stairs. I wasn't sure if it was Nicolas or Liam. One thing was for sure: I couldn't wait to see them in their tuxedos. Sliding the red lipstick over my lips, I spritzed on my favorite perfume and then headed downstairs. This was as close to Cinderella that I'd ever get.

When I reached the parlor, I stopped at the entrance. Nicolas was standing in the middle of the room. He looked devastatingly handsome in his black tuxedo.

"You look stunning," he said.

I felt the heat rush to my cheeks. The caterers made noise in the other room, but it was just the two of us in the parlor, as if we were in our own little world. Nicolas pulled out his phone and sat it on the table. The music streamed out from the little speakers.

"I wanted to have a dance with you privately before all the chaos starts." He stepped dangerously close.

I smiled, unable to resist his good looks.

"May I have this dance?" he asked, holding out his hand.

I placed my hand in his and he wrapped his strong arms around me. We swayed to the music and my heart raced. Nicolas placed his lips against mine and kissed me more passionately than I'd ever been kissed. I couldn't resist melting into a kiss when he looked at me with those blue eyes.

"Hallie, I can't deny my feelings for you any longer." He paused, then continued, "I've fallen for you."

This revelation sent my thoughts in a tailspin. I couldn't deny what I felt for him either. But I couldn't stop trying to fight it.

He caressed my cheek with his strong hand and gazed into my eyes. "I'm sorry if I haven't been completely forthcoming. I'm sorry if I've been keeping secrets from you."

I hadn't expected him to say that. My heart thumped wildly. What other kind of secrets did he have?

"What are you keeping from me?" I asked.

He held me in his arms. "I want to tell you everything I know."

"Okay, I'm listening. Please feel free to share everything with me. I think I've been waiting long enough."

He let out a deep breath, then said, "My mother was the previous leader of the Underworld."

It felt like someone had punched me in the stomach. I hadn't expected that news.

"Why didn't you tell me this earlier?" I asked.

"I just didn't want anyone to know that I was here." His eyes darkened.

"But Liam knew," I said.

"Yes, he did." Nicolas nodded. "I didn't want to burden you with my story, but now that I know and care so much for you, I had to say something." He took my hand in his.

"You can tell me anything," I said.

"I don't want the same thing to happen to you that happened to my mother."

I knew that his mother had died at the hands of Mara. Well, they had thought Mara had something to do with her murder. But would that mean I was destined for the same fate?

"Was your mother a vampire too?" It was a touchy subject, but I had to ask.

"She was a witch and a vampire. We were turned at the same time."

"Tell me about when you were turned?" I asked.

"My father died from tuberculosis. The vampires showed up one day and tried to take over our farm. We put up a good fight. My mother was turned, along with her sister too. Mara went with the vampires. She took the wrong path."

"It must be so hard for you," I said softly.

"Mara sold her soul to the devil years ago for reasons unknown to all of us. You know my mother was killed for the book. Thankfully she was able to hide the book with your aunt so that Mara couldn't get hold of it. I don't want the same thing to happen to you." His expression became saddened.

My heart sank. "What makes you think the same thing would happen to me? I mean, can't someone stop her?"

"So far they haven't been able to stop her. There is no proof that she did this, but I know she did and I intend to prove it somehow."

It all made sense now. Why had he been acting so secretive?

"I wish you'd shared this with me sooner. Maybe I can help you get Mara." A hint of frustration sounded in my voice.

"What do you mean?" he asked.

"There might be a way to get the proof you need to show that she did something to your mother," I said.

There was a slight hesitation in his eyes, then he touched my cheek again. "You'd do that for me?"

"You wanted to help me, right?"

He gave me a smile that sent my pulse racing.

"Then why wouldn't I want to help you?" I asked.

Nicolas kissed me again and I was instantly lost in his arms. I felt his fangs against my lips, but I didn't care. I just wanted to be lost in his arms. We continued to sway back and forth to the music.

"So when are you going to tell me how we can get the proof we need?" he asked.

The doorbell rang and I looked at the grandfather clock. It was already time for the party to start. I looked out the window and saw that there were several groups of people waiting on the veranda.

"The guests are arriving," I said. "I'll have to talk with you about this later."

He nodded and held my hand for a moment before finally releasing it. Butterflies danced in my stomach. I hoped the Coven didn't find out that I'd lost all my powers.

Candles flickered from every corner of every room. Tables with long white tablecloths and black gauzy material had been set up for refreshments. Black and white pumpkins had been placed around the room while faux black ravens kept sentinel over the crowd.

The Coven members were the first to enter. The women looked beautiful in their dresses and the men handsome in their tuxedos. People munched on the food and enjoyed the cocktails as I moved around the room like a good hostess should. Annabelle arrived and she was gorgeous in her green dress and matching mask.

"That is you behind there, right?" I laughed.

"It's me." She giggled. "How's it going?"

I grabbed her arm and pulled her to the corner of the room. "You're not going to believe what Nicolas told me before the party started."

I filled her in on what Nicolas had told me.

"You're kidding. Well, that explains a lot." She grabbed a glass of champagne from a passing tray and took a drink. "So what are you going to do?"

"Well, I haven't exactly thought of that yet." I nervously smoothed down my dress.

Annabelle took a sip, then said, "But I thought you told him there was a way to prove she did it."

I shook my head. "I told him that, but that doesn't mean I really have a plan yet."

"Of course not." She took another drink.

My mother entered the room, waving frantically at me from across the room. Her black silk dress reached to the floor with a small matching jacket. Her beauty products worked because she looked more like my sister than my mother.

"There's my mother. I'd better go say hi." I gestured at the foyer.

"I'm getting a snack," Annabelle said and walked off.

After assuring my mother that there would be no catastrophes, I scanned the crowd for Nicolas. He was nowhere in sight. Liam had been mysteriously absent as well. Where were they? Why hadn't I seen them? I was just thankful that the party had gotten off to a successful start. If I could just get through the rest of the night without any major disasters, then I could put this all behind me.

Annabelle was standing on the other side of the room, but with her hands placed squarely on her hips. I knew that stance meant that something was wrong. This could be the disaster just waiting to happen that I'd been trying to avoid. I wondered what was wrong. She was obviously pissed off at someone or something.

CHAPTER FORTY-SIX

I hurried over to her and touched her arm. "Is everything okay? What's wrong?"

She glanced over at me. Her face was completely red. That was not a good sign. I hadn't seen her that mad since someone ate her box of Thin Mints at work. She should have known better than to leave those things lying around.

She pointed at the group of women in the corner near to us. "Them. They were talking about you and I'm going to give them a piece of my mind."

She took off for the women and I grabbed her arm. I didn't get a good grip though and she got away. There was no stopping her at this point.

"Annabelle, it doesn't matter. Just ignore them."

She was mad enough that I knew she'd want to stomp on their witches' hats. The women looked over with shocked expressions when Annabelle approached.

"I heard what you said about my friend." Annabelle pointed at them.

She did realize they were witches, right? Had she temporarily forgotten? Stress had really gotten to her.

The woman with the stark blonde hair and black feather mask looked Annabelle up and down, then said, "What exactly do you think we said about your friend?"

"You said she was an embarrassment to the Coven. That her witchcraft had always been terrible and it would never change, no matter what house she lived in or who her great-aunt was." Annabelle clenched her fists at her side, ready to punch.

I looked at the women and then to Annabelle. "They said that? Well, now that is just plain old rude."

They were just lucky that I hadn't overheard their comments. Right now I had to worry about calming Annabelle down rather than being angry at these women.

"Annabelle, don't listen to what any of them have to say. They're insignificant." I glared at them.

Their mouths gaped open, obviously shocked at what I'd just said. The Coven could take a flying leap off a cliff with their ratty brooms.

The dark-haired woman glared back at me. "I'll just come out and say it to your face. It's the truth. You are an embarrassment. I can't believe they asked you to host this party. It was just because they thought you had some kind of special powers. We should have known that was all a lie."

So they knew about my diminished powers? I didn't care what they thought at this point. I didn't need them judging me.

Annabelle lunged forward and grabbed one of the women's dresses. She pulled on the satin sash around the woman's waist. She would have pulled it until it ripped right off if I hadn't stopped her. This was officially the disaster that I had worried about.

"Annabelle, please," I said, grabbing her arm.

She must have realized that everyone was watching us because she stopped resisting and ran out of the room. People had stopped dancing, drinking and eating all to stare at us. My mother had entered at that point. I didn't even want to have to answer her right now. If she wanted to be a part of this Coven then that was all on her. I wanted nothing to do with these women.

I stepped out onto the veranda after Annabelle. "Are you okay?" I asked when I grew near.

"I'm sorry, Hallie. I don't know what came over me. I just got so mad at those women judging you." She placed her head in her hands.

I touched her arm. Her whole body was trembling. "I've learned to ignore them by now. They are insignificant in my world."

She gave a half smile. "You're right. What difference does it make what they think."

I gestured toward the manor. "Exactly. I don't need people like that in my life. I've decided to just ignore them. They can think whatever they want, but I know what kind of her person I am."

"You're a kickass fun person," she said wiping away a tear.

I laughed. "Yeah, well, so are you. I'm sorry for even having the party here."

"You didn't know." Annabelle adjusted her dress, trying to regain her composure.

"Yeah, just the same. I should have never wanted the attention or acceptance of those women. I have all the friends I need... true friends like you." I wrapped my arm around her shoulders. "Come on. Let's enjoy the rest of the evening."

Annabelle had just given the Coven members a verbal tongue-lashing like they'd never had before. Obviously, she didn't care what kind of animal they could turn her into. At least she wasn't afraid of going back into the party.

When I stepped back inside, I searched the crowd for Nicolas or Liam. Neither of them were in sight. My mother was chatting with a group of women, probably telling them how my friend was crazy. I avoided them and turned the opposite direction.

"Where are your mysterious guests?" Annabelle asked when she caught up with me.

She had another glass of champagne in her hand. The flowing bubbly had probably contributed to her confrontation with the witches.

"I don't know where they are. I haven't seen them since the party started. It's very odd. I'm getting a strange vibe. It's not a good feeling."

I glanced at Annabelle and noticed that her eyes had widened and her mouth had dropped open. I looked in the direction that she was staring and I almost collapsed when I saw Isabeau.

CHAPTER FORTY-SEVEN

I couldn't believe this demon had crashed my party. She must have figured out how to break the spell that had banished her from the manor.

"How did she get back here?" I asked Annabelle.

I knew she wouldn't be able to answer, but I asked anyway. She just shook her head in response and continued to stare. Isabeau was arm-in-arm with Nicolas.

"What is going on? Why is she so cozy with Nicolas?" Annabelle stood beside me as we watched them.

He knew that she was a demon. He knew that she had partnered with the woman who had killed his mother. Had he lost his mind or had I been lied to? They didn't notice that Annabelle and I were watching them. They were engrossed in their private conversation. Nicolas' back was to me, so I couldn't see his expression. They walked out of the house and onto the veranda were other guests were mingling under the moonlight.

Lights had been strung up and twinkled in the dark sky. It would have been a romantic scene if I hadn't been following a demon witch.

I grabbed Annabelle's hand. "Let's follow them. I want to confront both of them and find out what's going on."

This party got worse by the minute.

Just as I was about to confront Isabeau and Nicolas, the Coven leader Misty Middleton appeared out of the darkness. She stared straight at me as she walked across the lawn.

Annabelle noticed her too. "Is she staring at us?" she asked.

I nodded. "Yeah, I think so. And she doesn't look happy."

"Do you think it has something to do with what I said to those women?" she asked.

"I don't know, but if she doesn't like it then that's just tough," I said, swallowing the bleakness in my throat.

Misty could be mad at me for not telling her my powers had been taken away before the party. It honestly was none of her business though. And I didn't care to tell her that either.

Misty walked right up to me and shot a cold look my way. "I want the books and I want them now."

Wow. She hadn't wasted any time letting me know what she wanted.

"I don't have the books," I said.

It was the same lie I'd told Nicolas and I was sticking to it. There was something weird about Misty's appearance. Her eyes kept changing colors, from blue to green, and then to a pitch black.

Annabelle looked at me with fear in her eyes. I was pretty sure she was ready to run away at any moment. I couldn't say that I blamed her.

"Misty, what is wrong with you? Why do you want the books? They are of no use to you. I am the leader of the Underworld now."

I didn't know if that was true, but it sure sounded good. It sounded like I knew what I was talking about and that was all I needed. Misty's face started to change. Her nose started growing out and her cheeks were higher. This wasn't right.

"Who are you?" I managed to choke out.

I felt Annabelle's tension beside me. I knew she was freaking out and so was I.

"I think you know who I am," she said with an evil grin.

Fear ran through my body. As soon as she said that I knew exactly who she was. Mara Abney.

She'd used her powers to take on a new image. This was not good. I was frozen. I didn't know what to do next.

"You didn't think you would get away with hiding the books from me forever, did you?" Her lips twisted into a cynical smile.

I didn't know what to say to her. I was never giving those books to her though. She'd have to kill me first. With the thought, I looked over to find Nicolas. He wasn't outside and neither was Isabeau.

"Now be a good little witch and go get the books for me." Mara cackled.

She really had that witch laugh down pat.

"What do we do now?" Annabelle whispered.

If I acted like I was scared Annabelle would freak out even more. I had to keep it together for Annabelle's sake. I knew this was going to turn into something that I wasn't sure I was prepared for. How did I fight a powerful witch like Mara? A witch who had already killed the last Underworld leader. Not that I was the leader anymore. I was sure the leader had to have powers to lead, and I had none.

I stood a little straighter and tried to come up with a plan. "The books aren't here."

Wind began to blow in the trees around the manor. Mara's eyes glowed a red hue. "I know you are lying to me."

"What are you going to do about it? Without me you can't get the books. I demand that you leave my property immediately." I pointed toward the gate at the end of the driveway.

The wind blew even harder. Annabelle stepped closer to me.

"Annabelle, why don't you go inside and get the other Coven members for me, okay?"

Annabelle didn't answer. She just turned and ran away toward the house.

Some of the Coven members had started a bonfire at the back of the property near the river to perform the annual ritual to their loved ones in the spirit world. The clouds had rifted enough to allow the moon to poke through. I kicked off my heels and ran in my bare feet around the manor toward the fire. I hoped someone could offer help for my fight with Mara.

The flames flickered high toward the sky as I rounded the manor. I glanced over my shoulder as I ran, but saw nothing. I found it odd that Mara wasn't running after me. I knew she was up to something though. She wasn't going to let me get away that easily.

Where was Nicolas? As I looked through the crowd of people gathered around the fire, I spotted a familiar face. I'd never been happier to see Liam.

He looked up and saw me. As I rushed toward Liam, he looked up, then ran over to me as I neared.

"What's going on?" he asked.

"Mara is here," I said in a panic.

He looked over my shoulder. "Where is she?"

"She was on the veranda, then I took off running around here. She didn't follow me." I looked behind me. "But I know she didn't go away."

Liam held my arms. "You have to get rid of her, Hallie."

I stared him in the eyes. "What do you mean I have to get rid of her? I'd love to, but how do you propose I do that?"

"You have to fight her for the power." He lifted my chin with his index finger to meet his gaze.

Looking down, I shook my head. "She took my power, remember?"

"She can't keep it forever. The spell she cast can only last so long. You can be stronger than her now. You've got the books, remember?" There was defiance and challenge in his words.

How could I forget? It was all that I'd thought about since the moment I found the first one.

"You have the power of the earth, air, water and fire," Liam stated.

That did sound quite impressive, but I had no idea what to do with these powers.

"You must destroy Mara once and for all and take over her power." His voice was firm.

"Nicolas said I need to destroy the books. That I shouldn't be the leader." I searched his eyes for a reaction.

Liam scoffed. "Of course he would say that. He has other motives for wanting you to do that."

My stomach was twisted into a knot. "Why do you say that? You two have done nothing but pull me to each side and I don't know who to believe."

"You can believe me. Nicolas is only there to steal your blood." Liam touched my arm.

My eyes widened. "What? What are you talking about? Why would he want my blood?"

"He wants your blood because it holds special powers for him," Liam said. "Vampires seek out witches' blood. I told you how the Underworld is in chaos. Stay away from him, Hallie. He is not good for you." He touched my chin.

My world was spinning. Liam's handsome face stared down at me.

The wind started to whip again. The tree branches swayed back and forth as if a huge storm was brewing. I knew that it was.

Liam pulled me close and held my chin in his hands. "You can do this, Hallie. I am here to help you."

"Get your hands off her," Nicolas yelled from across the lawn.

CHAPTER FORTY-EIGHT

Liam and I both looked over to see him running toward us. Annabelle was attempting to run in her heels behind him. Finally, she stopped and yanked the shoes off, then continued across the yard.

Liam let go of me and turned to face Nicolas. The last thing I needed was for them to fight. I had been between whatever weird fight they had with each other since the day they'd arrived. I didn't want to be in the middle any more.

"What is going on?" Nicolas demanded. "Is he hurting you?"

I shook my head. "Mara is here. Liam says I must fight her for her powers."

Nicolas shook his head. "No. No way. Don't listen to him."

"Why don't you stay out of this? You're going to get her hurt," Liam said.

"If anyone is going to get her hurt, it's you." Nicolas pointed at Liam.

Annabelle stood behind Nicolas. "Are you okay, Hallie?"

I nodded, but I knew that was far from the truth.

"Hallie, don't listen to him. You can't fight her. You can't trust Liam."

"I wish you all would stop telling me that. Liam has done nothing to make me not trust him. Tell me why I shouldn't trust him!" I demanded.

Nicolas stared at Liam, then looked at me. "Because Liam is out to destroy you."

I stared at Nicolas.

He continued, "He wants the books so that he can take over the Underworld. It was never for your protection. That's not why he came here."

They stepped closer to each other and I thought at any second they would reach out and grab each other. The wind whipped harder and the flames danced. Everyone was looking to the sky and staring at us.

I looked to Liam. "Is that true?" I asked.

"Of course not. It's all part of his lies," Liam said.

"Enough!" I threw my hands up. "I've had enough."

I turned around to run away, but I got halfway across the yard and froze. The wind blew so hard that I could hardly stand up. A strange light came from the side of the yard. It grew brighter and brighter as it came closer. I couldn't run toward the house. I looked to my left and saw the ghosts under the bright moonlight. They were at the edge of the trees, waiting for me to come near so they could grab me and take me away. They'd drag me away and I'd never be seen again. I had nowhere to go.

Liam and Nicolas called after me. I turned in the opposite direction and ran toward the water. The ground was slippery and I stumbled but righted myself and continued toward the water's edge. I didn't know what I would do next. Where would I go? If I jumped in the water I'd likely drown. The light followed me. For a moment, I was blinded by its brightness.

The area was washed in nothing but the white glow. Making out anything was extremely difficult. I had to stop running because I knew I was at the water's edge, even if I couldn't see the water. I turned around and looked directly into the light. The light began to diminish and a silhouette was visible through the light.

The long dress flowed with the fury of the wind and her hair whipped around wildly. The light finally vanished completely. Mara was standing in front of me. I looked behind me and stepped even closer to the water. I couldn't go much further before I'd fall in.

A wicked smile spread across her face. "I told you I would get the book. You have nowhere to go," she said with a cackle.

She was purposely pushing me closer and closer to the water. Why had I been stupid enough to let myself be cornered like this? I stepped back again. I couldn't go any further. The ground was wet and slippery. My feet slid in the mud and I fell to my knees. Liam and Nicolas watched nearby, but Mara was somehow keeping them at bay. It was as if we were in a bubble. She had me trapped like a wild animal.

"Go get the books and hand them over and I won't kill you. Doesn't that sound like a fair tradeoff right now?"

I struggled to get to my feet, but slipped again. I looked up at Mara. "Why should I believe a word you say?" I asked.

"You have no other options. They can't help you." She gestured at the Coven members with a tilt of her head.

"You can't hold off their powers forever. You're not that strong," I said.

"I don't need forever. Just long enough to get the books." She beamed, obviously proud of her words.

Isabeau had no problem walking through the protective bubble that Mara had placed around us.

"Give her the book now," Isabeau yelled. "She'll kill you if you don't."

I tried to conjure up enough energy to cast a spell against Mara, but nothing would happen. There had to be a way to hide her powers. Couldn't one of the many witches in the Coven help me? Or did they not want to help me? Where was my mother? My stomach turned. What if Mara had done something to her?

"I demand that you hand over the book now." Venom spewed from her words.

If I could hold her off long enough maybe she would lose her powers. I jumped up and began reciting the only spell that I could remember that might help my situation. Mara threw her head back in a big laugh. Isabeau joined in her merriment.

"Halloween, you can't stop me now," Mara said.

I slipped on the wet ground again and slid backwards. I clutched onto the ground, but there was nothing to grab onto. There was no way I could avoid falling into the water. My legs slid back into the water with a splash. I heard Annabelle scream out my name.

I clawed and kicked my way back up to the embankment. Mara and Isabeau were standing over me now. They looked down at me with their evil twisted faces. Would they kick me back in? Mara yanked on my arms, pulling me up. I was covered with mud. My dress was ruined, but that was the least of my concerns. I continued to recite the only spell that came to mind. Mara and Isabeau had my arms and were dragging me across the lawn. I struggled and broke free, running over toward the tree line. The ghosts were waiting there for me. Dodging around the trees, I came to the old family cemetery and stopped in my tracks. My great-aunt Maddy hovered over the old gravestones. She looked as she always had with her thick dark hair piled high on her head and a white gauzy dress.

She smiled widely, then said, "Use the power of earth, air, water and fire."

I wanted to stay and talk with her. There were so many questions to ask, but the sound of movement behind me let me know that Mara and Isabeau were close behind.

Running past the graveyard, I made my way back out to the same spot where I'd entered.

Mara and Isabeau were standing there waiting for me. I stepped backward and Mara and Isabeau walked after me. They were pushing me closer and closer to the water again. It looked as if my only way to escape was to swim through the river. The odds of me surviving that weren't good. I wasn't a strong swimmer to begin with.

Stepping closer to the water, I looked back, then took a deep breath and jumped in. My body instantly shivered as the cold water surrounded my skin. Even colder than I thought it would be. It sucked the breath right out of my lungs. I splashed and tried to remain calm, reminding myself that I had to swim or I would sink.

Words floated across the night air. "Use the power of the water." It wasn't Aunt Maddy this time. Nicolas called to me. I had to use the power of earth, air, fire and water. The water could possibly give me the energy that I needed.

Words came to me… words to a spell that I'd never performed before. I wasn't sure how I knew what to say but I did. I willed the water to work for me. Holding my head back away from the water, I recited the words. The swimming was effortless and the next thing I knew I found myself back at the edge of the water again.

I lifted myself out of the cold water. Mara and Isabeau seemed to be frozen on the spot. Neither one could move. When I looked over, Nicolas was standing by the trees. A wave of energy came off the trees through him and over to me.

I looked over at the fire as the flames danced high in the air toward the night sky. The moonlight cast a bluish hue over everything. I knew that magic was the most powerful on the night of the full moon, when energy spells were at their strongest. Tonight was a full moon and it held the energy that I needed—at least that was what I'd been told.

A wave of energy emanated off Liam and over to me the same way as it had with Nicolas. The fire crackled and popped. Were they sending me power? The power of earth, water, air and fire to cast the beings back to hell? I had to bind them from returning to this earth. They used every ounce of their power, sending the energy through the night air.

The light returned just as it had when it brought Mara. I hoped it was now taking her and Isabeau away. It came out of the sky around the trees and up from the earth. It was everywhere. This time the color was yellow and it wasn't as bright. The glow wrapped around Mara and Isabeau and in one giant swoop it carried them away. Scraping and grabbing at the earth, I wrestled my way up the embankment. I looked down at my muddied dress and hands. I could only imagine what my appearance looked like.

With Liam and Nicolas' powers to help me regain my new skills, I had been able to cast a spell and send Isabeau and Mara back to hell. I couldn't believe what I'd done. Liam had used his power to pull energy from the fire and Nicolas had used the power to pull energy from the earth. I hoped that they weren't just doing this so they could get to the books.

Liam and Nicolas ran over to me, each taking one arm and guiding me safely away from the water.

Annabelle ran over to me. "Hallie, are you okay? I was freaking out. You fell in the water and I thought you were going to drown. Not to mention those wicked women who were trying to take you away."

The more she talked, the faster her words came out.

"I'm okay. Try to take a deep breath." I patted her on the back.

She breathed in and out. "I'm okay now. I was just freaking out."

"It's understandable. I was freaking out a little," I said, trying to lighten the mood.

"What happened? How did you get rid of her?" Annabelle asked.

I looked at the men. "I had a little help."

It looked as if my grand ball was over for the evening. The Coven members were gathering around me though.

"What you did was amazing," a woman said as she walked along beside us.

I smiled. "I just did what I had to do."

As we neared the manor, my mother came running toward me. The real Misty Middleton was beside her. Tears streaked down my mother's cheeks.

"Where have you been?" I asked when she was near.

She looked me up and down, then grabbed my arms. "I was so worried about you. Mara confined us to the house. We couldn't get out." She hugged me until I thought the circulation would be permanently cut off.

A hot tear rolled down my cheek. Holding in the emotion was no longer an option.

CHAPTER FORTY-NINE

After going inside, I hurried upstairs to change out of my clothing. I wanted to get back downstairs to say goodbye to my guests and to apologize. It wasn't my fault Mara had shown up to cause problems, but I felt bad all the same. I had to slip in the shower though, I had caked-on mud in my hair and I smelled like the river. Not the most pleasant scent. And Cinderella thought she had problems. At least she'd only lost a shoe.

After dressing in jeans and an off-white sweater, I stood at the closet door. I was afraid to look. I knew I'd left the books there and apparently my powers had returned, but I still had that worrying feeling that they wouldn't be there. It would probably always be that way.

I had to make a decision. Did I really want to be the leader of the Underworld? There were pros and cons to the job, that was for sure.

I pulled my secret spot up. The books and boxes were still there. Apparently the books were mine now. I seriously needed someone to explain this whole 'leading the Underworld thing' before I officially accepted the job. Did I have to report to an office every day? Did they have an Underworld headquarters?

When I stepped out from my room, Nicolas was sitting on the front step waiting for me.

"Hi," I said softly.

"Do you feel better now that you got rid of the mud?" He flashed his devastatingly irresistible grin.

I nodded. "I ruined my dress."

"You look beautiful in the jeans too," he said with a smile.

He knew how to make me feel better. I stepped down then sat beside him.

"Tell me something," I said, looking over at him.

"Anything," he said.

"No more secrets. I want to know why there was so much animosity between you and Liam. And tell me the truth, because you said you'd be completely honest with me now."

He ran his hand through his hair and stared straight ahead. He didn't speak for a moment, then he finally said, "Liam was in charge of guarding my mother when she was killed."

I didn't know what to say, but it explained a lot. Why hadn't they just told me this to begin with?

"I'm sorry about your mother," I said. "What happened?"

"Liam didn't lie. He was the detective assigned to my mother. Her death happened on his watch and I accused him of not doing his job." He shook his head as his eyes glazed over. "There was no proof of that though. I was just taking my anger out on him. He was the easiest one to do that to, you know? I mean, I felt like he should have protected her." He searched my eyes.

"That's understandable." I touched his hand and he squeezed back.

"You can understand why I didn't want you to be involved with the Underworld. I didn't want to lose someone else who I care about. I now realize that Liam had no control over Mara or her demons. It was something that I refused to accept until now." He let out a pent-up breath. "There is one more thing."

"I'm almost afraid to hear what you're about to tell."

He ran his hand through his hair, then said, "Liam is my half-brother. We have the same father."

My mouth fell open. "That's why you look so much alike."

After a few seconds of silence, I whispered, "We should get downstairs so I can say goodbye to my guests."

He helped me up from the step. "You sure know how to throw one hell of a party."

I smiled. "I think I injured my side, don't make me laugh." I chuckled, then said, "Ouch."

"Are you okay?" He touched my side and it sent shivers through my body.

I nodded. "I think I'll have a big bruise tomorrow."

"You'll probably have several." He squeezed my hand.

When we got downstairs the crowd had disappeared. Only a few people had remained. Annabelle was sitting on the sofa with my mother, chatting quietly. They still looked a bit frazzled.

"Do you feel better?" my mother asked.

I nodded. "I'm sorry that I ruined the party."

"Are you kidding?" Misty had walked up behind me. "You're the leader now. Everyone in the Coven loves you. We'd like to welcome you into the Coven. That's if you'll have us." She smiled her sweetest smile.

I looked at my mother and she nodded.

"You are singing a different tune now. Earlier several Coven members had some not so nice things to say about me. How quickly things change." I shook my head. "Nope. I think I'm doing fine without the Coven. I think I'll stick with being on my own."

She frowned and stared at me for a moment, but didn't say a word. What could she say? Finally she said, "Well, thank you for hosting the party. We'd love to have another one here sometime."

I nodded. "I'll keep that in mind."

"Well, thank you again. I'll be going now. The caterers will clean up everything," she said in a clipped tone.

"Thank you, Misty." I tried to project a calm, in-control tone.

"I'm proud of you," my mother said when Misty stepped away.

"You're not upset?" I asked with wide eyes.

"Screw them. Annabelle told me what happened. You don't need them and neither do I." She folded her arms in front of her chest.

Wow, I couldn't believe my ears. My mother prided herself on her good standing with the Coven.

"My daughter is the queen of the Underworld now." She beamed.

Oh no. She was already bragging.

Annabelle stood. "Well, I'm going home and collapsing into bed."

"Thank you, Annabelle. You're one tough cookie."

"You call me tomorrow. We still need our girls' night. And I want to know everything about a queen's duties." Annabelle wiggled her finger.

"I don't think they call me a queen." I snorted. "But I'll make sure to let you know as soon as I find out."

After walking Annabelle to the door and watching as she drove down the driveway, I felt eyes on me. I peeked out onto the veranda. Liam was sitting on the step, peering out into the dark night sky.

"There you are," I said as I stepped outside.

He turned around and took in my whole appearance. "You clean up good," he said with a grin.

"Thank you," I said as I sat down beside him. "Thank you for everything."

He nodded. "Just doing my job."

"Is that it? You were just doing a job?" I searched his face questioningly. I wasn't sure what else I wanted him to say.

He glanced over at me. "No, it was much more than that. I think you know that."

My stomach flipped. I did feel that it was more than a job for him. I just wasn't sure how much more.

He reached over and held my hand. "I was never out to destroy you, Halloween. But I can see why you were so confused."

I touched his cheek. "Nicolas explained everything to me. How you were protecting his mother the night she was killed."

"He blames me for her death and I can't say that I blame him. She was my responsibility and I let her down. I let him down."

I shook my head. "I talked with him. He doesn't feel that way anymore."

"Halloween, you know he'll always feel that way," Liam responded softly.

I looked away. What could I say? Maybe he would, maybe he wouldn't.

"Are you ready for the job?" he asked.

I shrugged. "As ready as I'll ever be. I have to admit. I'm a little nervous about the whole thing. I'm not even sure what I'm supposed to do."

"The book will tell you everything you need to know. Some people will be by tomorrow to speak with you now that you've decided to take the position."

"I can't deny that this whole thing has been overwhelming." I picked at a loose thread on my jeans.

Liam's clean-shaven face gleamed in the moonlight. "I'm sorry we gave you such a hard time. It was complicated and there were a lot of hard feelings between us that we shouldn't have put you through."

I squeezed his hand. "You don't have to apologize."

Liam leaned over and pressed his lips to mine. My heart thumped wildly in my chest. His kiss was just as passionate as the first time he'd kissed me and with the same sense of urgency. My thoughts spun.

When he stopped kissing me, he ran his finger across my cheek. "I'll be leaving tonight. My work here is done. You don't need me hanging around."

I nodded. I would miss seeing his handsome face, but I knew there was no way he was staying. I had to see what my feelings were for Nicolas. And I thought Liam knew that without me even having to tell him.

Liam stood and reached for my hand. He pulled me to my feet and wrapped his arms around me. After one last hug, he grabbed his bag and stepped off the veranda toward his car.

"Aren't you going to talk with your brother before you leave?" My lips were still warm from his kiss.

"There'll be time for that another day," he said with a wink.

I watched as Liam drove down the driveway and pulled out onto the road. The thick cover of trees concealed his car soon enough and he was out of my life. But for how long? Surely I'd see him again, right? Would I need protection like Nicolas' mother? I hoped not. It was a scary thought.

He just wanted job security and to make up for not being able to save Nicolas' mother by helping me. If he helped me, he'd still have a place in the Underworld. Had Nicolas and Liam finally realized that their long feud had to end? Or had it ended for just the time being? I thought they needed to talk to each other and clear the air once and for all. It would have to wait for another time though.

The ghosts peered out at me from the tree lines. It didn't look as if they were going anywhere any time soon. I avoided looking directly at them and went back inside. My mother had Nicolas cornered and I knew I'd have to rescue him.

"Your mother was just telling me about the time you turned your date into an ass. I have to say this is a little disturbing." He scowled.

I chuckled nervously. "I'm sure your feet are killing you in those shoes, Mom," I said as I grabbed my mother's arm and ushered her toward the front door.

I said goodbye to the remaining guests and rushed my mother out the door before she could recount another embarrassing story. It was just Nicolas and me now. Well, and the ghosts outside, but there was no way I was letting them ruin what was left of the night. Life was going to be nothing like it had been before. Did I really know what I was getting myself into? Only time would tell.

So now I was the witch in charge? Take that, Coven! I wasn't sure what would happen, but I'd vowed to embrace my new talent for this day forward. But if I was the new boss, could I rewrite the rules that had been around for centuries? Dating a vampire might be frowned upon, but I was going to rewrite that rule. Would Nicolas want to hang around LaVeau Manor?

After everyone had gone, Nicolas took my hand and guided me into the parlor. He pushed on the music again. The steady melodic rhythm floated across the air.

"I think we need to finish that dance."

He held out his hand to me. We swayed to the music, but it wasn't quite the same now that I wasn't wearing my ball gown. Nicolas kissed me again and I was lost in his embrace. His hands moved across my body with ease. We were in our own world and this time no one would disturb us. Or so I thought.

Nicolas' cell phone rang, cutting off the music. We paused.

"I'm not answering that," he whispered, then planted soft kisses against my lips.

"What if it's important?" I whispered back through his kisses.

"It couldn't possibly be."

The ringing stopped and Nicolas continued his exploration of my body with his strong hands. The phone rang again. Still, Nicolas ignored the rings. Not that I was complaining because his touch made my skin tingle and my heart dance. The phone sounded again and Nicolas pretended that he didn't hear it. I couldn't ignore it so easily though.

I grabbed the phone and said, "Hello?"

"Hallie? Thank goodness. I've been trying to call your cell, but you didn't answer."

"Liam, is that you?" I asked.

Nicolas shook his head. "Perfect timing again."

"What's wrong?" I asked.

"The Underworld needs you," Liam said matter-of-factly.

"What do you mean?" My hands shook as I cradled the phone to my ear.

"I'm turning the car around and coming to get you." I'd never heard this much stress in his voice.

I looked at Nicolas. "What's wrong?" he asked.

I covered the phone with my hand. "It's Liam, he said he's coming to get me, that the Underworld needs me."

"Let me talk to him." Nicolas outstretched his hand and I handed over the phone.

After several 'uh-huh's and 'yes'es, Nicolas clicked off the phone. The sound of a car screeching to a stop sounded in front of the house.

Nicolas grabbed my hand. "Come on, we have to go."

Nicolas rushed me out onto the veranda. Liam was sitting behind the wheel of his idling car.

"Where am I being whisked away to?" I asked as I jumped in the passenger seat.

Apprehension took over. I'd never been in charge of anything before other than my mother's store a few times and now the bed-and-breakfast. I hardly thought those were worthy mentions on a resume. Why were the men being so quiet?

"When are you going to tell me what has happened?" I asked.

Liam hesitated as he steered the car out onto the road. He glanced in the rear-view mirror at Nicolas, who was sitting in the backseat. "Nicolas has been accused of stealing another witch's powers."

Uh-oh. This was going to be one hell of a ride.

ABOUT THE AUTHOR

Rose Pressey is an Amazon and Barnes and Noble Top 100 bestselling author. She enjoys writing quirky and fun novels with a paranormal twist. The paranormal has always captured her interest. The thought of finding answers to the unexplained fascinates her.

When she's not writing about werewolves, vampires and every other supernatural creature, she loves eating cupcakes with sprinkles, reading, spending time with family, and listening to oldies from the fifties.

Rose lives in the beautiful commonwealth of Kentucky with her husband, son, and three sassy Chihuahuas.

Visit her online at:
http://www.rosepressey.com
http://www.facebook.com/rosepressey
http://www.twitter.com/rosepressey

Rose loves to hear from readers. You can email her at: rose@rosepressey.com

If you're interested in receiving information when a new Rose Pressey book is released, you can sign up for her newsletter at http://oi.vresp.com/?fid=cf78558c2a

Made in the USA
San Bernardino, CA
28 June 2018